An America Reborn – 3

THE NATION REBORN

CARLTON JAMES

Black Rose Writing | Texas

ISBN: 978-1-68513-325-2
PUBLISHED BY BLACK ROSE WRITING
www.blackrosewriting.com

Printed in the United States of America
Suggested Retail Price (SRP) $21.95

The Nation Reborn is printed in Garamond

*As a planet-friendly publisher, Black Rose Writing does its best to eliminate unnecessary waste to reduce paper usage and energy costs, while never compromising the reading experience. As a result, the final word count vs. page count may not meet common expectations.

PRAISE FOR
THE NATION REBORN

"This is the third book in a riveting series. It is a compelling story, which further develops the theme of people emerging from a world catastrophe. An age-old struggle of good versus evil. It was definitely a page turner and I'm anxiously waiting the next book."
–Mary Anne Lamb, M. Education

"I loved the story and the characters. A marvelous continuation of a compelling saga ripped from the headlines that kept my interest from beginning to end!"
–Teresa McGuire, BS Education

"An entertaining, thought provoking, contemporary addition to the series. This thriller does not disappoint."
–Charles Monette, Pilot, Instructor, and FAA Examiner

"*The Nation Reborn*, Book 3 in *An America Reborn Thriller* series throws you smack dab into a world where the not-so-unthinkable has happened. Another brilliant, thrilling continuation from Books 1 and 2. Prepare yourself for a gambit of emotions as the Author breaches the barrier on Worldwide Devastation. He follows the journeys of each character coping with the aftermath of a deadly unleashed BioWeapon between Health, Heartache, unsung Heroes, and Hope for Humanity. You are going to read about unprecedented circumstances that bring out the best and worst in people. A true testament to the elements of survival, preparedness and military precision as individuals, communities and as countries give birth to new beginnings. Two questions for the readers: -Who would you trust or depend on when the SHTF? -What's your next step if you don't know?"
–Lana Bruce, Thriller aficionado

ACKNOWLEDGEMENTS

An America Reborn Thriller Series is based upon my observations over the past forty plus years as an officer in the U.S. Army Reserve and as an FBI Special Agent as well as being a student of history. Neither this novel nor this series would have been possible without the tremendous support and encouragement of my family, several close and brilliant friends, and my publisher, Reagan Rothe. Reagan provided just the right amount of nudge to get this book back on track. Special thanks go out to my friend and fellow author Arlynn. Your editorial assistance at several critical times down the stretch proved to be the difference in getting it done. Like our Founding Fathers I truly believe in our Republic and the grand experiment that guided the creation of it. Their brilliance can only shine, however, when strong leaders stand up and people see through the sweet lies promised by communism/socialism. I pray for our Republic and her oath keepers now, more than ever.

THE NATION
REBORN

CHAPTER 1
THE NEW YEAR - PLUS SEVENTY-THREE DAYS

Outside of Cronin, Kentucky
0845 Hours EDT

The Special Forces Staff Sergeant watched as the reject from a "Walking Dead" episode staggered up the road toward his checkpoint. He had his instructions, so with one carefully placed shot, the Sergeant fired a .300 caliber blackout round into the man's forehead. The body dropped into the ditch seventy-five meters down the road. The Sergeant sighed softly, resigning himself to meeting the man's un-diseased spirit the next time he tried to sleep. One more added to the dozens of spirits who visited him every night.

Even though the military rifle sported a so-called silencer, the crack from its muzzle was clearly heard for a couple of hundred yards. Suddenly, bullets from at least two long guns opened up to spray the edges of the bunker's sand bags. One sliced a hole in the sandbag next to the Sergeant's face, momentarily obscuring his vision, through the Sergeant's gas mask, with a cloud of dust. Suppressive fire started immediately from other members of the neighborhood security force manning the checkpoint. Unlike the shooters, the Sergeant and his security force were equipped with gas masks and chemical/biological protection suits. The Sergeant was well trained to fire with accuracy in "Full MOPP," or chemical/biological protective mask and clothing. The civilians in the security force were not, resulting in their inability to hit the unknown shooters.

Within three minutes, in accordance with the Standard Operating Procedures, or SOP, the backup tactical force arrived. They were a mix of civilians and two other Special Forces operators, including the Lieutenant in command. Thirty seconds after a quick briefing, they moved out, using short bursts of speed, to flank the unknown shooters. Approaching their last known position, they saw three figures, carrying rifles, running toward a nearby stone fence. A quick burst from an M-4 carbine dropped the larger man and shots from at least four other rifles dropped the other two.

Hearing the gunfire, Mike Broehm waited anxiously for his security chief to report. It was not enough that he held the fate of his friends and neighbors in his hands, but now he had to deal with whatever caused his people to shoot. He was still getting used to thinking of them as "his people." From the shot pattern he heard, he was fairly confident it was his people that fired the last round.

Linda Sharp, known affectionately among the security detail she commanded as "LT," walked into Mike's office area thirty minutes later wearing tight spandex shorts and a jog-bra. Her natural beauty and toned, well-rounded figure momentarily distracted him. She had stripped down in the makeshift decontamination shower outside the building where Mike had his temporary office.

"Commander, a zombie and three shooting fools dead, no friendlies injured. Although Hung received a few minor cuts on his neck from bullet shrapnel," Linda reported in her usual calm, concise voice. Zombie was the term they gave to those afflicted with the deadly virus and still able to walk.

Mike responded, "Details, please." His voice was deep, soft, but business-like, belying his internal reaction when learning of four people being killed.

"The zombie shooting followed your new standard procedure. I'll be working with Hung later, since he's been dealing with lots of demons since his wet work in the Sandbox." Linda knew dozens of Special Forces operators that either volunteered or were "volun-told," to go out and clandestinely kill enemies of the United States, resulting in serious Post-Traumatic Stress Disorder or PTSD. The orders did not include giving the enemy a chance or a fair fight. They were the enemy to be eliminated. Period. "When Hung took out the zombie, three fools attacked him with an AR-15, a .270 caliber deer rifle, and cheap 9 mm sub-gun. One was a big graybeard and the other two were young men. They were shot running toward a rock wall. Presumably searching for cover."

Linda tailored her brief for Mike, knowing he had no military or law enforcement experience and had ordered killing be kept to an absolute minimum.

"Were they related? You know, like father and sons?" Mike's question showed the anxiety he obviously felt about being responsible for someone's death.

"We don't know, Mike, but they had different last names and Indiana driver's licenses. This was a righteous shooting, Mike. They had already fired at us and were running toward a position of cover to shoot some more."

Mike nodded sadly. "Please let me know if anything else of interest is discovered. Did you recover their vehicle or means of transportation in the area?"

Linda's eyes flashed with surprise. She had somehow overlooked that detail. A very rare oversight on her part. "I'll send out a patrol right away to track that down. Thank you, Commander."

Mike watched her move quickly away towards the building entryway before turning back to his desk with regret. He would rather give some time and respect to the Indiana men that his people had killed, but he had more urgent matters to address; like which of his people would live and which might die.

The country had been on the brink of economic collapse, thanks to Chinese economic actions, the People's Republic of China (PRC) attack on Taiwan and President Katherine Fontaine's progressive policies. U.S. Department of Homeland Security hired goons were ordered to sweep the countryside in search of food and any useful materials for government soup kitchens and other "redistribution." At the neighborhood gate, the goons had been effectively repelled. Just when the country broke into anarchy, fifteen Islamic terrorists left Afghanistan, scattering into Europe, America, Russia, and China. Each man was infected with a nanotechnology enhanced virus so virulent it killed over 95% of those who became infected. Worse, the virus was transmitted through the air, killing its victim in two to four excruciating days. The President had ordered everyone to remain in their homes for an indefinite period in hopes the virus would eventually die out and/or they could develop a vaccine.

Until the virus erupted on the scene, Mike and his neighbors had relative control of their secure subdivision. The day before, Mike's brother-in-law, Marc

Baxter, arrived aboard a huge helicopter known as Marine One. Marc was the acting Press Secretary and acting Chief of Staff for U.S. President Katherine Fontaine, who he said was dead or dying. He carried with him 250 doses of a vaccine for the deadly virus and had privately pleaded with Mike to decide who should receive them.

Mike had no problem making decisions, but was terrified of serious decisions since an incident when he was a Boy Scout. Now he must decide who should get the vaccine. Worse, the vaccine required two doses to be most effective. The few remaining National Institutes of Health scientists believed one dose of the vaccine to be only about 50% effective. It was unlikely additional vaccine doses would be available anytime soon.

After using his usual prayer and opening himself to God's Will he still didn't decide on the correct answer, but felt the right answer would be revealed to him. The pressure was on, knowing that every minute he delayed would result in more people falling prey to the virus. He gave himself up to twenty-four more hours to ponder, collect additional information, and pray for the right decision.

***

Peter Worthington Residence
Outside of Cronin, Kentucky
0900 Hours EDT

Su Ling, known locally as Suzie, had just put down Volume One of The Federalist Papers. Her exotically beautiful Chinese features effectively concealed an extremely high level of intelligence. She and her best friend, Lisa, had arrived at "Uncle Peter's" house two months earlier at the direction of Lisa's father. Both young women had been Ph.D. candidate graduate students in biology before fleeing the Washington, D.C. area, for Kentucky.

When the virus struck, Mike asked both to collaborate with the Special Forces medic to develop recommendations on how best to survive. They researched the emerging virus diligently until Internet access ceased, along with publically available electricity, water, and other utilities. For Suzie, this left far too much time to think about the life she had escaped. For some reason, she was drawn to studying the history of the American Republic. This was not the history of the United States they had taught her at the very secret and brutal Chinese Intelligence special operations institute known as the "Charm School" outside of Shanghai, but the accurate history, as confirmed by several sources. Considering what she had endured during MSS training, someone with less intelligence and discipline would have suffered from nightmares, terrors, and chills. Suzie took it all in stride, focusing her mind on the task at hand, except for…

Just then Lisa walked into Uncle Peter's great room and saw Suzie sitting in her corner reading by the light of the large picture window and enjoying the warmth of the enormous fireplace.

"Heh, girl," Lisa said cheerfully. "Whatcha readin'?"

It took Suzie a moment to decipher Lisa's Southern accent, which had grown much more pronounced since her return home to Kentucky. "Your Uncle Peter recommended I read this book of essays written by three of America's founding fathers when they were trying to sell the new U.S. Constitution to the original thirteen colonies. Fascinating!" That brought a giggle from Lisa after she momentarily envisioned Suzie as a Chinese version of Mr. Spock from the Star Trek TV series.

Suzie's enthusiasm for the American "Great Experiment" was giving her life new meaning. Mike Broehm requested they also examine the founding of the country and give him some suggestions on how to better guard against another communist/socialist rise to power. All government functions had shut down over a week earlier as the sickness spread across the country like no plague in world history. When not providing guidance for the neighborhood to survive the virus, this was a great project to fill in the time.

"Lisa?" Suzie asked nonchalantly, "What can you tell me about this Marc Baxter that came in yesterday afternoon?" Su Ling, as Suzie was known before her arrival in Kentucky, had a legendary reputation within the limited number of MSS handlers who knew she existed. Her ability to clandestinely obtain information was unlike any other female or male they had encountered. None of her techniques seemed to work on her new best friend, Lisa.

Eyes twinkling, Lisa said, "Why Suzse. I think you LIKE him!" The exclamation brought instant giggles to both young women. "I knew you could judge character quickly, but have you decided you like him based on first sight?” Lisa’s smile and flashing eyes passed an entire conversation. She then read the response from Suzie just as quickly.

With a sigh, Suzie muttered, “You know I have been told who to fuck and pump for information for so long, well, that doesn’t mean I haven’t dreamed of finding someone…” She let the phrase peter out as her eyes dropped.

Lisa moved immediately to Suzie’s chair, squeezed in beside her and gave her a big hug.

“I know, sister.” After a brief pause, Lisa said, “You know, someone very smart once told me it’s proven that under great stress, humans are genetically driven to procreate.” The twinkle and smile reappeared on Suzie’s face.

“You mean in times of high threat, we fuck like bunnies?” Suzie said with a smile.

Lisa was still trying to get used to Suzie’s somewhat crass and direct word choice regarding sex. “I’m sorry Su, I mean Suzie. I didn’t mean to bring that up.”

Now it was Suzie’s turn to comfort Lisa. “You no worry about it,” Suzie said in slightly broken English. “That just a job I no longer have to do. You and your father have given me freedom for the first time. And I like it!”

CHAPTER 2
THE NEW YEAR - PLUS SEVENTY-FOUR DAYS

Peter Worthington Residence
Outside of Cronin, Kentucky
0830 Hours EDT

It was light outside when Marc Baxter awoke to find himself sleeping on a cot in a strange greenhouse. He did not know what time it was, only that it was obviously after dawn. Standing right outside the outer door of the greenhouse was a soldier in full MOPP gear, watching him intently. Clearing his throat, Marc asked the soldier where he was supposed to use the restroom. The soldier merely pointed at the five-gallon plastic bucket with a specially fitted toilet seat.

Sitting on the field toilet, Marc's groggy mind contemplated what had happened to him over the past two years. Finishing his business, he glanced up and saw an observation window in a home attached to the greenhouse. It was raining steadily and ice was forming on everything but the warm roof of the greenhouse. At the window of the house, a beautiful oriental girl stood watching him. Seeing his glance, she pivoted and walked away. Her facial expression had gone from fascinated delight to surprise at having been caught watching to mild embarrassment.

"Excuse me," Marc said to the soldier, "how long have I been out?" It shocked him to learn he had been sleeping for over thirty hours.

The oriental girl must have alerted someone that he was awake because within a couple of minutes, his sister Lauren appeared in the window, along with Mike. "Marc, honey! You're finally up!" The tone of her voice conveyed both concern and love through the temporary microphone and sound system. "Peter's wife, Elizabeth, is preparing a breakfast tray for you right now. I'm sorry it isn't what we you'd normally get, but she thought after whatever you have been eating added to over thirty hours asleep, you'd probably need something fairly bland and not too heavy. How are you feeling?"

"Hungry, and like I've finally left the gates of hell to land in this little Garden of Eden." The grin forming on his face made Lauren remember the mischievous brother she raised after their parents died.

"By the way," Marc asked, "when do you think I can get out of quarantine and actually give you a big hug? I figure that's why the armed guard in Hazmat gear is here. Oh, and you guys know I've had my vaccine, right?"

"Well, Marc," Mike said with a faint smile, "that has been a topic of discussion since you arrived. Shaving your head is standard operating procedure out of the military chem/bio handbook, but there were one or two that thought you should have your entire body shaved." With a twinkle in his eye, Mike continued, "You owe me one, buddy. I shut down that idea straight away. Certain indignities no man should have to go through! And not only that, I imagine the itching, while the hair grew back would be miserable!"

Laughs and giggles were heard from almost everyone but Marc.

"You can't be serious," Marc said with exasperation, not sure if Mike was being serious or not. His hand had unconsciously begun rubbing his now bald head.

"After consulting with our military friends, said Mike, "we figured between your thorough decontamination and the other considerations, forty-eight hours should be enough. We waited until now to see if you'd be showing any symptoms of the virus. If you had it you would be showing symptoms by now."

"But, hell, Mike! I got two vaccine doses!" The delay exasperated Marc, who felt the need to repeat himself.

"I know, I know. But assurances by the CDC on an experimental vaccine are not exactly the gold standard that the damned thing even works. A year after the COVID vaccine came out, study after study showed it neither kept someone from getting the virus nor spreading it. Whether it made it less likely someone would die from COVID was questionable at best. I know you're impatient, but please go with me on this. Okay? This bug is reported to kill over 95 percent of people it infects. We just want to have an abundance of caution. You've slept through over thirty-six hours of your quarantine, so by this evening you should be able to physically join us. With Peter's wife Elizabeth's breakfast under your belt, you may even want to take another nap before your time is up. Damn, son, looks like death warmed over!"

"Okay, everyone, let's give this poor man some privacy for his meal and nap. That is, after I've had a word." Mike's tone, used with everyone that had gathered at the window, clearly said it was time for them to find somewhere else to be.

Once everyone had gone, Mike said, "Before I leave you to your food and another nap, what can you tell me about this damned virus and the package you brought with you?" Having been awakened only a few minutes earlier after a fitful night of wrestling over who should get the vaccines, Mike's tone was strained with frustration and backed by anger.

"Mike," Marc said quietly, "I think it's pretty easy for all of us to want to dump the big decisions off on those we trust, forgetting the loads they carry. I just came from such a pressure cooker and presume you are involved in most of what goes on around here?"

A quick glance confirmed his guess was correct.

After a deep breath Marc said, "Believe me, my world has been completely nuts since before the election, but none of that compares with what has happened in the past several days. But those are my burdens, not yours. Here's what I know. Forgive me if I go over things I told you when I first got here. This girl Julie Carrithers, whose blood was used to develop the vaccine, was rescued by U.S. Special Forces in Afghanistan. Someone with more than half a brain, which is far more than anyone in the White House seemed to have, decided to fly her back to the Centers for Disease Control, or CDC in Atlanta. I think it was a Captain Schneider, who was one of the rescuers. Anyway, when she got there Schneider had a laptop belonging to the raghead monster that had taken the Chinese virus and, using nanotechnology, changed and improved it into what we're seeing now all over the world. She overheard a couple of the raghead scientist's assistants talking about getting the virus from the Chinese."

Marc drank an entire bottle of water before saying, "The few remaining scientists there were able to use the information on the laptop, which was in English of all things, combined with a couple pints of Julie's blood, to come up with the vaccine. She somehow was blessed with at least partial natural immunity. Apparently, the CDC scientists were dropping like flies at that point and there was some type of accident. They could only produce a limited number of doses of the vaccine and sent 1,500 to the President. She had 1,250 distributed to government officials and top Pentagon brass, though it was too late to do much good, and minus a couple of dozen for herself and the surviving White House staff. They kept the remaining 250 doses close to Katherine until she and her top assistant…"

Marc looked down and his voice gained a husky, choked-up tone as he thought of Susan.

"Anyway, after running messages over to the Pentagon from the President I was stopped at the outer door by White House security, given the pelican case with the vaccines and a letter from Susan explaining she and the President had the virus and I should take the vaccines and find someplace safe to go."

Tears were running down Marc's face.

"There was also a Presidential Executive Order that Marine One was to take me to wherever I said to go. Mike, I couldn't think of anywhere else to go."

Compassion for his brother-in-law flooded Mike as he watched Marc standing, trembling slightly. "Heh, Marc. You done right, son." The words were said softly, but with feeling.

"Now can you do something really tough like stay awake long enough to eat some breakfast? I'll touch base with you later today." Mike's positive smile was infectious, brightening Marc's mood immediately.

Mike turned away before letting his own problems reenter his mind. It was 8:45 a.m. and it felt like he had been up for a week.

Having been cooped up in Peter's house for several days, Mike decided he needed a change of scenery to help him make his decision. With the help of the Special Forces soldier assigned to watch over Marc, Mike climbed into a military protective rubberized garment known as a SCALP suit (suit, contamination avoidance and liquid protection) and put on a gas mask with hood. "My God," he thought, "How do people breathe in these damned things?"

Walking outside behind Peter's bunker house through the freezing rain into the wood line, he slipped three times before finding a stump and sat down to contemplate. Watching a poor sparrow flit from branch to branch momentarily distracted Mike from the task at hand. Should he vaccinate 250 people or only 125? If he vaccinates 250 people and half of them die of the virus, then the 250 made little sense.

Mike sat quietly, falling into a deep, meditative prayer, when he heard insane screaming coming from somewhere close behind him. Suddenly, the staccato bark of a three shot burst from an M-4 rifle brought him completely out of his meditation. Off to one side stood Linda Sharpe, in full MOP gear, with her rifle barrel smoking. Looking over his shoulder he could see on the ground an obviously sick, quivering, convulsing woman breathing her last breath with a death rattle from punctured lungs. Without a word, he stood up, nodded calmly to Linda and walked back to the decon shower to prepare to re-enter Peter's house.

CHAPTER 3
THE NEW YEAR - PLUS SEVENTY-FOUR DAYS

Peter Worthington Residence
Outside of Cronin, Kentucky
0945 Hours EDT

In his underwear, Mike walked into the area off the family room that was designated as his office. He was still dripping from the decontamination shower and carried his outer clothes in his arms. At least the warmth from the roaring fire in the open-pit family room fireplace had taken the chill out of the air. He had made the decision of what to do with the 250 vaccine doses after having talked to Marc and remembering delay cost lives. With gallows humor, he thought about how just a few days earlier he was gravely concerned about the neighborhood being overrun by Homeland Security thugs on a pillaging mission. This decision seemed to be even more vexing because there was no one else he could lean on. His attempt to bring in his security chief Linda Sharpe and her fiancé U.S. Army Special Forces Lieutenant Colonel (LTC) Sean Callahan into the decision-making process failed miserably.

The previous evening, Mike had called in Linda and Sean to discuss it. That lasted five minutes. Linda gave him an update she had got from the last transmission from Special Forces Command in Florida. Sean summed it up as he rose to awkwardly walk away on his artificial leg.

"Commander, you have your options and none seem right to you. Time for you to sleep on it. Decide and we'll make it work."

At least, Mike thought, last evening he had a night to sleep on it. Yeah, right. So much for sleep.

The discussions with Lisa and Suzie, his best available scientists, didn't help either.

When he asked his normally sage and practical wife, all she would say was, "Honey, go with what's in your heart, mixed with what your practical brain says is right. Nobody here will ever second guess you." Well, that was a lot of help!

Although he didn't feel good about it, he nodded his head and called his runner, a nine-year-old boy named Kevin, and sent him off to gather the people who would be involved with the vaccine. Like so many children, Kevin's entire family had died of the virus. With almost everything encased in a half inch of ice, it would take the boy twice as long as usual to deliver the message. Man, he thought, this ice storm was going to cause all kinds of problems for people, especially since there was no power or running water available for those without generators or wells.

Peter Worthington's great room had a crowd of twelve, each called to the meeting by Mike. Since the virus had struck the world, most gatherings of over two or three were frowned upon. Except for those living in Peter's house, everyone else had to go through decontamination and strip down to skivvies to enter. They wore a mish-mash of bathrobes from Peter's closet. Those present included Mike, Lauren, Lisa and Suzie, who were living there along with Peter and his wife Elizabeth, Sean and Linda, Sean's father, Police Chief Fred Callahan and his Korean-born wife, Penny, and the two most senior Special Forces Operators, one of which was their medic, known by his Team nickname "Doc."

"Thank you for coming on such short notice," Mike said with some resignation in his voice. "I think everyone here is aware of the virus vaccines that were brought to us by Lauren's brother Marc Baxter in Marine One day before yesterday." Glancing at everyone in the room, Mike couldn't help but show some of the anger, frustration, and sarcasm he felt. "And each of you has been most helpful in guiding me in how to decide who will get what."

Reactions to Mike's frustrated words varied. A few felt ashamed at having dumped the decision entirely on his shoulders. Those who had made life and death decisions felt sympathy balanced by annoyance at their leader. Peter was simply angry, but carefully swallowed all the things he wanted to say. Shouting out, "show some balls, boy," wouldn't be productive in this situation. All knew Mike was still growing into his position.

With a deep breath, Mike continued. "After a lot of thought and prayer, here's what I came up with. I want the folks in this room to draw up a list of 200 people who are healthy, and most of them adults, that should get the vaccine. Of the handful of children on the list, they should be exceptional in some way that will help us survive. No sympathy names here. I will choose seventy-five from the list that I believe will be most beneficial to everyone's survival. Those seventy-five will receive two doses of the vaccine. I will then draw lots from the remaining one hundred twenty-five people from that list for the fifty remaining double-doses of the vaccine. There will be no single doses. I don't want to waste a vaccine on a fifty percent chance of immunity. Also, all the vaccine doses will be dispensed. I will not waste a single life among us on speculation a few doses might be useful later. 'Might' doesn't cut it with me this time. We will assign those receiving the vaccine to do everything possible, such as delivering food and clean water, to those that did not. The rest of the folks who did not receive the vaccine will want to stay sealed in their location until it is determined to be safe for them to come out. I will conduct these actions in front of three witnesses, two of whom will be Fred Callahan and Linda Sharpe. The rest of the folks here are to pick the third. We will make no announcement of these actions. Questions? Comments?"

Mike surveyed the face of each person present. A few gave him a simple thumbs up, while most just nodded their head. Each knew and empathized with him. Each would support the decision from now on. No one had anything to add.

"All right," Mike said in a heavy voice. "Please come up with the list of 200 people. When that list is complete, I'd like Fred, Linda, Sean and Peter to bring it to my office around the corner."

Mike again took a deep breath, walked around the corner and closed the door to the small sitting room that was converted into his office. All he could think about was the leather couch against the wall. In only a few moments, he was fast asleep.

***

In the great room, Peter looked at everyone and said, "Okay, then. Let's get started on our list. Any suggestions where to start?"

Linda pulled out a notebook from her backpack. "I think this might be a good place to start," she said. "A while ago, I asked Doc to build a list of everyone in the neighborhood and the neighboring farm families who signed on with us. I've been scratching off those who have died. Oh, and we could add a handful of names from the National Guard and Governor's office we think might be worthy of consideration."

Less than four hours later, Elizabeth took a deep breath and said, "I think that's it. Anyone feel strongly about someone we left off the list of 200?" The response was silence, with many dropping their eyes. Whether they had made life or death decisions in the past, they had all just done so now.

"Anybody have issues with the top 100 names on the list? You may have noticed that when writing out the final list, I cherry-picked names and put those I thought should be given the most consideration." Smiles were seen around the room. Everyone had watched Elizabeth do that and were grateful she was the one to do it. Anything to help Mike's job of narrowing down the list met their approval. None were surprised to see their own names were at the top of the list. Modesty/humility be damned. They each knew their own value.

"I have a suggestion," Fred said. "Why don't we take a thirty-minute break and revisit the names of those left off and see if anyone has additional thoughts? We only have one shot at this and I, for one, don't want to think I overlooked the obvious." All agreed and wandered into the kitchen for a snack.

After the thirty minutes, they removed two names from the list and another two were added. Fred, Linda and Elizabeth then knocked on the door, waking Mike up, and entered for the final decision.

***

Basement in a Home
Outside of Frankfort, Kentucky
1205 Hours EDT

Kerry DuBois was shaking a little, having retreated to a corner of the basement. Jerry, "the Tank" Monahan, had thrown him to the ground after nearly crushing his throat with both of his thumbs. Tank just had no sense of humor. Hell, there had been only five warm cans of beer left in the basement fallout shelter before Kerry decided he just had to get a buzz before they were all gone. Unfortunately, Tank had heard him pop the top on the last one and became enraged when Kerry wouldn't stop chugging the rest down his throat.

Kerry glared over his shoulder at Mickey Blondiac, known by everyone as Blondi. Softly under his breath, he hissed, "Shit, Blondi, were you gonna stop him before he killed me?"

With some disgust, Blondi said, "Kerry, you're lucky he didn't just snap your neck like a twig. Hell, one or two of those should have been mine!"

All three men had been cloistered in the home-made fallout shelter for the last eight days.

The shelter had been prepared by one of Blondi's journalist friends in the home of his mother, ten miles outside of Frankfort. That friend had been an early casualty of the virus. Blondi collected Kerry and Tank and brought the two men to the house, where the old woman refused to let them in. In frustration, they turned to leave, then Tank wheeled around and shot her five times before she could raise the hunting rifle she held in her arms. All three hurried into the house and were surprised at the quantity of survival supplies in the basement.

***

Presidential Emergency Operations Center (PEOC)
Beneath the East Wing of the White House
1330 Hours EDT

Presidential Personal Assistant Susan Cassel held the President in her arms as she faded in and out of consciousness. Blisters had formed on the face of President Katherine Fontaine, revealing the deadly Chinese virus had even penetrated the air filtration system of this secure facility. Susan noticed a few blisters were forming on her own arms, so she didn't mind fulfilling her duty to the end. She felt an immense amount of pride at having given her best, and only friend, Marc Baxter, a way to escape this death hole with a Presidential Order directing Marine One to transport him to safety.

Throughout the first year of the Fontaine Presidency, Marc was the one bright spot of reason and rock of stability Susan could always depend upon. He was the de facto Press Secretary, and just a few days earlier was appointed Katherine's Acting Chief of Staff, when the appointed Chief of Staff, Burt Combs, had disappeared. This all made Marc the only person in the world she could confide in, and take to her bed for her physical and emotional needs. Marc, being fifteen years her junior caused her to giggle silently a little, thinking she would be considered by some to be a "cougar." Marc was a truly decent man that had no aspirations to collect or wield power.

Two days earlier, Marc had returned to the PEOC after having carried another Presidential Directive to the Pentagon on the Presidential Helicopter. When he attempted to enter, one of the remaining Marine guards had stopped him and given him a sealed Pelican case containing vials of the vaccine and two envelopes. Susan had written her brief letter hoping he would feel her level of appreciation and admiration and would understand she was doing what she could to help him survive. The last 250 doses of vaccine the CDC had sent to the President should guarantee his acceptance wherever he found shelter. The President's Order should get him there.

The dwindling number of Pentagon reports received at the PEOC painted an incredibly bleak picture of what the Chinese virus was doing to the entire world. Enhanced by nanotechnology, it floated through the air and attacked humans with over a ninety-five percent mortality rate. Analysts believed a majority of the survivors would probably perish because of hardships following a total collapse of society and essential services. People weren't prepared to survive without modern conveniences. Government services at every level had ceased. Power, water and every other public service previously available to the American people had stopped. Hospitals no longer functioned, and those afflicted with the virus found whatever corner they could, suffered horribly, and died. A small percentage that were still ambulatory staggered around in delirium, further spreading the virus, until they fell down and died. A few pockets of people shut themselves off from the rest, but there were no reports of how they fared. The virus had even penetrated the not-so-secret government shelter in the Greenbrier Resort in West Virginia. A little satisfaction crept into her after she read the report that Chinese General Secretary Song was killed by his own virus.

Katherine moaned a little through the morphine haze before she suddenly stopped breathing. A flood of relief flowed through Susan. She gently laid the older woman's body back on the bed and reached for the morphine to give herself an injection. She really didn't care how much was in the syringe, so long as it was enough that she wouldn't wake up. Susan's last thoughts before she lost consciousness were about the girl, Julie Carrithers, at the CDC. It was her blood that contained antibodies targeting the virus which had been what made the vaccine possible. Was she going to turn out to be the Second coming of Christ for the human race?

CHAPTER 4
THE NEW YEAR - PLUS SEVENTY-FOUR DAYS

Peter Worthington Residence
Outside of Cronin, Kentucky
1400 Hours EDT

It took Mike nearly fifteen minutes and one of his carefully horded Energy Shots to wake up and get his mind functioning. Fred, Linda and Elizabeth waited patiently.

"Okay, what do you have for me?" Mike asked with more power and authority in his voice.

"Mike," said Fred, "here's the 200 names you asked us to give you. You might notice Elizabeth has placed around eighty to one hundred names at the top of the list that she, and frankly, the rest of us, think you ought to give special consideration."

Looking into Mike's eyes, Fred could see understanding and appreciation blossom. "We included only the able-bodied, with a couple of exceptions having useful skills, and only eight children. Have to say, we used your mandate as the excuse to not make most of the list children. Those kids on the list all came from Linda's security force and all have the potential to become excellent leaders."

"One other thing, Mike." Elizabeth added. "We knocked around some logistics of how to actually administer the vaccine without getting anyone's knickers in a twist. Several people can either be summoned or brought here and Doc will give them their shots, one week apart. We kinda figured a security team, with Doc, of course, could go out and interview the rest who will get the vaccine, one at a time. If they're around other people, they'll be told Doc is looking to identify potential volunteers for a secret mission. They will then be taken to a private room, given the vaccine and told they were hand-picked by you to receive the vaccine. They'll also be given a cover story. No negotiation. They should keep their mouths shut about it and if they can't do that, they will not get the second shot. What do you think?"

After a deep breath, Mike bowed his head and thanked each of them. While discussing each name, except for the most obvious, Mike agreed to their recommendation regarding getting the vaccine administered.

***

One of Linda Sharpe's security team entered the great room and approached Mike. "Mike, there's a very pushy, somewhat distraught woman outside in the greenhouse that insists on seeing you right away. She won't say what it's about, only that it's critical she speak to the man in charge."

With a sigh, Mike nodded and walked around to the window overlooking the greenhouse where Marc was still sleeping. Standing just outside of the greenhouse door stood a mature, attractive brunette with dark hair and veiled eyes, fidgeting noticeably. Mike keyed the microphone and softly asked the Special Forces operator guarding Marc and the greenhouse if the woman looked or acted sick. In his chem/bio suit, the guard motioned negatively. Mike then instructed the guard to invite the woman to the door and to hand her the microphone. He further cautioned the guard to have her be as quiet as possible. Marc continued to sleep peacefully in the corner of the greenhouse.

"Hello," Mike said softly. "Can you hear me? I'm Mike Broehm. As softly as you can, please tell me what is so important it won't wait until tomorrow morning?"

The woman in her middle 40s, with dark hair, flashing brown/gray/hazel eyes and wearing an oversized Army combat jacket and bib-overalls took the microphone in her hand, and after a deep breath said softly, "If you don't make good on your promise and get me some help right now, our deal is off. Do you get me?"

"Frankly, madam. I have no idea what you're talking about." Mike's frustration with everything going on and his new leadership position was wearing on him.

"Okay, your people came to my family farm over two months ago and said if I wanted to join with your neighborhood, they would protect me and help me out whenever I needed extra help on my farm. I agreed and I haven't even had contact with your people since then. I'm on my family farm by myself with almost a hundred head of cattle, chickens, a dozen goats and this goddam ice storm just broke legs on two of my steers! It's all I can do to keep the animals cared for without this! Where's all this damned help you promised? You people can probably use the meat by now and if you don't send anyone over to butcher it and haul it out, leaving me some choice cuts, the coyotes are going to get it all. What's your word worth?"

"What's your name, please?"

"Anna. Anna Boesch. I live about a quarter mile that way." She pointed off to the side of the Worthington property.

"How are you feeling, Anna?" Mike asked out of concern, seeing that she looked exhausted and like she hadn't been eating very well lately.

"Well, I already got over the goddamned virus over a month ago, if that's what you mean. Your guard over there doesn't have to be wrapped up in a space suit on my account." Anna's frustration was also running high. "I mean it about butchering those steers right away, like right now, before the coyotes get 'em. I also need a couple of healthy men for one or two days a week to fix fences, and other farm chores. I've been working my ass off twenty hours a day, since my hired man and his wife died of the virus, with no help, and I just can't keep up! And I'll trade some eggs for flour and any canned vegetables I can get. My pantry is just about bare."

Through the frustration, Mike could tell Anna was a decent, hard-working woman feeling overwhelmed and that she obviously hadn't been eating well lately. "Anna, what did you do before the virus turned the world on its head?"

The change of topic stopped Anna for only a second. "I'm a paralegal and office manager that keeps, I mean, kept a law office full of eight attorneys and six overworked staff members from killing each other, and maybe giving their clients the services they expected. God, I could use a bourbon Friday right now, in the worst way!"

Mike chuckled and said, "I'm sorry I can't help on the bourbon Friday, though it sounds appealing. What I can do is send someone back to your place with you to help butcher the steers. It'll take about an hour to get this together. Would you mind waiting there in the greenhouse until I get that arranged? There's an old, overstuffed chair to your left. I can have some water brought to you as well."

"Okay," Anna said cautiously, "but I shouldn't be away too long. I've already killed half a dozen coyotes on the farm in the last two weeks, and the pack can tell when I'm not around."

Mike turned away to go look for Linda Sharpe when he discovered she was standing behind him, just out of sight from the greenhouse.

"Oh, Linda," Mike said, startled, "I was just going to look for you. Did you hear what the lady down there had to say?"

"Yes, I did, Mike," Linda said. "I think a couple of my Operators can handle the butchering detail pretty quickly. This neighborhood will very much appreciate the meat, too. My butchers can take care of that distribution. You might want to ask Elizabeth to put together a quick meal for Anna. And I'll have the guys gather a care package of some long-term storage food for her as well."

"That would be great, Linda. Thank you," Mike said with appreciation. "Just a thought. My truck has a hand-crank winch that attaches to the trailer hitch receiver. I can get it for your guys to use for the butchering. I know it has made my life a lot easier whenever I field dress a deer."

***

Denali National Forest, Alaska
2015 Hours Local Time

Sitting in a comfortable, overstuffed, easy chair in his snug rental cabin, Major Cho Chong of the MSS thought about the bizarre events that had brought him to the last frontier of the United States. He landed in Fairbanks, Alaska, almost three weeks earlier, traveling on a forged American passport. Upon arrival, he had purchased a used Chevy Suburban, lots of supplies, two hunting rifles, ammunition, and a one-month package at a hunting lodge/cabin outside of the

Denali National Forest. Though it was already late February, winter continued to exert its firm hold, with several feet of snow and temperatures hovering near -40 degrees, which was coincidentally the same in Celsius or in Fahrenheit. Though the electricity stopped working a week earlier, someone thoughtfully placed an abundance of candles and oil lanterns in the cabin cabinets. The fireplace roared with nicely seasoned wood burning merrily, taken from the covered woodpile a few steps outside of the door. All he had to do was shovel the snow from the path and carry in several loads of wood twice per day.

Since being released by the leader of the terrorist group Jihadists of the Prophet, (JOTP) in Kabul, Afghanistan Cho had indulged his creative streak more than at any time in his life. If what the JOTP leader had told him was correct, and he had no reason to doubt him, his superiors in the MSS had planned to have him killed right after he had arranged for the JOTP martyrs to be infected by the virus and dispatched to all countries affiliated with the West, plus China. His analytical mind could see the reasoning for his death in keeping with cleaning up all the "loose ends," particularly those with full knowledge of how such a plague was unleashed upon humanity all over the world. To quote a popular American phrase, it did, however, piss him off. Unfortunately, this also meant the highest leaders in the MSS very much wanted him to be and remain dead. He could no longer enjoy the benefits and support of being a very high-ranking spy within the MSS. News he had heard through the ham radio traffic showed humanity was rapidly dying all over the world, including the Chinese Premier and American President. This was speculation by unknowledgeable voices over the radio, but potentially promising for his own position.

Despite being extremely angry at his MSS bosses, Cho's practical side quickly asserted itself and he looked at the events as an opportunity. The entire world was completely shut down, including the organs of the MSS and the Chinese government. Therefore, when the survivors raised their heads, they would need strong leadership to pick up the pieces. He set to work drawing up a framework for seizing control and operating the next Chinese Dynasty. With Cho, or at least someone who looked exactly like Cho, but with a different name and background, directing things from the shadows.

CHAPTER 5
THE NEW YEAR - PLUS SEVENTY-FOUR DAYS

Peter Worthington Residence
Outside of Cronin, Kentucky
2015 Hours EDT

Mike had spent the past two hours going through reports. Tired as he was, he had specifically asked various members of his "staff" to compile the reports, like the one Linda Sharpe had delegated to her security team leaders to count and provide a daily status of the survivors in the neighborhood and those surrounding farmers who had joined them. Each Team Leader was given a basic format to compile the report, none were done in the concise, informative and logical style Linda used. Mike learned another lesson in leadership that each task, or report in this case, should be compiled into a summary report at the beginning, followed by the body of the report containing all the relevant details. He made a note to ask Linda to provide a summary from now on.

Suddenly from the other room he heard a cheer go up from the dozen people that had stuck around for dinner, followed by an adult beverage (if they brought their own) or just good conversation, if not. Walking into the room he saw the completely shaved head of Marc Baxter being subjected to pounding on the back and a near roar of questions from several directions.

Several minutes into the mild chaos, Mike's wife, Lauren, raised her voice and quieted everyone. "Okay, people! Okay! Okay! Okay!"

Those asking questions and others engaged in their own conversations got the hint and gradually everyone stopped talking. Lauren continued, "I know everyone is excited to see my brother up and about. Just like you, I'm dying to hear everything he can tell us about what happened in this crazy world and what's happening in Washington. That being the case, Marc, honey, would you mind filling in a few details for, say, five or ten minutes, and then it'll be time for everyone to answer your questions?"

Thinking about it for a moment, it surprised Marc his sister's request wasn't a bother for him. It didn't have any type of feel like the pressure cooker he had left in Washington where everyone in the Administration wanted the "Wonder Boy," as Chief of Staff Burt Combs used to call him, to adjust press releases that were both acceptable to the President and sounded at least moderately reasonable to the critics in the press. Instead, everyone in the room projected a feeling of genuine support and curiosity. He had to stop looking at the Asian girl, though. God, she was drop-dead gorgeous!

"Thank you, and I mean each of you, for the wonderfully welcoming entrance. You don't know how incredibly sweet it is to actually be among friends who aren't trying to use you or stick a knife in your back at the first opportunity." Marc's words were spoken softly, but with obvious sincerity.

"For those that don't know, I was brought into President Fontaine's Administration," a low growl momentarily interrupted Marc's words coming from the room. "… After working on her campaign. For the record, I was a fool who bought all the progressive bullshit shoveled out at the Columbia University School of Journalism. By the time I spent two months in the White House, starting as a flunky in the Press Office, I could see how many lies were required to support the President's agenda. The original Press Secretary was hospitalized with Lyme's Disease and her deputy was incompetent, owing her position to her race, so I ended up being brought into things someone with so little experience rarely got to see."

Looking around the room, Marc could see everyone was hanging on every word. Then it suddenly occurred to him this briefing would take hours if he didn't speed it up.

"Because of details I won't go into, I ended up privy to a majority of the inner workings of the White House. Frankly, looking back, it disgusts me. After that first two months of all the shine of being there wearing off, me, and I have to say most of the staff in the White House, spent their sixteen plus hours each day simply trying to minimize the amount of damage being done by the administration to the rest of the country."

Glancing at his listeners, he looked for some level of sympathy for his predicament, but saw none.

"Everything I saw and did was classified Top Secret, though I'm not sure any of that matters anymore. I would appreciate it if everyone here would do me that favor of keeping the stuff that may still be sensitive to yourselves."

Again he was met by stony looks and veiled anger.

Mike chose that moment to interject. "All right, everyone. Listen up. Marc here says he did everything he could to minimize the damage the Bitch was doing to our country. I know more than he has told us and when and if it all comes out, we are all going to thank him for everything he did. There's not a single one of us who hasn't been taken in by someone along the way, especially when we were young."

Looking around, half of those shook their heads in agreement.

"I will not go into a lot of what I know, but there are a bunch of other reasons we need to be thankful Marc dropped out of the sky to join us. Just take my word for it. Marc brings with him an accurate history of how we got where we are today and has given us all the tools we're going to need to rebuild this country and even this planet of ours." His look around the room garnered nods from almost everyone present. "I want you to know that I trust him and will lean on him from now on, as well as the rest of you here, to make sure I don't screw up too often. Who's willing to take my word on this?"

Mike hadn't been satisfied to overcome the obvious hatred for the Fontaine administration, and by extension, Marc. He just wanted to convince everyone present to feel the same way he did about Marc. There was something about the way Mike communicated with people that brought automatic trust. The reaction to his words was immediate. Literal applause, similar to what had happened when Marc first entered. It still surprised Mike.

"Well, thanks," Mike said with mild embarrassment. "Now, Marc, what questions do you have?"

Marc was also embarrassed, but said, "Ahem, can someone please tell me what you folks have going on here? I mean, like, you know, is this, like, everybody in your group? Have you lost many to the virus? What's going on here?"

Everyone looked at Mike for the answer, but then looked at Lauren, who had laughed softly. "So this is how you use that Columbia degree. Like, like, like. Somehow, I don't think you used that word to communicate in the White House."

"Aww, Lauren, hell! Gimme a break!" Marc's reversion to little brother status brought much needed humor to the room.

Mike said, "Peter, can you give Marc a Reader's Digest version of what we have here?"

"Sure Mike," Peter said. He then provided a concise situation report (sitrep) to Marc describing what local politics had become and how the neighborhood came together for survival. He saved the description of how the Special Forces operators had found themselves outside of Cronin, Kentucky, for a later time. In fifteen minutes, Peter had finished up and many in the room were much better informed than they had been. This included Lisa and Suzie.

"So Uncle Peter, or anyone, is the Lieutenant Governor in charge of the state since the Governor was assassinated? Or did that pass entirely to Homeland Security and that skunk Coyote Collins who had been appointed by the President's people?" Lisa posed the question. She had been spending much of her time with Doc, dealing with managing the virus threat.

Sean Callahan spoke up. "I think I can take that one." He nodded toward first, his dad, Cronin Police Chief Fred Callahan, then to his fiancé, Linda Sharpe. "Dad has maintained liaison with the existing government structure, at least until about a week ago, when the virus began dropping people like flies."

Winces were seen on several faces around the room at the fly reference.

"We don't know if the acting Governor is alive or dead at this point. Contact with the National Guard in Frankfort stopped four days ago. We, I mean Mike and his staff," Sean received an approving nod from Mike, "have let things settle down for two more weeks in hopes much of the virus floating around in the air will have died in the sunlight or literally blown away. So really, we don't know what the status is of the Homeland Security thugs. I can say that realistically, if the 95% kill rate is anywhere near accurate, we won't have anything to worry about regarding any organized government. For me, personally, I think we're really looking at the man who will rebuild this state and possibly even the entire country."

Sean's piercing gaze at Mike didn't bring the head drop and embarrassment he expected. Instead, he received the confident, penetrating gaze Linda had described to him, but that he had not yet seen himself.

Mike paused and then said, "I guess this is for everyone, but I don't see that we have anything to view as a threat, besides this virus, for the rest of this year and maybe even for a few years to come. In that opinion, I know I am in the minority and I truly pray that I'm correct. I will say that when threats do come, they will probably come fast and furious."

Mike hoped his wishful thinking was working overtime.

***

Peter Worthington Residence
Outside of Cronin, Kentucky
2315 Hours EDT

Laying on her double bed in Uncle Peter's house, Lisa recalled having caught Suzie thinking wistfully about Marc Baxter. Though she had gently teased her best friend about her growing desire to "fuck like bunnies," she privately thought about how Suzie was probably right. People under stress are programmed to want to reproduce to perpetuate the species. She hadn't felt a physical desire for any man, at least not regularly, since breaking up with her boyfriend last year in undergraduate school. Looking back, he had been more of a boy than a man. Cute, horny, immature. He had been fun to play with but not very experienced or someone she felt was a "keeper." Now, probably because of the intense circumstances, she found herself checking out almost every man she encountered. Unfortunately, that number was quite small, having been cloistered in Uncle Peter's house as she was. At least Suzie hadn't caught her watching the tall, young Sergeant that pulled a guard shift while Marc was in quarantine. At one point, he had stripped off his shirt and began knocking out multiple sets of fifty pushups, followed by several calisthenics. He had well sculpted arms and shoulders and an extraordinary "six-pack," which her friends at school would have described as a "twelve-pack."

Lisa asked Linda about him and was surprised when Linda smiled, almost regretfully.

"That's a very interesting, complex and damaged hunk of a man." Linda's words were chosen with care. "Don't get me wrong, he's as good a man and person as any you're likely to run into, but like many people who have killed in combat, he will spend his life fighting demons those actions created."

Linda paused while looking carefully at Lisa for an uncomfortable length of time. She then said, "Lisa, you're very bright and courageous in your own way."

Lisa's stare back at Linda changed to one much more guarded than before.

Linda could see Lisa's reaction, took a deep breath and said, "Because you're as bright and perceptive as you are, you're used to being able to fix or figure out any problem you've encountered. Correct?"

The question startled Lisa, but she nodded.

"Okay," Linda said, "two points here and I'll shut up and wish you well. First, I strongly suggest you don't pursue this kind of man if you're not going to approach him for the long haul. No dalliance here or you'll end up hurting, or maybe even killing him and he could take you along with him."

Lisa's look of shock was as strong as Linda hoped. "Second, hitching your wagon to him will be a wild and difficult ride, but from my perspective, it could be well worth it."

Linda was silent for a full minute as Lisa mulled over what she had said. "Lisa, honey," Linda said with a much more motherly tone, "Hung has been through things you could never imagine. That being said, you are smart and, I hope, patient enough to both gain his trust and understand at least part of what he goes through every single day. He'll move mountains for you, kill for you, and make you the center of his world. Many girls, or even people in general, can't fathom or even tolerate that level of emotion and devotion. If you can, it would be the most beautiful thing to ever enter your life. Coupled, of course, with many terrifying moments to come. But what it really comes down to is if you earn his trust, you must never, ever break it. To break it is to break him. Then the demons come out."

Linda unscrewed her water bottle, took a long drink, and said, "I didn't mean to get all hot and heavy on the subject. Just wanted you to understand, at least a little."

Lisa stared into Linda's eyes for a few seconds before responding, "Thank you."

There was determination and deep thought behind the stare, which made Linda smile.

CHAPTER 6
THE NEW YEAR - PLUS ONE HUNDRED TEN DAYS

Peter Worthington Residence
Outside of Cronin, Kentucky
1015 Hours EDT

Mike looked out the window of his/Peter's office at the deluge of rain falling outside. It was times like this that he really missed the ability to call up the weather radar on his computer. Mike remembered the floods of 1997 and 1998 clearly. He and Lauren had just moved into their new home in January when a week later Central Kentucky experienced its highest-ever rainfall total in 24 hours. Several hours into the torrential rains, he walked down the steps to his new basement only to discover four inches of spring water floating the wall to wall carpeting and dozens of moving boxes that were not yet unpacked. Even though his house was on a high spot at the top of a knoll in the rolling hills of the neighborhood, it had no sump pump and the water table temporarily rose above the floor of his basement. Roads in the area were cut off and flooding was everywhere.

Linda walked into the room as Mike gazed out the window. "I didn't even bother to suit up to come over here this morning, figuring all the viral spores will have been washed out of the air by God's shower. Is this normal for it to rain in Kentucky like this?"

"No," said Mike thoughtfully, "I was just thinking this reminds me of the pattern during the flood of 1997. A storm system trained over us for almost thirty hours, drawing moisture up from the Gulf of Mexico. We had over ten inches of rainfall, with flooding cutting off roads and even washing away some bridges. Fortunately, nobody in this neighborhood lost their homes to the flood, so hopefully that will hold true this time as well. Who do we know that might have access to boats? Although people drown trying to take boats out into flood waters all the time, so let's not set ourselves up to do something dangerously stupid."

Hung walked into Mike's office, dripping wet in his lightweight uniform and boots. Seeing Linda, he said, "LT, there's a little boy that says his momma is about to be washed away in the flood. Can we help?"

Mike answered, "Yes, we can. Four doors down from my house to the west is where Rollie McDermott lives, or used to live, before the virus got him and his family. In his garage is a twenty-one foot fish and ski boat that handles rough water like a dream and has a big 150 horsepower engine on it. It's winterized, but I can get it fired up in a couple of minutes, with fresh gas. Linda, how about you and Hung come with me?"

"Okay, Mike," said Linda. "Hung, are you a good swimmer?"

"Yes ma'am," said Hung. "I was a lifeguard before joining the Army."

Linda shouldn't have been surprised, but she was. Linda was part fish, having just missed out on making the U.S. Olympic swim team. "Okay then, let's go, Mike. Hung, please gather up the boy. We'll take him with us."

Twenty minutes later, Mike's truck backed the boat trailer down a driveway into a slightly calmer eddy of the rushing water of the stream that had turned into a wide river. The motor was already purring loudly with a thick lead rope securing the boat to the trailer. Mike, Hung and the boy climbed into the boat, which had its bilge pump running full speed. The rain continued to come down in sheets, but, fortunately, was bearably warm in the 78 degree heat. Mike's waterproof ball cap kept the water out of his eyes, but the rest of him was soaked, despite him wearing a full rain suit.

With Mike taking the mid-boat control wheel and throttle, he lowered the motor and motioned for Linda to release the lead rope and throw it toward the bow of the boat. The rapid current instantly took control of the boat, but Mike expertly brought it under control with steady throttle and moving it directly into the current to hold it in place. The boy pointed across the fifty-foot channel, upstream to where his one-story ranch home was half submerged in water. Mike slowly fought the raging water, avoiding the larger floating debris as it passed by, and pulled up to the house.

"Hey, Mike," Hung shouted above the roar of the water and rain, pointing. He then turned to the boy and asked, "I see someone waving from that window high on the roof. Boy, is that your mom waving at us?"

The lad excitedly said, "Yes! She and my sister are probably up in the attic. That's an attic window."

Sure enough, Mike and Hung could see a soaking wet woman and small girl waving frantically in the window. Hung waved back at her and turned to Mike. "What do you think?"

"Hung," Mike shouted, "I'm gonna take the boat around to the side of the house in the breakwater, where that window there is above the water. I'll get the boat up close to the window and we'll break it out. You should be able to break or pull out the window with the boathook there and maybe anchor the boat to the windowsill. You may need to go in through the window to bring them out."

Hung responded with a quick thumbs up.

Mike maneuvered the boat to the side of the house where, as he had predicted, the current was much weaker, with the house breaking most of its force. He moved the boat next to the house, giving Hung the chance to ram the boathook through the glass and pull out the entire aluminum frame of the window. He then put the boathook through the opening and lashed it to the anchor points on the side of the boat. A quick spring into the window was followed by Hung disappearing into the house. Three minutes later, Hung reappeared at the window with the mom and little girl in tow. Mike didn't dare leave the boat controls, so Hung climbed back out of the window into the boat before lifting first the little girl and then her mom into the boat.

Once the boathook was released, Mike quickly maneuvered the boat toward the front of the house. Suddenly, the house foundation seemed to crack and the entire house began to drift toward the boat. Seeing this, Mike gunned the engine to shoot back toward the middle of the torrent, just missing being swept downstream by the accelerating house. Another house and a tumbling trailer home could be seen sweeping down the stream in their direction. The rain was too hard for Mike to see much further than these two obstructions moving down the stream. In a quick judgment, Mike gunned the boat across the stream and toward Linda and the waiting trailer. He could see Linda's eyes widen at the speed of his approach. He raised his hand and began moving it in a rapid "saddle up and get moving" circle. Linda jumped down from the trailer and entered the truck and started the engine.

Mike yelled at Hung, "Get ready to snap the nose of this boat to the trailer when I run it onto the skids!"

Hung understood instantly and unsteadily moved toward the bow of the boat. The timing had to be perfect. Mike ran the boat up onto the waiting trailer ramp that was still halfsubmerged in the stream. When the bow touched the front tie-down point, Hung snapped the D-ring into the eye and motioned to Linda. She immediately touched the accelerator, pulling the boat and trailer out of the water. The tumbling trailer home smashed into and was drug along the temporary bank of the rushing water, just missing the precariously balanced boat.

While Mike and Hung were out securing the boat firmly to the trailer and Linda comforted the family inside the truck, Mike said to Hung, "Now THAT will be one to tell your grandchildren!"

Hung rewarded Mike with a big smile.

***

Arriving back at Peter's house, Mike changed into dry clothes and then watched the rain continue to fall. He thought about how blessed he was to be living in a place that had backup power, even if it was only turned on for a few hours each day. Clean running water pumped out of a well, with hot water a few hours of the day, lights and access to a computer with printing capability and fans to at least keep the air moving. Almost everyone else he knew was doing without these luxuries, to include refrigeration. Everyone was spending their entire waking hours avoiding the virus, getting clean water, finding food, and just managing to keep living. It gave him a genuine appreciation for his blessings.

Thinking ahead, when he and Lauren moved back into their home, after the quarantine, he would need to turn on his whole-house propane fired generator and get his water collection system operating. He had a series of fifty-five gallon drums in his basement that were filled from rainwater collected by his roof gutters and could be pumped into his kitchen, two bathrooms, and his master bedroom shower. Despite these flooding rains, he foresaw times when it would not rain enough to fill his needs and he would have to ration drinking water and even hand-carry buckets of water inside for filtration and to run his toilets. Food should never be a problem with Lauren growing a large garden every year plus all the long-term storage food he had purchased from Peter. But again, he had prepared for these things and most had not. What about them?

Little Kevin, Mike's runner, came into Mike's office, in a panic and gulping for air. "Mr. Mike! Come quick. A lady is about to have a baby!"

"Where, Kevin?"

"In the greenhouse," said Kevin.

Mike stopped to check Lisa and Suzie's workspace but did not find them. He then hurried to the greenhouse door and into chaos amid the continuous screams of a woman in labor. The Special Forces Operator standing guard at the door had brought the Hispanic lady into the greenhouse and had her sit on the couch. Obviously, her water had broken, and she was lying on the wet couch with her legs spread, screaming loudly, in between panting heavily. Mike took one quick breath, thought about the mandatory first aid class he had taken during his orientation to be an instructor at the Community College, and barked at the soldier, "Get me some clean towels, soap and water, rubbing alcohol and something to clamp off the cord. Can you do that for me?"

The obviously uncomfortable Operator nodded and moved out to comply with Mike's orders.

"Kevin," Mike said. "I want you to go find Doc, or Lisa and Suzie if you can't find him. Go!" Off Kevin went at a dead run.

Mike walked over to the woman and asked, "What's your name, sweetheart?"

Through her panting, she said, "Maria. You have done this before, Senor?"

Mike gave her a reassuring smile while patting her soaking head with his hand. "Sure, I've had lots of training at this. Now, how long has it been between contractions?"

"I don't know! A few minutes ago and they started coming quicker and quicker!" she said between gasps.

The soldier brought a case of bottled water, a bar of soap, a bottle of rubbing alcohol and some clean towels. Mike said, "Okay, Sergeant, I need you to take one of those towels and quickly wipe down the couch, then help me put another towel underneath her. Got it?"

"Yes sir, Mike." He did as directed and actually had a look of satisfaction on his face when the towel was smoothed under her bottom and between her legs."

"What about the clamp?"

The Sergeant held up a woodworking spring clamp.

"That'll do just fine," said Mike. "Please rinse it off with the rubbing alcohol and set it on a clean towel."

"Maria," asked Mike, "is this your first child?" She nodded yes. "Did you take any classes for this?"

"Si, Senor Mike. I take classes where they taught us to breathe and push, but not too much unless they say to. My husband would be here to help, but he died." She broke into tears until the next contraction and she temporarily forgot all about losing her husband.

Mike gave Maria all the coaching he could remember from his First Aid class until he could see the child's head poking out. "Okay, Maria," Mike said, "time to really push." She gave one mighty effort and out popped the newborn boy, being trailed by the bloody umbilical cord and, after a few seconds, finally the placenta came out. Mike deftly grabbed the spring clamp and affixed it to the chord before wiping the baby's mouth with a soft microfiber towel. The child didn't move. Then it started to turn blue. After a few seconds, Mike turned the baby over to help loosen umbilical fluid and then began to give soft puffs into the baby's mouth. He then began to gently press on the baby's chest in a regular rhythmic motion. Seconds later, the baby coughed and cried loudly, then began to return to a normal pink color.

Doc burst into the greenhouse and stopped in amazement at the sound of the crying baby and the sight of Mike holding the child in his hands while wiping it off with the towel. Doc's eyes took in the wood clamp on the umbilical cord, still attached to the placenta. With a huge smile, Doc said, "It looks like you've got things very well in hand, Mike. Would you like some help?"

"Thank God, Doc! Never happier to see someone before. I've about run out of the First Aid Course instructions I remember."

Maria looked at Mike with a mix of amazement and consternation. "Senor Mike, I thought you said you had done this before?"

"Maria," Mike said kindly, "you and me and God just delivered your healthy baby boy and now there's a real medical person to make sure things are all right! It's a miracle!"

"Thanks be to God," said Maria reverently.

Over the next two days, Linda and her security force affected two additional rescues. Five deaths by drowning were reported in the area and over a dozen survivors had to abandon their homes and move into homes no longer occupied and on higher ground. Following the events of this day, word of what Mike and his group in the neighborhood had done for their neighbors would quickly spread by word of mouth. Mike's own reputation grew by leaps and bounds.

CHAPTER 7
THE NEW YEAR – PLUS ONE HUNDRED TEN DAYS

Hunting Cabin
Outside Denali National Forest, Alaska
2015 Hours Local Time

Cho sat, quietly meditating in the rustic, but comfortable hunting lodge. He had almost returned his heart rate and breathing to normal after having worked for two hours on his intense martial arts training routine. For the first several weeks, he had spent most of his waking hours working strictly on survival. From cutting and dragging wood for the massive fireplace to hauling water in from the stream, there was almost always something to do, particularly during the expanding hours of daylight. Spring was slow to come to the area of Alaska around Mount Denali, formerly known as Mount McKinley. Although there were a few days that crept above freezing, there was still plenty of snow and the icy winds that required him to wear the heavy-weight long underwear underneath his clothes and parka, even inside of the cabin. Power, of course, had been lost shortly after news of the virus swept around the world.

Two weeks earlier, he had driven the Suburban into the small town of Healy, where the tourists frequently boarded small planes for sightseeing in the area. There he learned the Governor had ordered the Alaska National Highway blocked fifty miles north of Anchorage to prevent the virus from infecting everyone in the state. All stores and shops were closed in the area and the crucial, life-sustaining boat and truckloads of supplies that were regularly shipped in, had stopped completely.

Cho spent approximately two hours daily listening to the shortwave radio he had purchased. All commercial communications had ceased when the electricity stopped, so rationing of the gasoline allowed for about 2 hours per day, every other day, of power to charge the backup batteries. At least it could continue for another month or so.

Cho had begun to plan his exit from the area as soon as reports filtered in that the virus deaths were slowing. Semi-official announcements to stay in place for two years had been changed to only a year. Unofficial speculation was that the more realistic time was six months, so long as they kept a careful distance from other people who were not verified as "clean."

***

Basement in a Home
Outside of Frankfort, Kentucky
1210 Hours EDT

Kerry DuBois woke from unconsciousness, wondering if he was alive or this was a terrible dream. He croaked, "Hello? I need some water." No one responded. God dammit, he thought with bitterness, someone should be there to help him!

Breathing deeply through his nose, since his throat seemed to be only partially functional, brought more focus to his mind. He remembered he was in a basement outside of Frankfort and all the terrors of the past couple of months came flooding back into his memory. The most recent terror was Tank choking him into unconsciousness, although at the time he was convinced Tank was simply killing him. Waking up to being alone was far worse than if Tank had actually done so. Kerry was never alone. There was always someone around that he could convince, cajole, or otherwise serve him whatever he needed or wanted. Adding insult to injury, when Tank choked him out, Kerry had lost bodily control in his pants. He had to crawl over to the laundry area of the basement and found another ill-fitting pair of jeans, but no underwear.

Cursing his luck, Kerry crawled to the foot of the stairs and, on hands and knees, climbed up to the main floor of the old lady's house. The door at the top of the stairs was open. Even though there was still plenty of food and water in the basement, and the threat of the virus was immensely strong outside of the house, he couldn't bear to contemplate staying there by himself. There would be no one to talk to or verbally jab into doing something interesting. He simply could not bear to be … alone.

At the top of the stairs Kerry carefully peeked over the edge and could see the front door, twenty feet away, open to the outside with sunlight streaming in. There was a foul smell coming from the left of the front door where the decomposing body of the old lady, mostly just bones, lay crumpled on the carpet. He didn't like awful smells, which motivated him to raise from a crouch to stand hunched over and move quietly to the open doorway. The air coming into the door was much better, but the stench to his left was also stronger. Not seeing anyone visible through the door, he took a chance and stumbled quickly outside to crouch behind the brick and wood railing making up the front edge of the porch. It was a cold, clear day, causing him to look up at the unfamiliar sky like a fool watching a shiny object. It only lasted a few seconds before his paranoia pushed him back in fear.

The road out in front of the house was quiet, with nothing visible coming in either direction. His eye caught a flying bird, some type of small sparrow, flutter into view to snatch a bug out of the air. The smells of early spring were wafting through the air, making him doubt any of the virus was still a threat. He took his first steps outside of the porch overhang when he heard something approaching down the road from the right. Returning to the dubious safety of the porch, he finally detected a person's giggling, gurgling voice before he saw what used to be a woman staggering in his direction. In absolute terror, he disappeared back into the house, slammed the door to the basement stairs behind him, and fell down the stairs, landing in a heap. It was several minutes before he remembered he hadn't locked the door. This caused him to sprint/stagger back up the stairs to lock himself in.

Treating his cuts and bruises with the first aid kit, he shuddered as he thought about the apparition he had seen. The staggering figure would haunt his memories forever. It was as close to a real-life zombie as he could imagine. He vowed to remain in the basement for at least another month, maybe more. He also sealed the door with a hammer and nails, just to make sure none of them could break through.

***

Outside of Frankfort, Kentucky
1405 Hours EDT

For the third time, Tank was becoming disgusted with Blondi and his whining. His stern warning to the sniveling coward an hour earlier had apparently only sunk in for forty-five minutes. They had left the safety of the basement because Tank wasn't sure Kerry was dead, but either way, he didn't want to smell the slimy excuse for a human being any longer. He had planned to leave alone, but Blondi convinced him that four eyes were better than two to spot threats and dangers in the now unknown world. That had proven to be correct, as Blondi had seen the zombie staggering in their direction from between two houses when Tank's attention was focused on a thin trail of smoke visible one quarter of a mile down the road. Blondi's warning gave Tank time to draw his pistol and kill the pitiful creature twenty yards from where they stood. Both blessed their lucky stars they were standing upwind from the thing and quickly walked away, adjusting their course and ensuring they walked into the wind.

"Tank, tell me again where we're going. Please?" Blondi caught himself. His first few words were spoken with a demanding tone brought on by fear and frustration. Tired and frightened as he was, he was cagy enough to know how quickly Tank could kill him. Like a child who knew he pressed his dad too far, Blondi tried his best to walk on eggshells around Tank.

Tank let the question hang in the air as he surveyed the road that meandered down the gentle hill to a curve at the foot. In an abundance of caution, he stood motionless behind the trunk of a tree just beginning to sprout buds from the tips of its branches. The thin column of smoke originated right around the bend, just out of sight. The shot killing the zombie a hundred yards behind them would have alerted whoever had lit the fire. Remaining motionless, Tank finally softly said, "I told you, Blondi, I'm heading in towards town to a small warehouse I leased. Ya know, full of important stuff for redistribution."

Tank continued, "You remember, before this damned Chinese virus started killing almost everybody on the planet, I had a great contract to store lots of essential things for our wonderful Regional Governor, Coyote Collins when he was appointed by the Fontaine Administration. Was working on collecting stuff for redistribution and storing in my warehouses even outside of Kentucky when the fuckin' virus hit. Well, I'm headed to one of those warehouses now. It should be another couple or three miles down this road toward town. Now shut yer trap, and…"

Tank stopped abruptly as his eye caught a slight movement at the bend of the road below. After another minute's careful examination, Tank chuckled softly in appreciation.

"I got you, you sonofabitch!" What Tank had seen was the momentary reflection off of a stainless steel rifle barrel. It was in a tree blind screened by a brown, black and muted green camouflage tarp and held a sniper dressed in a mishmash of camouflage clothing with a black knit cap. "Without the sun on yer barrel and that bright black cap, I'da missed ya."

Tank turned to Blondi. "Now here's what we're gonna do." Tank had Blondi's full attention now.

"I'm a gonna work my way around to that line of piney trees and get up nice and close to that ole boy's tree stand. In exactly one hour from now, go ahead and set the stopwatch on your fancy wristwatch, yer gonna step out and start walking slowly down the road in his direction. He ain't gonna shoot at ya till you get within fifty yards or so, hell, why should he? You got over a hundred yards to walk to keep his attention fixed on you and, shit, he's probably only hunting zombies, anyway!"

With every word Tank spoke, Blondi's eyes got bigger and his fear grew. "Shit, Tank! You're using me as bait? Well, fuck that!"

In one motion, Tank's enormous paw grabbed the front of Blondi's shirt, drug him to his feet behind the tree trunk, and with his other hand slapped his face, hard.

Blondi could feel the hot breath in his face from two inches away as Tank said, "Listen to me, you fuckin' little worm. Without me, you're a dead man anyway, so do what you're told or I will hunt you down and kill you my-own-self. Got it?"

Not trusting his voice as he barely avoided peeing in his pants, Blondi just nodded.

"Good. Now, one hour, you start walking."

Tank turned and stealthily moved away from the tree and toward the row of pines.

Blondi quivered for most of the time as he waited for the hour to expire. When his watch alarm went off, he jerked, thought momentarily about running away in the opposite direction. Instead, he began trudging toward the thinning smoke from the fire. He hadn't gone fifty yards when he heard a shot followed by two more quick shots. He jerked reflexively at each one, before it occurred to him he hadn't been hit. A few moments later, he could see Tank walk around the corner and motion him vigorously to hurry and join him. He broke into a trot and covered the one hundred yards in what seemed like only a few seconds. His breath came in gasps.

"Here," Tank said brusquely, "carry these." He shoved a shotgun and a 9 mm pistol rudely into his hands and Tank started hurrying down the road.

Near the small fire, Blondi could see the figure of a mid-sized boy laying in a pool of blood, his head having been partly blown off by Tank's heavy pistol. In the tree stand, another larger boy's body was briefly glimpsed by Blondi with blood dripping from it. Before he could even think about the horror, Blondi was on his knees puking out everything he had eaten that day, plus probably the past three. The gags and shudders came in waves and continued for over a minute before he again felt Tank's rough paw grab the back of his shirt and neck, dragging him to his feet.

"Grow up, pretty boy. You're in a real jungle now, so you're gonna hafta get used to the look and even smell of blood. Now pick up those guns and come on. There's probably some other yokels heading this way to see what all the shooting was about."

CHAPTER 8
THE NEW YEAR – PLUS ONE HUNDRED TWELVE DAYS

Peter Worthington Residence
Outside of Cronin, Kentucky
0915 Hours EDT

Lisa and Suzie were excited about the prospect of going outside for the first time since the virus began its devastation. They, along with Doc decided that since they had been vaccinated for over two weeks, there had been no reported new infections in their community for several weeks, and early spring had been uncharacteristically warm and sunny for two straight days it was time to smell fresh air once again. Just feeling the sun on their faces and fresh air coming into their nose was heavenly! Their first stop was the security post at the entrance to the neighborhood. It was being manned by Security Detail Team 3, led by Sergeant Hunter "Hung" Jenkins.

Hung had gotten his nickname during his initial Special Forces training for being particularly well endowed below the waist. In the all-men environment of training it had been kind of funny and he just sloughed it off even though it was not something he liked. The name had stuck like Velcro to him and he had to admit; it had definitely helped his reputation with the ladies. "Hell," he thought, "with most of these girls, I don't have to say a word to end up in bed with them."

Hung was selected, along with seven other operators, to provide security and an initial staff for Sean Callahan's TOP SECRET covert operation inside of the United States. While he recovered from the loss of his lower leg through an

IED, Sean had been recruited to command a Special Forces Battalion that was to operate inside the United States against "subversives." He had only agreed to the job because his unwritten orders, conveyed by a very squared-away Command Sergeant Major, were to drag out formation of the Battalion for as long as necessary.

No one at SOCOM wanted to see the Special Forces operating against American citizens. The virus struck the world before anything more than preliminary organizational plans could happen, stranding the SF Operators and Lieutenant Colonel (LTC) Callahan at his parent's home outside of Cronin, Kentucky.

Hung had initially been terrified when he arrived in Kentucky and was introduced to the LT. She was a civilian member of his SF Security force for LTC Callahan's operation. He knew she had been one of the first female "A-Team" leaders in Special Forces who also had an outstanding reputation. He could see political correctness and even court martial in his future as soon as she heard his nickname. Fortunately, like every soldier that came in contact with Linda Sharpe, he found her to be totally professional, but was also someone easy to trust. She had a way of asking questions with no pre-judgment or personal prejudice. The LT was an officer, of course, but she had been in combat, sent enemies to meet their maker, and had received a Purple Heart. She had "walked the walk." During the few weeks he had known her, she was one of the few he felt he could talk to, at least a little. When he confided in her he had lost his girlfriend after nearly choking her out during an intense PTSD flashback, she had looked him in the eyes not with horror, but with compassion and empathy. That sealed the deal and his trust in her. Something civilians couldn't understand.

"Put it back in your pants, boys," came a voice from behind Hung and three civilian members of Security Team 3. Hung immediately recognized the voice as the Doc. Two of his younger team members were momentarily shocked at the words, especially considering two of the prettiest girls they had ever seen were accompanying the medic. Their faces melted from minor shock to hesitant pleasure at being included in authentic SF banter.

"Who have you got there Doc?" Hung asked with a widening grin. Over his shoulder Hung ordered, "At least two of you better have your eyes watching for trouble. Got it?"

"Yes, sir, Sergeant," both young men shouted out in unison.

The other team member, married and in his early 30s, nodded approval and divided his attention between the two young security members and the newcomers.

"These two ladies," the Doc lingered on the term ladies for emphasis, "are part of my medical team and advisors to Mike on this killer bug. They are the reason you're not wearing masks and SCALP suits anymore. Both Ph.D.'s in biology and the smartest ladies you're ever likely to meet."

Hung's jaw nearly dropped open. That much beauty with that much smarts all in two packages?

The Doc chuckled softly. "Relax, Sergeant. They don't bite and can even hold a respectable conversation with someone like you and me. Let me introduce you to Lisa and Suzie. They're getting outside in the fresh air for the first time since this whole viral mess started." Hung quickly introduced his three team members to the visitors.

"Is everyone feeling okay here?" Lisa asked the friendly question in a normal conversational tone, but was watching everyone in the security team closely. She hoped Hung didn't notice her gaze had lingered on his smiling face a little longer than the others. It was natural to spend more time looking at him since he was the leader of the security team. Wasn't it?

Lisa couldn't help but blush a little and averted her eyes before hearing Suzie snicker softly under her breath. Damn that girl! She missed absolutely nothing! At least Lisa hadn't allowed her eyes to drift below his waist during the inspection. She wasn't a virgin, but was far from someone she would consider experienced with men. She just hadn't met someone she was comfortable exploring on that level.

"Nothing new to report, Doc." Hung launched into his typical oral brief, presuming Doc would carry it back to Linda. "No people out wandering around today, but we're really appreciating the sunshine. And, of course, not wearing any MOPP gear.

Hung moved his gaze away from Doc to Lisa. "Where you folks headed next? The rest of Team Three is out patrolling the perimeter, so make sure you don't try anything that looks evasive. They'll see you clearly so long as you walk around normally. Wouldn't want anybody getting shot at unnecessarily." His smile said he was kidding, but only a little.

"I wouldn't want to get shot either," said Lisa. "Still a lot of things I want to do and see." Finishing the last word, she immediately found her eyes begin to drift below the level of Hung's eyes before she caught herself. Thank God she hadn't continued THAT line of view.

"Lisa, Suzie, you ready to continue our tour?" Doc was one of the more perceptive SF Team members, all of whom were very observant.

At their nods, Doc led them along the perimeter of the neighborhood, following the wellworn pathway used by the security teams. He made a mental note to remind LT the patrols shouldn't use the same pathway every time they made the circle around the neighborhood. That's poor operational security or OPSEC and could set them up for an ambush.

"Everything looks so peaceful," Lisa said as they came to the creek along the back side of the neighborhood.

"Enjoy it, ladies," Doc said softly as his eyes moved constantly around the perimeter.

"But don't let its looks deceive you into complacency. Consider this a training walk as well. You tell me, what should you be looking for?"

Suzie responded quickly to the question. "Any movement first, then anything out of place. Going from nearest to furthest before focusing additional attention on any potential surveillance or ambush positions."

Doc stopped suddenly and looked Suzie over carefully. "It sounds, young lady, like you've had some training. Have you?" The question was asked casually, but with an edge to it.

Without missing a beat, Suzie smiled and chuckled. "Growing up, my grandfather, who emigrated here from Taiwan, was an infantry officer for Chiang Kai-shek. He and my grandmother raised me. I think since he didn't have a son, he constantly drilled me with military tactics and how to handle any threat. He even taught me some hand-to-hand combat combinations, many of which are lethal and, some very messy. He always said, 'there are threats behind every blade of grass. If you want to survive during hard times, remember these lessons!'" Suzie had repeated the quote using her notional grandfather's heavy accent and gravelly voice, in heavily accented English.

Lisa looked at Suzie with a little shock and wonder.

Doc visibly relaxed, accepting her explanation and smooth delivery. "Okay, sounds like your grandfather knew what he was talking about. Now, maybe you ladies can tell me what dangerous animals are likely to be in our vicinity?"

It was Lisa's turn to grin. "Oh, you mean the two-legged kind or the slimier ones like copperheads or fiddler spiders?"

"Copperheads?" Suzie asked.

"Copperheads are venomous snakes partial to these here waters." Lisa had slipped into her Kentucky drawl to add emphasis. "And fiddler spiders are technically known as brown recluse spiders, and were first identified in Kentucky, but got the name fiddler spiders because of the dark patch on their back in the shape of a fiddle, or violin. Those things are very poisonous and can kill a child or unhealthy adult, but will certainly make their victim very sick."

This brought a soft laugh from Doc. "LT warned me you two were quick and you don't disappoint."

Both girls looked at each other before breaking into soft laughter. Doc looked them over approvingly, basking in the sound of people laughing with enjoyment for the first time in a very long time.

***

Hunting Cabin Outside Denali National Forest, Alaska
1010 Hours Local Time

Cho pulled his Chevy Yukon into the driveway of his cabin and, with more than a little frustration, slammed it into park. He had driven South on Highway 3 to see if it was clear only to find the roadblock still in place. Whatever devastation had happened to the rest of the world, the Alaskan governor's quick actions had stopped the virus from moving much North of Anchorage. Cho had spoken with the National Guardsmen blocking the road from a distance of 50 meters, where he encountered the bright yellow saw horses blocking the highway and a sign that said, "STOP OR YOU WILL BE SHOT."

When Cho got out of his car with his hands up, a soldier with a bull horn casually told him the road was closed by order of the Governor and he should turn around. He had heard the same message when he tried to drive North of Healy. This time Cho shouted, "Heh, friend. I'm starting to run out of food. Any idea when the road might open up? And who is in charge these days?"

Rather than the, "I don't know," that Cho was expecting, the soldier said, "Well, since most of state government, including the Governor, have died from the virus, our National Guard Commander, now up in Fairbanks, is running things. He may open the roads to those that want to leave Alaska in two to three weeks. Can't say for sure. Guess he wants anyone that wants to get out the state to do so before they eat any more of the available food. Don't know what to tell you, but you may want to come back this way in three weeks or so. That is, if you've got enough gas to return if it's still closed."

"Should I just come back here then, with all the food I have left, and camp out and wait?" Cho's question brought a troubled look to the soldier.

"No, orders are to let no one set up camp near the road. Sorry." The soldier didn't sound sorry, merely polite.

Safely back at his cabin with enough gas left to refill his gas tank one more time, Cho decided he could give it another month. He had killed a moose and caribou with his rifle and was able to drag back a lot of the meat. When he went back to the carcass for a second load, he and the bear that was feeding on it decided he had gotten enough on the first trip. He might also stop by the Healy airport first and see what opportunities might be there to fly out.

CHAPTER 9
THE NEW YEAR – PLUS ONE HUNDRED TWENTY-FIVE DAYS

Peter Worthington Residence
Outside of Cronin, Kentucky
1015 Hours EDT

Only a few days after Suzie and Lisa enjoyed their first tour of the neighborhood, the weather turned unusually harsh. Freezing temperatures and even several bouts of a few inches of snow fell on Central Kentucky, making life both hungry and miserable for the survivors. Lisa complained, "Damn it! I was just getting used to wearing short sleeves and really looking forward to letting my legs breathe fresh air, and now it's snowing again! What the hell!?!"

Suzie glanced up from her chair by the window. She had been reviewing a book detailing the history of the Founding Fathers. "Did you know," abruptly changing the subject, "that Alexander Hamilton was a bastard orphan from the British West Indies and was an aide-de-camp to General Washington during the Revolutionary War? He wrote most of the Federalist Papers!"

Suzie's enthusiasm for American history always amazed Lisa.

"Okay, I get it," muttered Lisa. "Quit complaining when I'm sitting here with my best friend, in a warm house with enough food to eat and free of a deadly virus. Honestly, girl, sometimes I need a real kick in my tushy to appreciate what I have."

"Tushy?" Suzie asked curiously.

This brought a laugh from Lisa. "Yeah, you know, Tushy. Ass? Booty? Butt? Buttocks? Bum? Backside? Bottom? Hind end? Gluteus Maximus? Derriere? Fanny? Posterior? Rump? Tail End? Place for a 'Kick me' sign?" Running out of synonyms off the top of her head, Lisa giggled and couldn't restrain her smile.

"Kick me sign?"

"Never mind," Lisa said with another laugh. "Did you finally get to corner Marc and actually talk to him?" Lisa's question was given in a soft, conspiratorial tone to keep her words from carrying to the nearby kitchen.

Suzie's face instantly froze into what Lisa thought of as her 'inscrutable face.' Almost as quickly, she dropped her eyes and allowed a small smile to appear on her face. Lisa was the first and only genuine friend she had ever had. She reveled in the joy of being able to trust someone completely, but still had to remind herself that was even possible.

"Yes, sister. I talked to him for sixteen glorious minutes in the greenhouse last evening. For someone so smart and who has bedded many girls, he was almost like a little boy. So innocent, yet one with his eyes wide-open. He has been taken advantage of and emotionally hurt before and prays that I will not do that."

"What?" Lisa whispered the question with wide eyes and dropped jaw.

"Yes, he has decided he wants me, even though he knows at least some of my background." Suzie measured Lisa's reaction. "Just before two of the soldiers entered the greenhouse, he told me Mike told him they had forced me to become a spy for Chinese intelligence and to do unspeakable things for that work or they would kill me. His response was if anyone, anyone ever threatened me again, he would kill them." Suzie paused, then said, "And he would. I am certain. Efficiently, and very brutally."

Both women looked at each other, thinking about this revelation.

Suzie continued, "I have done nothing to or for Marc to make him feel this way, but he does."

Lisa had known Suzie had an innate ability to tell if someone was lying to her, but that skill or gift obviously ran a lot deeper.

"I have met no one, including my parents that felt that way about me. Yes, Lisa, I love him and can tell that he loves me."

"Well, what did you say when the guys walked in on you?" Once again, Lisa was amazed how quickly Suzie seemed to adapt instantly to any situation.

"I said, thank you for doing that for me, Marc. Can we discuss this sometime tomorrow? After I have had time to do some research?"

"He looked me in the eyes and I could see understanding, just like I see in your eyes. Lisa, He's not even a sister!" With that, Suzie rose and gave Lisa a big hug.

***

Peter Worthington's Residence
Outside of Cronin, KY
1520 Hours EDT

Mike looked up from his desk and saw Linda Sharpe enter his office after a quick knock on his door. "Come in, Linda. Please have a seat."

Of course Mike didn't want to see the worst days of the virus come back, but he did sometimes wistfully think about when Linda and a few other very attractive ladies used to come into his office wearing only underwear or a thin robe after a decontamination shower. Unlike Lauren, Linda oozed sensuality, he thought regretfully.

"What news from Frankfort?" Mike knew Linda had taken a patrol to the state Capitol in Frankfort to determine the situation involving Kentucky State Government.

"Commander, there is no longer an organized government in Frankfort or anywhere else we could determine. When we stopped by yesterday, the Capitol Building's door was swinging open with a hideous smell of death coming out of it. In another month or two, we may want to send in a team in full MOPP gear to search for survivors, but I doubt we will find any. The Governor's mansion was locked up, but showed no signs of life. Any semblance of government has gone off to the hills to wait things out. Just before dark, we drove over to the Boone National Guard Center and the State Emergency Operations Center. Both the National Guard Headquarters building and the EOC building were shut and locked, with no one answering our knocks. Just to be sure, I had the SUV drive away and sent a two-man patrol back to check out both for lights. They spent the night and saw no movement or sign of life. I suspect the surviving National Guard guys loaded up whatever food would fit into their military vehicles and drove off to find their families."

"Did you see any survivors during your trip?"

"Yes, Sir, we did. There were only a handful, and they looked pretty pitiful. They appear to be immune to the virus, but had been going into houses containing dead people to find food. Most seemed to suffer from serious dysentery, so the doc gave them some pills and told them to get soap to wash their hands and their bodies, then to be sure to boil water before drinking it. They wanted us to 'take them home' with us, but were told that wasn't possible. I'm not sure what you want us to tell this type of survivor from now on and I didn't have an appropriate answer off the top of my head other than learn to be self-sufficient."

"Linda, what are the odds one or more small groups of NG guys loaded up weapons and food and moved somewhere else to stage for future pillaging operations?"

"Truthfully, Sir, I'd say they would be low considering the small number of probable survivors and that most men will only want to go home to take care of their own. Doesn't mean there wouldn't be one or two individuals or groups, though."

"Okay," Mike said. "That being the case, what would you think about coming up with a plan between you and Sean to send out an expedition to go there and collect some military equipment? I'm thinking that under the circumstances Sean, as active U.S. Army, would be expected to collect unused resources for the benefit of whatever constituted authority is available. I think we're the constituted authority, and I'd much rather see that material and supplies brought under our control before someone else decides to pillage and cause trouble. Thoughts?"

Linda's face brightened and even showed a new level of respect. "Sir, I think that's a great idea. Let me discuss this with Sean and we can get back to you. Tomorrow late afternoon soon enough?"

"Sounds good to me. Thank you, LT." Mike's smile and first use of her nickname stuck in her mind as she walked toward the door.

"Oh, and Linda," Mike asked. "Please have the team leader of whatever security team is on duty come to see me? I think it's time to distribute some plants we have available for gardens."

"Yes, Sir, Commander."

***

Ten minutes later, the team leader found Mike, Lauren, and Elizabeth "Liz" Worthington going over a listing of all the plants and seeds that had been carefully nurtured and stored in the greenhouse outside the Worthington house.

"Mike," Lauren said, as they both looked at the large binder containing the accounting sheets. "These are great for what we have just here in Peter's warehouse and greenhouse, but they include nothing being kept by the surrounding farms affiliated with us or even in any of the neighborhood homes. Don't you think it should include their stuff with ours?" Lauren stopped to cough, showing ugly congestion in her lungs.

Just then, Peter Worthington dropped in.

"Peter," Mike said with enthusiasm. "Just the man I was looking for."

"Uh, oh. That sounds ominous and like something involving a lot of work all rolled up into one." Peter's comment was accompanied by a cautious smile.

"We've run into a problem I hadn't expected, but should have," Mike said. "So far, everyone around here has been pretty much living off of food and stuff they have stored, supplemented by food you had stored here. There have been no issues with people having big hearts and sharing what they have. But…"

Mike let the word trail off, leaving the elephant in the room.

"But," Peter said, "that won't continue indefinitely and since I have the vast majority of the long-term food stored here, when will I start being picky who I'm willing to share it with?"

Mike smiled and chuckled. "No, that isn't my concern. I'm looking at the bigger, longterm picture. Affiliated farmers and others among the survivors have things they don't need or will trade for things they need more. What we have now is a de facto bartering system, since money is essentially worthless."

Peter's face lit up. "Now I'm following you! Yes, we need to develop a system of credits to use to exchange goods and services. I shun from using the Federal Reserve as an example, but that's the type of thing you're looking for?"

"Yes, I think so," said Mike cautiously. "I'm not really sure what, exactly, I am looking for, but I see the problem of surrounding farmers having seeds and other means for everyone to plant to add to our food supply. And I don't think I want to demand anyone to do or give up anything without just compensation. Would you mind gathering whoever you need to work on the problem and get back to me?"

"No problem, Mike. It may take several days to come up with one or more workable options."

***

Peter Worthington's Residence
Outside of Cronin, KY
1920 Hours EDT

"Heh, big guy," Lisa said in her best Humphrey Bogart movie voice, "think you'd have time to show a girl around the area sometime soon?"

When Lisa saw Hung enter Uncle Peter's house and give Mike a quick briefing, she seized her chance to talk to him and waited outside the great room in ambush.

Hung turned to Lisa with first a look of surprise, quickly followed by amusement.

"Why sure, sweetheart," Hung responded in a hilarious copy of Groucho Marx. "Where, exactly would you like to go? Paris? London? Versailles?"

This time it was Lisa who was surprised. "Do you have access to an airliner now, or are you talking about Versailles (she pronounced it Ver-sales), Kentucky?"

"Oh, so you have seen a local map or two?" Hung asked with a big, knowing smile.

This entire conversation threw Lisa off track. She had not expected him to be articulate and obviously well educated. Not to mention his ability to engage in playful social sparring. Suddenly, Lisa felt herself to be the one lacking experience in this situation.

Hung assessed her reaction quickly and in his normal deep voice said, "It's Lisa, right?" When she nodded her head, he continued, "I actually have tomorrow off from assigned duties, so if you would like to scout around the area, I'd love to provide you with an armed escort. It begs a question, though. If I can't get access to a motor vehicle, would you prefer to hike the area or are you up for a bicycle ride?"

Lisa had spent her entire life being quicker and brighter than virtually everyone else she met. Suzie was, of course, an exception, as were Mike Broehm, Uncle Peter, Doc and Marc Baxter. She was stunned, intrigued, and surprisingly turned on to find this gorgeous and reportedly well-endowed man was that mentally sharp as well.

"I think by foot would be fun, if a vehicle isn't available," she said slowly. "I could probably borrow some kind of vehicle from Uncle Peter."

"No, don't bother," Hung said quickly. "I'm pretty sure I can get one of the SUVs from our motor pool, so long as I'm willing to run some errand or other. That shouldn't take much time."

They agreed to meet outside the Worthington residence at 0800 in the morning.

At 8:00 a.m. a black Chevy Suburban with dark, tinted windows pulled up in front of Peter's house. It had hardly come to a stop when Hung jumped out and walked swiftly to the front door. Lisa had been waiting just inside, wearing tight, mid-calf high pale stretch-pants, a tank top and thin short sleeve blouse. She opened the door and greeted Hung with a big smile.

"M'lady, your chariot awaits," Hung said, returning her smile and offering his arm.

"I true gentleman, I see," Lisa said with a small smile.

They walked down the short flight of steps from the porch. "I'm impressed to see you in hiking shoes instead of other choices you might have made."

"Why thank you, Hunter. Oh, what would you like me to call you?"

For the first time in her presence, Hung actually blushed. "Well, M'lady, most everyone has been calling me Hung or Sergeant for so long, you're welcome to use that. Or Hunter, or whatever you name would like to use.

Hopefully, that isn't something profane, but for you, I'd even answer to 'duffus,' but if anyone else were to use that it would cause a fight." His smile was infectious, with his twinkling blue eyes.

"For now, I think I'll call you 'Huntsman,' until something else comes to mind. You know, after the movie Snow White and the Huntsman. Did you see it?"

The look on his face shadowed his negatively shaking head.

"It's a Sci-Fi/Fantasy action movie modeled after the Snow White story, combined with a former soldier battling an evil queen. You kind of remind me of Chris Hemsworth, the actor who plays the Huntsman."

The confused expression on Hung's face deepened.

"He's the hero of the story. You know, he played Thor in the Marvel Comics movies? Oh, never mind. I'm just being silly."

This rewarded Lisa with a smile from Hung. "M'lady, you can call me whatever you like. Shall we set forth on our quest?"

Hung held the SUV door open and closed it after she was seated inside. "How about a slow drive around the neighborhood, then around the surrounding area?"

"That sounds nice. It's been years since I've been here visiting Uncle Peter."

"Just a reminder, any movement or people that you see, please let me know right away. And don't leave the vehicle without checking with me first." Lisa gave Hung a surprised look.

"These are all just security SOPs, or Standard Operating Procedures. For this trip, I'm treating you like one of my Protectees; VIPs I would provide top-level security for when moving around hostile territory."

"With all the death, is there really a security threat out here?" Lisa's surprise was expected by Hung.

"Yes, ma'am. There is. There are still some zombies wandering around and we've gotten some intel from a few survivors of shootings and anarchy within the surrounding 100 klicks or so."

"Klicks?"

"Oh, that's military shorthand for kilometers," Hung said with a chuckle. "The military is famous for having almost another language."

Lisa was struck by seeing the countryside completely barren of cars or movement by humans of any kind. Hung drove the SUV West along meandering country roads through horse farm country. On two farms along the road, Hung stopped the vehicle and got out.

"You're welcome to get out, if you like, but it'll be a little unpleasant," Hung said in a sad voice.

Hung walked to a very small pasture where two starving horses were standing, heads down. Lying dead in the pasture were half a dozen horses, including a small foal. Hung went directly to the gate and opened it and propped it to remain open. He then returned to the truck, holding the passenger door for Lisa go get back in.

"Aren't you going to do anything for those poor horses?" Lisa's voice showed both her horror and concern.

"I just did what I could," Hung said sadly. "If they are alive enough, they will find grass to eat and water to drink outside the fence. If not, then at least they had a chance. There are pent up horses all over the area that don't have any way to get out of their waterless fields or where they've eaten the grass down to the dirt. In normal times, farm workers would regularly spread out hay and alfalfa for them to eat and fill water barrels in the pasture. We're under orders to do nothing more than release them from the field, otherwise all of our time would be spent caring for horses and not keeping our own people alive."

They stopped at two more pastures to open the gates and then stopped by a coral next to an old, broken-down shack where an older, black horse was standing. Hung asked Lisa to stay in the vehicle. When he got out, he shouted, "Hello, in the house!" Hearing no response, he got out of the truck and walked to the coral gate.

"Okay, mister! Don't you move or do nothing! I got me a good deer rifle with you filling up my sight!" The voice came from the shanty and Lisa could see the barrel of a rifle sticking out through a partially open front door.

Hung said, "Howdy. I'm only checking on your horse, in case he was trapped in the coral with no one to care for him. You doing okay?"

"Who the hell are you, boy?" The man's voice was full of fear and distrust, mixed with a little bit of hope.

"Sir, I am Army Sergeant Hunter Jenkins. I'm out surveying the area for my commander. One of the things he wants us to do is release horses from fields or corals if they're trapped and will die there. That's all. Are you aware of how things are in the world? I can sit down with you for a few minutes and tell you what I know, but I need to move on to the Boone National Guard Center in Frankfort shortly."

"Thank the Lord," said a woman standing behind the man. "Jerry, put the rifle down and let's hear what the man has to say!"

Jerry didn't move, but asked, "Who's the woman in the truck?"

"That's Lisa, advisor to Mike Broehm. Like everyone else she wanted to get out and smell the fresh air. So long as you're no threat to us, you can put the rifle down and I won't hurt you or anyone else here."

Jerry sized Hung up quickly and lowered his rifle. "I still don't trust anyone with this sickness killin' everyone, so how 'bout you just tell us what you can from there?"

"Okay," said Hung. For the next ten minutes, Hung gave Jerry a thumbnail sketch of what happened in the world and where things were now. "The best we can determine, the virus has mostly died out in the air. That's how it spreads through the air from infected people and their dead bodies. Sunlight kills it, so if you can stay away from anyone alive that's sick or any dead bodies, you should be relatively okay. There's a group of healthy people over near Cronin that's organizing for safety and that wants to rebuild things. Mike Broehm is in charge, so if you hear anyone that's working for him, they will be a lot like me. What Mike is recommending we tell everyone is that they should get together with any survivors that they can trust and help each other. Be respectful to folks and follow the golden rule, like we all used to. I have to go now and, by the way, thank you for caring for your horse. I've seen hundreds of starving and dead horses, and that's just awful."

"Now wait a minute," said Jerry. "My girl here could really use a doctor, and we're running low on a few things. Can you help with that?"

"Jerry," Hung said sadly, "we just stuck our heads up for air a couple of weeks ago. What I believe will happen is Mike wants to rebuild the government, with all the normal services, like medical and the like. I won't lie to you. It's gonna take months or years."

Seeing Jerry's face falling, Hung said, "But, heh, I know you need this help now. If you were ever in the military, you know I can't and won't make promises I don't intend to keep. What I'll do is get your address here and try. The operative word is try, to get one of …"

Just then, Lisa walked up behind him and said, "Jerry, I'm Lisa. I'm not a medical doctor, but let me come in and see your wife and try to figure out what she needs. Okay?"

Jerry's wife pushed Jerry out of the way and came out on the porch. "Out of my way, Jerry. Let this lovely girl come on up here."

Lisa saw the bandage on the woman's arm that smelled terrible. "Hunter, would you please get that medical kit out of the truck for me?"

Lisa put on the surgical gloves out of the kit and carefully unwrapped the bandage. She rinsed the wound with saline and discovered it to be covered in grubs, but was amazingly clean of infection.

"Where did these grubs come from?" Lisa asked, amazed.

Jerry said, "Well, my Grandpa used to tell us young'uns that if something got infected, just put some grubs on it and they'll eat the infected stuff and leave the good flesh alone. So that's what I done."

"Wow!" Lisa said to Hung. "Wait until I tell Doc about this one!"

Lisa continued to clean off the wound with disinfectant before adding an antibiotic ointment, then re-wrapping it in a clean dressing. She set aside a spare dressing and several antiseptic pads to change the dressing. "Okay, now, I think you should leave this dressing on for two days before taking it off for a look, to see how it's healing. When it looks to be healing properly, you can leave the dressing off for a day and see if it'll scab over. Make sure to rinse it off with sterile water, which you can make by mixing a little bit of salt in boiling water."

"My God, you're an angel," said Jerry. The woman was crying happy tears.

When Hung and Lisa drove away, Lisa cried softly, causing Hung to pull over two miles from Jerry's farm.

"I'm sorry, my Huntsman," she said. "This new reality and helping people like that, well, it's a real first for me."

Hung grabbed her shoulders and pulled her over to him and held her for a few minutes. Suddenly, Hung pushed Lisa away, grabbed his M-4 rifle and got out of the truck. Staggering down a driveway fifty meters ahead was an obviously sick woman covered in sores. She fell down and then got back up to stagger toward the road. Hung's rifle barked once with a bullet ripping through the woman's skull. He lowered the rifle, placed it on safe and re-entered the cab of the truck. Gruffly, he said, "Time to head back."

For the next ten minutes, they said nothing. Lisa mentally smacked herself in the face to get her act together. "Heh, handsome. Have you always had those rugged good looks, or is that something the Army beat onto you?"

Almost instantly Hung's mood shifted, and he said, "That time my drill sergeant from Basic Training kicked me in the face obviously had an unintended effect. I think he was going for the opposite, to take away the shit-eating grin I seemed to always have on my face."

"Well soldier, let me tell you, I LIKE that shit-eating grin!"

Hung's eyebrows raised, then he pulled to the side of the road and kissed Lisa with more passion than she had ever experienced. He then surprised her even more by moving back behind the wheel and driving a meandering course through horse country toward the neighborhood. Over the next hour, the ride provided nothing but a peaceful summer day in the countryside outside of Cronin. Lisa jumped on the opportunity to ask dozens of questions to get to know more about this paradoxical man. On the one hand, he had killed hundreds of fellow human beings. This level of violence was outside of her ability to comprehend. But he was also an extremely gentle, caring, and thoughtful man. Linda's description had been spot-on. It would take the rest of her life to truly understand and unwrap even a majority of what made Hung the man he is. Is that something she wants to tackle?

When Hung drove by the checkpoint at the neighborhood entrance, one of the other Operators flagged him down. "Heh, you ugly bastard." Looking at Lisa, the Operator said, "You're a brave and compassionate lady to hang out with this one, ma'am! Lisa, isn't it?"

"Oh," Lisa said, "you know my name?"

"Of course, ma'am. Make it a point to know the names of all the beautiful ladies. Say, when you get bored with this guy, …"

"Okay, Buck Sergeant. What's up, other than your libido?"

"Oh, yeah, Hung. Sorry, got distracted. The LT wants to see you. Something came up."

Hung took a deep breath and sighed. Turning to Lisa, he said, "I'm sorry, M'Lady. Duty calls."

Back at to the motor pool Hung opened Lisa's door and provided a courteous hand-out. She stepped out of the SUV and walked right into his arms for what, this time, was a lingering, luxurious hug and kiss.

"Thank you, my Huntsman," she said as she pulled away and caught her breath. "When can I see you again?"

Hung grabbed her up in his arms again and gave her the most spectacular kiss she had ever experienced. "Interest you in a walk this evening after chow?"

"Yes, I would like that."

CHAPTER 10
THE NEW YEAR – PLUS ONE HUNDRED THIRTY DAYS

Boone National Guard Center
Frankfort, Kentucky
1025 Hours EDT

It frustrated LTC Sean Calahan waiting outside of the Boone National Guard Headquarters building. Unlike the rest of his team, his SCALP suit, with gas mask, did not fit well over his prosthetic leg, making him a potential liability during the initial search of the facility for either survivors or casualties of the virus. After a tense twenty minutes waiting outside of the building, two of the Special Forces Operators, including Doc, came outside gently but firmly, escorting an emaciated and terrified young Buck Sergeant.

"What do we have here, Doc?" Sean asked in his professional but kind tone of voice.

"Sir," Doc responded, "we found this sergeant hiding in a locked storeroom with an M-4 in his hands but no magazine in the rifle."

Sean, with gas-mask pulled up onto the top of his head, focused his attention on the Sergeant and said, "Sergeant, I am Lieutenant Colonel Sean Callahan assigned to SOCOM. You know, Special Operations Command in Florida?" He waited for the sergeant to nod his head.

"You're obviously aware the virus has swept the country and the world and that Kentucky State government is not currently functioning?" Again, the Sergeant cautiously nodded his head.

"As the Senior Officer currently in Central Kentucky, I am taking command of the remaining military forces and assets. Are there any more National Guardsmen alive that you're aware of?"

The Sergeant looked carefully at Sean, and after a moment and deep sigh, he seemed to make his first serious decision since the virus. In that instant, he accepted Sean as his Commander and to "hook his wagon," to this confident LTC.

"Sir, I know of at least a dozen soldiers and one Captain that have survived as of yesterday. I can help your guys find them if you're willing to take them and their families into your command and protection."

The pleading look in his eyes said it all.

"Son," Sean said gently, "I am looking for all the good military men and women I can find to bring into my command and I WILL take care of them and theirs as part of the deal. In case you haven't noticed, everything has been turned upside down and you, me and the folks under my command will be part of making sense of it all and bring order and organization to the survival and rebuilding effort. So long as I can count on you and those that you can bring with you, we will all get through this and start to rebuild."

With those words, Sean fully realized, for the first time, the enormity of the situation and what his role would be in it. He trained in the U.S. Army for most of his adult life, but had never imagined being in this position. Nor did he know where he had found the words he knew would now guide the rest of his life.

"Yes, Sir," the young man said in his best basic training voice.

Sean took his highest ranking Special Forces Operator aside for a moment. "Master Sergeant, I want you to stay with this man and help him gather as many of the National Guardsmen as possible over the next forty-eight hours. Let me know where you decide to set up the garrison. While that is ongoing, have Hung locate, gain access and catalog everything they have that may be useful. Particularly all weapons storage, vehicles and any crew-served systems. A decision to be made ASAP is whether there are enough reliable soldiers to guard what's available and what we can transport and store on or near our current location outside of Cronin.

You know the drill, Master Sergeant. It's like we discussed last night. Step one in rebuilding civilization. With fewer assholes to deal with."

The Sergeant chuckled. "Colonel, you really think Mike is up to rebuilding everything? Might-maybe you be better equipped to do that job? Then you could kinda hand over the reins after the dirty work is done?"

Looking at the Master Sergeant closely, Sean could see genuine admiration and allegiance coming from this twenty-nine-year veteran. Both men had recruited, developed and mentored men and a few women to take leadership in situations all over the world, so for this challenge, they were uniquely well trained.

"No, I don't think so. You haven't had the chance to be around Mike much or see both the intelligence and common sense he has, along with that intangible leadership skill. You know, the one you always look for, but rarely find? Mike's got it to a level higher than I've ever seen. It's no exaggeration to compare him to the likes of a George Washington. He makes everyone around him just want to trust him and believe in him. I think God just decided he was the right man to deal with this incredibly fucked-up world. You know there will be the usual assholes that survived the virus, and we'll have to deal with them."

"Okay, Colonel. I haven't known you very long either, but I can already see what you're made of. And, truth be told, me and the other guys all figure that if you're good enough for the LT, we'll follow wherever you lead."

His comment brought a surprised look to Sean's face.

"Oh, really?" A smile broke out on Sean's face. "You trust Linda's judgment over the high-falootin' Academy education and training I've had?"

"Colonel, she's made quite the impression on everyone. Word to the wise, don't ever fuck that lady over. She's got a lot of friends."

The smile of appreciation grew larger on Sean's face as he thought of how lucky he was to have Linda here, now, and soon to be his wife. "She has that effect on me, too, Master Sergeant. Has from the moment I first saw her."

***

Peter Worthington Residence
Outside of Cronin, Kentucky
1220 Hours EDT

Peter sat on the leather couch next to Scott Shelby, Peter's financial advisor and good friend taking a final look at the papers laid out on the table. Sitting in a chair across from the table from both men was Mike, looking slightly harried.

Peter looked at his project partner and asked, "Soooo, you think you might have a solution for us, Scott?"

Scott looked down briefly and smiled. "Well, I have a place for you to get started." Looking at Mike, Scott continued, "Peter asked me to A, don't waste your time, and B, to leave out all but absolutely essential details in describing this to you. Mike, the devil is in the details and that's how we ended up in the extraordinary mess our financial system was in at the time of the virus-induced collapse. But, let me begin by a short description of how early banking worked. In the days of our nation's founding, banks were privately owned and operated on a simple ledger system. Banks would take in items of value, such as gold or silver coins, property certificates to livestock or really anything of value and place a description of that in a ledger. They would use a separate ledger book for different types of property. That's how the expression, 'Me and the bank really like this house, land or other property.' This ledger allowed the customer to draw monetary credits, in the form of dollars and cents, against the value symbolically held by the bank."

"Okay, Scott," said Peter. "Let's cut to the chase. Mike doesn't need to know how the ingredients of the pie are grown, collected or even mixed. That's your job and mine. He just needs to know enough about the pie to sell it to customers."

"Okay, Peter. You're right. That's the problem with economics. The old see the trends and the youngsters don't think any of it applies to them."

Looking at the two men, Scott sighed. "Okay, guys. For now, Peter and I will put together a simple ledger system for a new bank. Any ideas of what to call it? I'll work with Peter and have something put together in three or four days to get started and we can start issuing paper credits based upon whatever assets you and Peter tell me are available to Mike's new government. Then we can start buying, with those credits, what the government needs to operate and kind of feel our way from there. I know it sounds tenuous, but really, it should flow pretty well when we get started. Now, Mike, you okay with being the original guarantor of these credits until the system gets running properly? It'll make it a lot easier 'cause folks around here trust you."

Mike rolled his eyes and muttered, "Well, shit. Guess I'm in for a penny in for a pound."

***

Lisa walked into the kitchen and found Liz going through a basket of potatoes from the previous season. Lisa said, "Oh hi, Aunt Liz. Are those potatoes still good?"

Liz reluctantly dug her hands deeply into the basket and said, with resignation,

"Unfortunately, almost half of them have spoiled. I'm trying to rescue as many as I can to cut up in pieces and plant the eyes later this week. I heard you had an interesting trip with Hung a few days ago."

"Oh yes," said Lisa enthusiastically. "He's not what I was expecting at all! Smart, articulate and a real gentleman! Speaking of that, eventually, would it be all right with you if, when the time is right, I asked him to stay overnight in my room?"

It felt like a winter chill had suddenly invaded the kitchen. Liz looked at Lisa with a face of total consternation. "Lisa, honey, if you feel the urge to have sex with that or any young man, you will need to find someplace else to do it. NOT anywhere in MY home. My home, my rules." Liz dropped the towel she was using to dry her hands and walked from the kitchen.

Lisa was aghast. "How dare she treat me like a child," she thought. "Yes, it's her home and her rules, but hell, she wouldn't even talk about it! No questions, no discussion, nothing! If that's the way she wants it!" Lisa walked out of the kitchen and back to her little table that functioned as her work station.

***

Basement in a Home
North of Frankfort, Kentucky
2300 Hours EDT

Kerry Dubois awoke in a cold sweat, shivering in fear. It had been nearly a month since Tank had choked him almost to death and then left him to die. The cold sweat resulted from his dreaming of the zombie he had seen the last time he had tried to leave the house. He had promised himself he would wait at least one, maybe two more months, to let any of the creatures die off before leaving again. Shivering in his own stinking sweat, Kerry decided he would put together a pack of food and water and find some other people.

Kerry woke again to sunshine coming in through the filthy basement window not long after dawn. He gathered up whatever he thought might be useful in a dirty pillow case he tied around the end of a baseball bat. He figured he could use the bat for defense if he needed to. When he got to the top of the basement stairs, he cursed loudly when he found the door nailed shut. He had put in over a dozen nails to prevent any zombies from getting to him in the basement. It took him almost an hour and three bloody knuckles before he pried open the door with a crowbar. Walking to the open front door, Kerry's heart almost stopped when he noticed the body of the old woman had two turkey vultures on it, digging for any remaining tidbits. At least it didn't smell as bad. The turkey vultures complained loudly on their way out the front door, chased by Kerry's approach.

Deciding his best bet would be to find people in a population center, Kerry struck out toward what he hoped was the direction of Frankfort. Two miles down the road, he saw a man coming toward him, pushing a shopping cart loaded with convenience store snacks and small food containers.

"Good morning, my good man," said Kerry, giving the man his best, winning smile. "You look like you might know where a man could find some food and water. Would you mind telling me where you got all of those good things?"

The older man, wearing a dirty thin jacket over a dirty flannel shirt and jeans, looked up at him dully and said, "Nope. Find your own shit, boy. I ain't sharing my secrets with the likes of you." He then spit on the street next to the cart.

Kerry's anger erupted, and he said, "Why you nasty, motherfu…"

The man cut Kerry's words off, grabbing a machete from the cart and swinging it at Kerry's stomach. At first, Kerry thought the man had missed him. Then he noticed the blade had sliced through his shirt and open jacket and had sliced a red line across his stomach, causing a small section of whitish intestine to peek out of the opening in his skin. At the sight, Kerry immediately screamed and fell to the ground. The pain had not even reached his brain yet, but the sight of his blood and especially his intestine completely horrified him.

The old man held the machete toward Kerry as he trudged past him on the road. He spit on Kerry as he lay on the ground, then said, "And don't think about following me or I'll turn back and finish up on your thieving ass." The statement was said in a calm, normal voice that lent credibility to the threat.

Kerry laid on the ground until the man walked out of sight. It was only a matter of thirty seconds before the pain hit him. He doubled over, but somehow had the wherewithal to reach into his pillowcase and pull out a semi-clean white towel. He pressed it tightly against the wound as the pain increased to agony levels, just before he passed out.

In the middle of the night, Kerry awoke shaking from the Spring-time chill in the air. Everything came back to him in a flash and he could feel his blood soaking his hands where he held the towel across the slash. For the next two hours Kerry called out, demanding someone come help him. He then fell asleep again with the cut feeling as if it were on fire.

Soon after dawn, a skinny dog licking his face awakened Kerry. He lashed out his hand at the dog and instantly regretted it as his stomach wound partially tore open again. After another hour of calling for someone to come help him, without success, Kerry decided he would either have to get up and walk somewhere or just lay there and die. It took him three tries to roll onto his knees and finally get up. He used the bat to both support the pillowcase full of his possessions and as a crutch to hobble down the road toward Frankfort.

Over what felt like hours, but was actually only about thirty minutes, he had only hobbled about a quarter of a mile. On the breeze coming from his left, he suddenly smelled the aroma of cooking food. Instantly, he turned toward the house, opened the gate in the picket fence and staggered to the front door. Kerry could tell he was now running a fever and was almost delirious. He pounded on the front door, shouting, "Help me! I've been stabbed!" He shouted various other demands for help, including babbling about his having been attacked.

From the other side of the door, a muffled woman's voice said, "Go away. I have a gun!"

Kerry fell to his knees and then onto his side and passed out. He dreamed of his mother making chicken pot pie for him and having a chocolate cake for his birthday. Stupid old woman. He had only contempt for her.

Two days later, Kerry woke up to find himself in a small twin bed with clean sheets in what looked like a little girl's room. Sun flowed into the windows. Checking himself over, he found he had no clothes on under the covers and that apparently someone had washed his naked body. Mystified, he debated on whether he should call out when he heard footsteps in the hallway outside the open doorway. A short, dark-haired woman in her late forties walked into the room and, seeing his eyes open, immediately smiled. "Well, good morning," she said cheerfully. "You gave me quite a scare. What's your name, handsome? I'm Alice Smallwood."

Alice had been quite obese before the virus, but between taking care of her mother and rationing the food stocks she found in her childhood home, she had dropped over fifty pounds over the past year, leaving her with draping folds of skin hanging from her face, neck and arms.

"I'm Kerry," Kerry croaked, before Alice handed him a glass of clean water. He drank, coughed several times, and asked, "How long have I been asleep?"

"Oh, sweetie, you passed out on my doorstep two days ago. Since then, I first had to decide whether I was even going to open the door or just let you bleed out and die on my front porch. Since I'm a surgical nurse, I guess I just couldn't let you die, so I drug you in, stitched you up and, using techniques I learned at nursing school, somehow got you into bed. Not before, however, cutting off your clothes and cleaning you up. The clothes I burned and truth be told, you really didn't weigh all that much. I'm guessing you, like the rest of us, have dropped quite a bit of weight over these last few months. Anyway, what happened to you?"

Alice's rapid-fire babbling came at a rate Kerry could barely understand. Kerry had had time to get his wits about him, at least a little, so he quickly came up with a story to her question. "I spent the first three months after the virus struck in a basement bunker stocked with almost everything I needed." He decided not to mention anything about Tank or Blondi. "Gosh, I'm starving. Do you have anything to spare that I could eat?"

"Oh, just what was I thinking," said Alice. "Let me warm up the soup for you. You shouldn't have anything heavy after the wound and infection you had, which fortunately, I had some antibiotics to give you, but you used up the last of them, so don't get gashed again or you're in real trouble!" Alice walked out and down the hallway.

Ten minutes later, Alice returned with a tray bearing a diluted chicken noodle soup with a few crackers on the side. "Here, Kerry honey. Try some of this. Are you strong enough to handle the spoon?"

Kerry momentarily glared at her before changing his expression to a smile, remembering his circumstances. "Thank you, Alice. I think I can do that."

One taste of the soup made Kerry want to complain bitterly. It was barely edible, being watered down and nearly tasteless. It never occurred to Kerry that Alice was sharing what little she had. Instead, he smiled and thanked her as he shoved the three crackers into his mouth greedily. She smiled in return.

"Kerry, that was a nasty cut across your gut that went through the all the layers of skin and cut the muscle and membrane that holds your insides where they belong. It took both of the suture kits I had here to close up the muscle and then the skin. So long as the antibiotic does its job, you will knit back together over the next few weeks."

"Next few weeks?" Kerry practically shouted the question.

"Now don't you get all worked up about it," Alice said with her 'calm the upset patient' voice, "you will heal and be up and about in just a couple of days, but you won't be able to do much for at least four to six weeks. Baby, you were badly hurt and nearly died! There's been enough death around here, and I couldn't allow another one if I could save you."

Finishing his soup, crackers, and water, Kerry promptly fell asleep.

CHAPTER 11
THE NEW YEAR – PLUS ONE HUNDRED THIRTY-FIVE DAYS

Non-Descript Warehouse
Outside of Frankfort, Kentucky
0705 Hours EDT

Blondi's eyes snapped open from his fitful sleep at the sound of rustling close by. There were stacks of cardboard boxes containing everything from food to clothing to other useful items, like flashlights and hand tools. They were less than neatly stacked haphazardly around the concrete floor of the warehouse. When Tank broke open the lock on the side door to the building, Blondi had seen dozens of rats scattering in the sudden onslaught of the light pouring through the doorway. Anything that was not encased in a thick plastic or metal container had been pillaged by the rodents.

Blondi let out a short, strangled scream as he looked up to the rope supporting the head of his sleeping hammock to see the beady eyes and black fur of a very large rat trying to figure out how to get around the large plastic garbage can lid preventing the rat's access to his hammock. The rat jumped down the five feet to the concrete floor and scurried off.

Tank had found and broken into the warehouse over a month earlier to discover what he had called his "nest egg." He added the thirty-five guns and cases of matching ammunition taken from a gun store a mile down the road.

"What the fuck…" Tank's words had been hushed as he pushed open the door to the tightly woven wire mesh of the tool crib room, holding his shotgun in both hands while standing there fully naked. He was clearly visible in the early morning light pouring through the skylight of the warehouse.

Using soothing words, Blondi said, "It's okay, Tank. Goddamn rats were trying to get past the rat block you made for me on the hammock!" Tank had fashioned the rat block out of the garbage can lid when he threw Blondi out of the tool crib. That happened when Tank "took in" the starving woman that was now his sex slave. Blondi wasn't happy being evicted from the tool crib, but it was better than having to watch and listen to Tank repeatedly using the girl. Now he just had to listen.

Standing behind Tank was a short, thick, large-breasted woman in her early 30s. She was naked, wearing a dog collar with a chain leash clipped to it. She attempted to look sultry, as Tank had repeatedly instructed her to do, but this morning, she just looked tired and beaten. It was obvious she had been overweight before the virus struck. Based upon the folds of skin on her belly, arms and neck, as well as her dangling breasts. She had lost over thirty pounds in the past two months.

Blondi briefly glanced at the girl with a little pity, but mostly bored derision. He couldn't help but look at Tank's naked form that had hardened over the past two months. Even though Tank was in his 60s, Blondi found a strange attraction to him, especially since seeing his naked profile. Blondi had always been attracted to the rough, confident, well-endowed men he came across. He had even quietly offered to give Tank a blowjob two months earlier, after Tank had choked Kerry out cold in the old lady's basement, but had been rebuffed. "Too bad," he thought wistfully.

"Well, shit, Blondi," Tank said roughly as he turned back into the tool crib. He took the girl's leash. "Come here, honey. You're gonna see if you can't milk another couple of ounces out of me before it's time to check out the two new girls. If you're real good, maybe I won't want to replace you!"

Tank's laugh turned Blondi's stomach, almost as much as listening to Tank take whatever sexual pleasure he wanted from the girl every night for the past two weeks. Yesterday, Tank had "taken in" two more girls who had survived the virus. They, too, were starving, but had been slender before getting sick with the virus, leaving them almost skin and bones. Both had been college freshmen at Kentucky State University. The fact they were black made no difference to Tank, who promptly fed them, had them stripped down and washed up by Blondi, then shackled, using restraints Tank found in a police car that was abandoned nearby.

When Blondi assessed his own situation each night, after crawling into his hammock, he had to be realistic about how much he owed to Tank. No, Blondi was sure if he ever parted from Tank's leadership, he would end up dead - or wishing he was.

***

Peter Worthington Residence
Outside of Cronin, Kentucky
2220 Hours EDT

Suzie came instantly awake to a tapping on her bedroom door. "Uh, hello?"

"Suzie?" Elizabeth's concerned voice said through the door. "Can I come in?"

"Sure."

Elizabeth came with a candleholder and lit candle in her hand. "Have you seen Lisa? No one seems to know where she is."

Suzie's smile instantly eased Elizabeth's fears.

"Lisa is okay. She's with Hung in his new place tonight." After a pause of five seconds, Suzie asked, "Is there anything else?

Elizabeth said, "Ohhh. No, I guess not. No, wait, can you tell me which house is Hung's new place?"

The stern look on Suzie's face surprised Elizabeth.

"I can," said Suzie, "but they are not to be disturbed without very good reason. Agreed?"

Elizabeth stood in the doorway, stunned, for several seconds. "Okay, dear. If that is how she wants it." Elizabeth resolved to corner Lisa the next time she had the chance. "Would you please tell me which house she's in now?" There was an icy demand in her question.

Suzie ignored the tone and said, "She is in the fourth house, South of Mike Broehm's house, on the same side of the street."

Elizabeth closed the door and walked away down the hallway without another word.

***

The Rhapsody
Port of Alaska, Anchorage, Alaska
1955 Hours Local Time

Cho sat on the bunk in the Captain's cabin on the 915 foot luxury cruise ship Rhapsody as it raised anchor in Seward, Alaska. Two and a half weeks earlier, he was finally allowed to drive South on the Alaska Highway by the National Guard. He then drove directly into Anchorage to the docks. He was looking for a good-sized ship that was already provisioned with food and fuel adequate to take him to Shanghai, China. What he found was devastation and rotting cargos sitting on hundreds of ships scattered around the port. In only a few hours he found two men, Ho Chin and Michael Kim, who seemed to have a reasonably informed view of what was going on around the port and in Alaska in general. In less than an hour, Cho had recruited them to join him in building a new world. Considering the world situation, bringing the men into the fold was relatively easy. Years in the spy world had cultivated Cho's skills and served him well.

Cho learned only two cruise ships were in an Alaskan port and had been fueled and partially provisioned before the virus struck. They were both in port at Seward. Chin would find and load a small trailer for Cho's Suburban with several necessary items including weapons and ammunition from an abandoned gun store, food for several weeks and twelve five-gallon fuel containers for the two-hour trip from Anchorage to Seward.

Kim explained that on the first ship, The Rhapsody, several of the crew, to include the First Mate, Pilot and a Second Mate, had survived. They were organizing and carefully vetting and selecting new people to join the crew and making plans for how to survive long-term. They had also recruited a few survivors from shore to remove the dead bodies and conduct a thorough cleaning of the ship. The second ship only had a Second Mate and a dozen foreign born hospitality workers that survived. Kim believed it likely that someone had, or soon would, take over the ship and either killed the crew or simply pillage it for what it contained.

It had required Cho over a week of conducting carefully orchestrated meetings with The Rhapsody's officer corps to convince them to join him. Though his initial goal was to arrange for his passage to Shanghai, China, Cho never missed an opportunity to further other goals. Taking control of a large, well-supplied cruise ship would certainly prove to be beneficial in this new world.

Cho was impressed to see the First Mate had ordered all surviving passengers to disembark from The Rhapsody before beginning interviews to see who would be allowed to come back on in a working capacity.

"Captain Gao," the First Mate said to Cho, using his new name, "I have recalculated our travel time to Port Honolulu. Sailing at 20 knots per hour, which is two knots below our usual cruise speed, it should take us about six days to get there. You mentioned possible travel on to Shanghai?"

"Yes, but let us see what we find in Hawaii," Cho said. "You believe your Second Mate will be able to operate a fuel transfer boat once we reach there?"

"Yes, Sir! He was raised in Vancouver and worked on a fueling vessel owned by his uncle for five summers while in school."

"Very good. Prepare a plan for everything that needs to be done once we arrive in Port Honolulu. Also, task an appropriate crew member to compile for me a list of not only the names and citizenship for everyone on board, but also include where each one has lived and what secondary skills they have. Oh, and is the male Pilipino nurse the only one with medical training on board?"

"No, Sir," the First Mate said. "Besides the male nurse, we picked up Doctor Nostrodomos from the National Institute of Allergy and Infectious Diseases (NIAID) at the U.S. National Institutes of Health. He and his mistress, who didn't survive, had been on an Alaskan cruise/tour. And also a Nurse Practitioner who worked for a front line doctor group dealing with the COVID-19 pandemic. The doctor is really an asshole. I was initially going to put him in charge of the ship Infirmary, but a day later I had to change things up and give that duty to the Nurse Practitioner, who is really a talented lady. Nostrodomos raised holy hell for about a minute before I had two crew members face plant him on the deck. He was informed the next, similar outburst like that from him would earn him a swim overboard. I assured him there would be no second warning. I then informed him that if he caused any trouble for the NP or anyone else on board, he would get similar treatment."

The First Mate paused a moment to gauge Cho's reaction. He received an approving nod from Cho. "Well done. Keep me informed about this doctor. I have seen many men like him before. Just the type who has brought our world to the state it is in now. Have this Nurse Practitioner come see later this afternoon, when everyone gets into the routine of being at sea."

"As you wish, Captain." The First Mate nodded and smiled as he withdrew from the cabin. He approved of this new Captain.

CHAPTER 12
THE NEW YEAR – PLUS ONE HUNDRED FIFTY DAYS

Marc and Suzie's New Residence
Outside of Cronin, Kentucky
0645 Hours EDT

Marc Baxter woke with a start, heart racing and sweat pouring down his face and chest in the early dawn light. He looked wildly about before his eyes fell on the most beautiful face he had ever seen, looking at him with concern.

"It is okay, my love." The words came soothingly from Suzie's lips, though she kept her distance across the king-sized bed.

The bedsheets were tangled in disarray around his lower legs, with the rest of his naked body exposing a prominent display of morning wood. Suzie was boldly eying the display with appreciation, before asking, "What were you dreaming about?"

The confusion in his mind took a few moments to settle before he said, "God, you are so incredibly beautiful!" He continued to be in wonder that Suzie had suggested they move in together ten days earlier. Three days later, they decided on their new home.

Suzie's hands had been clutching the bedsheets up to her chin. At that moment, they slowly, sensually dropped to expose her perfect breasts. Her eyes were hesitant, with a look of nervousness she had not felt around any other man in years.

A hint of suspicion crossed Marc's face before he reached over and hugged her with a passion reminiscent of the prior evening, when their lovemaking had seemed to go on for hours.

She instantly spread her legs and guided him into her. Words were unnecessary for the next several minutes as she climaxed first, then expertly built him to a tremendous crescendo.

Both lay breathing heavily, luxuriating in the afterglow of their bodies' perfect harmony.

Two full minutes later, Suzie said softly, "My incredible lover, what was troubling you before, well, you know?" Her smile said playfulness, but there was serious concern in her eyes.

"Sweetheart, I can definitely tell it will take me a while to get used to what an amazing woman you are."

Marc glanced away and when he looked back into her eyes, he saw the concern building in her eyes.

"That's exactly what I mean. The getting used to part. I've never met anyone who could virtually read my thoughts and feelings like you can, even before I'm able to understand what I'm thinking and feeling myself. Your mind goes so fast, you're way ahead of me, so please, just give me the time I need to catch up."

Marc rolled over to her and pulled her against his sweat-cooling body. "You know I love you completely, totally and without reservation, right?" He glanced down to look into her eyes.

Suzie nodded, before snuggling against him and beginning to trace her fingers first around his face and then moving through the hairs on his chest. This brought about another sensual reaction and his demand, "Tell me what you want me to do."

For the next twenty minutes, Marc learned several new and exquisite things to do to her body to bring pleasure to them both.

Marc stood in the bathroom shower stall of his new (to him) house, washing up from water in a five-gallon bucket of cold water. Suddenly, he felt Suzie's hands take the sponge from his hands, followed by a soapy sponge rubbing all over his body. This began another twenty-minute session of the most sensually delightful bath Marc ever experienced.

Marc and Suzie had just moved into the comfortable ranch home right next to Mike and Lauren Broehm's house a week earlier. It had taken three intense days of cleaning to remove the smell of death left from the prior owner's passing, but it was now a very nice home and fairly well-set-up for post-apocalypse living. And it was very close to Peter Worthington's house, which now functioned as the center of the neighborhood government.

An hour later, Suzie walked into Peter's house to find Lisa waiting for her to go over work schedules for the cleanup crews tasked with removal and disposal of virus infected bodies.

"Heh, girl," Lisa said. "Sleep in a little, did ya?"

The question brought a rare blush from Suzie, who was the least bashful woman Lisa knew.

"Oh, you did," Lisa giggled, which brought a giggle followed immediately by a full-on laugh from Suzie.

Just then Mike walked into the Peter's Great Room and asked, "Well, well, what are you two…" One look at the girls' mischievous grins stopped Mike in mid-sentence. "Ahem, never mind. Where are we on getting at least the neighborhood free of the virus?"

"The best I can say is we're making progress," Lisa said. "The two teams we've formed have been actively working on clearing out the bodies."

In a serious tone, Lisa continued, "Mike, it's really tough on the team members to deal with bodies and especially with the ones inside of houses. Gas masks don't even begin to stop the smell and we can only use people that have received both doses of the vaccine. Each of us went out with a team for the first three days and, I have to say, I've had nightmares every night since. God, I don't know how morticians can do it. Some of them have to be scooped out with a shovel! We've decided not to use anyone under twenty-one for the detail, which limits the number even further. Have to admit, all this 'adulting' really sucks. At least for me," she glanced at Suzie and received a concurring nod. "Let's just say the cloistered world of school and the university did little to prepare us for this type of thing."

Mike nodded his understanding.

"Speaking of that," Mike said, "Have you talked to your Uncle Peter and Aunt Liz?"

Mike had spent nearly three hours earlier in the week listening to Peter vent on the impetuousness of youth and just because the kid has a world-class intellect doesn't mean she can thumb their nose at authority.

Lisa hadn't spoken to Peter or Liz since the day Liz had reprimanded her for asking to allow Hung to stay over. "Mike, I'm not sure they ever want to talk to me again."

It amazed Mike that someone so smart could be so emotionally dumb. He moved over to her and gave her a big hug.

"Lisa, honey, your Uncle Peter and Aunt Liz still love you very much. In fact, since you arrived unannounced on their doorstep, they have tried to be surrogate parents for both of you two girls. Uh, I mean young women. Part of that includes feeling responsible for any big, lifealtering decisions. Rumor has it that moving in with a man, especially a complex man like Hung, probably qualifies. Don't you think?"

"Mike, don't worry about that," Suzie interjected on behalf of her best friend. "We did research and have over five years of pills that will keep us from getting pregnant. At least until we want to be." Suzie said this with a scheming grin.

Lisa looked at Suzie with surprise and Mike looked at Suzie with mild shock that she had gleaned the underlying point he was just beginning to move toward making.

"Well, uh, Lisa, since your parents aren't here and you really don't have anyone but Peter and Liz to keep a watchful eye… and don't give me that look, you two! Everyone, and I mean everyone, needs someone with life experience at least available to keep them from goofing up their lives too badly. Lord knows I have enough folks watching and second guessing me every minute of every day, and I don't mind it, at least not much. We all know you're both extremely smart, but that doesn't mean you can deduce the right decision from your readings or simple logic. And Lisa, you're dead wrong if you think Liz wanted you to move out of their house. She just didn't want any youthful hormones getting you into things, like falling head over heels in love or having a child that will have lasting consequences. Hell, there's a whole Romance Genre dedicated to people falling prey to their emotions. Life throws enough unexpected variables at us to not avoid those we can control."

"Now, enough lecture. You're both of age and responsible young women. It looks like I will also have to remind you both that I have responsibility for everyone in this neighborhood and we haven't seen a tenth of the hardships we're all going to face going forward. We all need to work together and that includes you two and Peter and Liz. Now Lisa, will you please walk over and talk to Liz sometime today?"

Mike stopped and waited for Lisa's response. It took several seconds before Suzie playfully smacked Lisa upside of her head, before she grudgingly said, "Yes, Sir."

"Thank you." Mike thought about all the additional counseling he wanted to give her, then nodded his head.

"Now, back to the cleanup project."

Lisa said, "On the plus side, we have been able to reclaim over a dozen houses that are available for new folks to move into. And Mike, Hung and I have chosen one of them just down the street from your place. That will not be a problem, is it?"

"No, not from me or Lauren."

"Okay," said Lisa. "Back to the cleanup. Each house will, of course, have to be completely cleaned and sanitized by whomever is moving in, but at least they're available within the protection of the neighborhood. That number should triple within the next week or so. Do you know how many people we have living in the neighborhood now, Mike?"

Mike thought about it and said, "Linda told me a couple of days ago that we had about 160 people living inside of the imposing fence of the neighborhood." The statement brought smiles since they all knew the "fence" was actually just an old, single-strand of formerly electrified cattle wire, attached to metal fence poles, to mark the boundaries. Hanging on each fence hung strategically placed "NO ENTRANCE" signs.

"Besides that number, we have over 200 living on farms surrounding this area that are associated with our group, to which we provide protection and support. Anyway, anything else for me, ladies?"

Lisa smiled. "No, not right now, Mike. I know where to find you if I need you. Oh, are you and Lauren happy to have the house back to yourselves after Marc moved out?"

Another big smile broke Mike's lips as he looked over at Suzie. "Yes, and thank you Suzie for making it possible to get rid of that foghorn of a snore."

Suzie rewarded him with another blush before saying, in her best fake Southern accent, "Well, suh, whatever do you mean? I haven't heard a peep from that lovely man!"

"Yeah, Suzie," said Lisa, "maybe he just hasn't gotten to sleep yet!" The giggles of both girls began again, resulting in Mike beating a hasty retreat to his office.

Suzie walked over to Lisa and gave her a not so affectionate punch in the arm, followed by a smile. "You did that just to embarrass him, didn't you?"

"That obvious?"

"It was to me," Suzie said. "Speaking of which, are you about finished helping Hunk clean out the two-story house down the street yet?"

"Yes, just have the bedroom left, where the husband and wife decided to lie down and die together. We got the mattress and box springs drug out and down to the designated contamination dump. That was quite a job by itself."

"And? Did you try out one of the other rooms?" Suzie's question brought serious embarrassment to Lisa's face.

"No, we didn't. He wants to do this right, in the master bedroom of our new home. Hell, I half think he wants to wait until we get married, but sister, I'm not waiting THAT long!"

"You know, Lisa, you can take him anytime you want him. I'll even show you how if you like. That's what sisters are for, right?" The earnest seriousness of Suzie's statement and question touched Lisa deeply.

"No, I don't think so. I can tell this is pretty important to him and, like Linda said, he's worth it, but it's gonna be a wild ride! I can wait for that kind of wild for a little longer." Almost as one, both girls gave knowing sighs.

***

Peter Worthington's Residence
Outside of Cronin, KY
1120 Hours EDT

"Hi Mike," Sean said as he walked confidently into Mike's office, expertly using his prosthetic leg.

"Heh, Sean! Just the man I wanted to see. How're things going on the Frankfort/National Guard front?"

"I wish I could say they were moving along flawlessly, but then again, that's not realistic. Linda did her usual detailed report last week, so I'll just cover anything new since then. Though, in a nutshell, we have access to so much highly lethal equipment, I'm more than a little nervous about being able to secure it all. I had the men bring two of the M1 Abrams tanks and two self-propelled 155 mm artillery pieces, with several truckloads of corresponding ammunition, here for storage and maintenance by our security forces. We also now have two of the Up-Armored Humvees sporting assorted heavy weaponry, as well as two Bradley fighting vehicles."

"What's that?"

"Mike, the Bradley is basically a light tank that can go most off-road places using tracks instead of tires. It has a 25 mm cannon for a main gun, TOW anti-tank or bunker buster missiles and one or two machine guns. The TOW is kinda like an old time bazooka that has pinpoint accuracy out to over two miles. The Bradley is pretty bullet proof and can carry several men into combat for fighting from the inside or dismounting. I don't foresee us needing any of these over the near term, but if any small groups of marauders or rogue military units roll into our area, it will be very handy to have a ready show of force."

"That sounds good to me, Sean. Do I remember from Linda's report a similar type unit is set up in Frankfort right at the National Guard Center?"

"Yes, Sir. They have about the same amount of equipment in an active status. The rest is being systematically disabled to be able to use the parts or rehabilitate it, as needed. We've currently got a full company of men and a few women, totaling over 200 people that were active National Guard, Reserves or former Army, Marines, etc. Their surviving families add another 250 or so, that are now living in housing on or nearby the Center, as well as some of them providing administrative support for the Guard. They are all being commanded by a National Guard Captain who seems to be pretty squared away with a competent retired Command Sergeant Major to help keep him out of trouble."

"Damn, Sean, that sounds pretty impressive!"

"But there's a big BUT, Sir. The captain has had to deal with a small but vocal number of troops that seem to think we should implement the old woke culture in this new world order. Unless you've got some ideas on how to deal with those malcontents, I've got a couple of my team non-commissioned officers (NCOs), making their presence felt to support the Captain and Command Sergeant Major, but I don't think they'll be needed very long."

"I see what you mean, Sean. Something tells me in Green Beret 101, they have probably taught you how to deal with this type of thing. That being the case, I presume you'll let me know what you plan to do and how it works out? You also won't have any second-guessing from me. But, I presume you already knew that."

"I appreciate that, Sir. And yes, that is exactly what I planned to do with this, and most of the other kinks in the military portion of our rebuilding. I do foresee some arrests and a trial coming up within the next few months for what will amount to treason. I expect you will either preside over this trial/military tribunal or designate someone to do so?"

Mike sighed heavily. "It never ends, does it?"

"No, Sir. It sucks to be in command."

CHAPTER 13
THE NEW YEAR – PLUS ONE HUNDRED FIFTY-TWO DAYS

The Peter Worthington Residence
Outside of Cronin, Kentucky
1945 Hours EDT

Lisa was totally shocked to see this absolutely gorgeous man, with his huge puppy-dog eyes boring into hers, on one knee in front of her, holding an open ring box. Inside the box was a HUGE diamond set in white gold. He had tried to say something before giving up and proffering the ring instead. Tears began flowing freely down her face just before she literally jumped onto his chest and rode him straight back onto the floor in Uncle Peter's great room.

"Yes, I will marry you," Lisa squeaked in a little girl's voice. "And you better get used to having me jump on you! This has just become a regular thing. Understand?"

His puppy-dog eyes had gone from surprise and a little fear, to the happiest and most pure smile a man can have. "Lisa, you can jump me anytime you want to. And God help anyone who tries to say different!"

Lisa then buried him in kisses.

A respectable two minutes later, Mike walked around the corner from his office and cleared his throat. "Ahem, okay you two, you can either take this to your place, or let me pour and toast to this wonderful occasion."

Lisa looked at Hung while he looked in her eyes for what seemed like an extraordinary length of time.

"Okay," said Mike, "since you two can't decide, I'm gonna pour and we can get this engagement formally started! You can properly," Mike drew out the word slowly, "start the engagement later."

Mike opened a bottle of Peter's finest bourbon. Glasses clinked and Mike said, "To the happy couple and the beginning of their new lives together!"

"Heh! What's going on that involves my finest bourbon?" Peter's attempt at false outrage devolved into warm laughter, followed by, "Really, congratulations, you two! Just don't drink all of my best bourbon. Save some for the wedding!"

***

Hung and Lisa's Residence
Outside of Cronin, KY
2110 Hours EDT

Later in the evening they lay in the brand new Tempurpedic® king-sized bed in their new home. Hung had obtained the bed from the furniture store in town and, as a surprise for Lisa, had smuggled it into their bedroom. Lisa snuggled into Hung's arms, feeling sated, sore, and content. Her husband to be was like no other man she had ever experienced. Gentle, masculine, affectionate and patient, AND he lived up to his nickname. She promised herself she would hit up her bestie for some creative ways to give him some new experiences. After, of course, she had some time to recover a bit. Her man was huge and virile! Thank God she had gone on the pill seven days earlier!

Lisa felt fortunate Suzie had prevailed on Doc to take her and Lisa into a pharmacy in nearby Cronin for a scavenging trip a week earlier. There were three pharmacies in town, an independent one, one in the big chain discount store and the third in the big super-grocery store. The independent one was the only one that was not already pillaged. Besides sanitary needs, they broke open the locked sliding metal gate to the prescription area and took all the birth control pills, antibiotics, and whatever Doc felt might be useful. The twelve shopping carts full of items easily fit into the covered military pickup truck. Doc left a note taped to the pharmacy window informing the owner the U.S. Army contingent,

Central Kentucky, had taken the items. Contact would be made to pay for the them at a later date. He even thoughtfully closed and re-locked the door.

Hung lay next to his fiancé, thinking he had found a real, honest-to-goodness angel. Of all the terrible things he had experienced over the past few years, she enveloped him with her love and seemed to crave everything he desperately wanted to give her. The way she cooed when he stroked her soft, firm butt, to the firm, but soft pinches and nibbles on her nipples, she seemed to love it all. More importantly, she seemed to love him. Broken, confused, and clumsy as he was, she still loved him enough to want him forever. He would kill anyone that ever threatened her. Tonight he would just lay next to her and hold her. Sleep wasn't allowed for him as he protected the love and purpose for his life from all threats, including him.

***

Peter Worthington's Residence
Outside of Cronin, KY
2130 Hours EDT

Peter Worthington crawled into bed next to his wife, Liz, after another long day. He could see she was laying there awake with a thoughtful expression on her face in the candlelight. Though he had a backup generator for the entire house, it remained unused a majority of the time to conserve the LP gas fuel. In his initial planning for extraordinary times he did not expect to have access to propane when the shit hit the fan (SHTF), so he had two 10,000 gallon tanks installed, each in its own well-vented, but secure, underground concrete bunker. At Mike's direction, the Security Force had gone to the company in Cronin that stored and delivered Propane and brought two of their large trucks to the neighborhood, leaving a note on the door of the company. Still, Peter didn't like to waste any propane when a candle or firewood would do.

"What are you thinking about, my dear?" Peter was tired, so he did not ask with an expectation of receiving a significant answer.

"Peter, do you think I did the right thing driving Lisa out like that? I mean, it is a brave new world and all, but I just couldn't bear the thought of what my mother would have said if I had wanted to take you to bed in her house, and feel the same way about Lisa humping Hung in my house. Just down the hallway from this very room!"

After thirty-five years of marriage, Peter could clearly recognize an unwinnable topic of discussion, but being as tired as he was, the caution flags were ignored.

"Honey, Lisa is a grown woman, even though you consider her a daughter and a little girl." Seeing Liz's eyes blaze, he continued, "but she's also a guest in our home, and if you don't approve of what she's doing in it, you have every right to just tell her to get the hell out! Isn't that what you did?"

"I did not! I mean, you know I would never say a thing like … dammit Peter, you're no help at all!" She grabbed a pillow and whacked him in the face with it.

Rolling out of range at the far side of the bed, Peter continued, "Well, have you talked to her since she moved out? Mike's got her and Suzie working on clearing out the infected bodies from the …"

"Yes," Liz said, interrupting him. "Three days ago, she found me in the kitchen and asked to talk. I have to admit, I was pretty frosty to her, but I'll give her credit for gumption. She neither apologized nor backed down on her decision. She confidently informed me she and Hung had chosen a new home to live in and she would try to, quote, 'respect my rules,' of all things, when she was here working for Mike. Smart assed, horny little bitch!"

Peter could hear Liz's teeth grinding as she folded her arms across her chest in disapproval.

Peter watched her for a couple of seconds, fighting the urge to smile. "Well, you know, honey, I seem to recall some pretty erotic moves you put on me before we were married."

"But we were almost engaged," Liz almost shouted at Peter across the bed.

Peter could no longer suppress his chuckle. "I know you were out working on another food project until a few minutes ago, so I guess you haven't heard the news. Hung proposed to Lisa about three hours ago down in our Great Room. They are now officially engaged."

Liz burst into tears and buried her head in her hands.

***

Alice's Home
North of Frankfort, Kentucky
2300 Hours EDT

Kerry laid in the bed feeling very sorry for himself. Alice had just tucked him in after removing the dressing and cleaning the wound and exclaiming on how well the scab was healing. He still wasn't steady on his feet yet, despite her constant nagging that he get up and move around. She had even started to wear shirts without a bra under them, unbuttoned halfway down her front to interest him in her flabby, sagging-skin body. Kerry didn't know what it was, but he had lost all interest in sex since the virus had struck and was particularly repulsed by Alice's clumsy advances on him. Maybe if she wasn't so fat with skin hanging off of her. It really frightened him when she would insist on washing him between the legs every day. Two days earlier, he had even felt a slight stirring down there before thinking of the skin dangling off of her arms.

He tolerated all of this because she had actually gone outside of the house and found food at other abandoned homes and even a gas station mart down the road. He guessed she should thank him for forcing her to go out and forage for food. Otherwise she might have starved, sitting by herself moping in her house. He was careful to keep all these opinions to himself, though he wondered if she wasn't beginning to catch on. She had preached at him about appreciation of God and particularly about God's helpers. How none of us could get by in this world by ourselves without the Lord and his helpers. She even asked him how long he thought he would have lived if she hadn't dragged him in off of her porch. He only shut her up when he asked her how long he would have survived if she had shot him, as she promised to do. That made her all defensive and backed her off, at least for the rest of the day.

Kerry contemplated his next move when Alice walked into his room and informed him she would no longer be serving him meals, or washing him, or otherwise caring for him. He would need to get up off his lazy ass and start doing those things for himself. Also, how did he propose to find food for them both?

Kerry allowed his shocked facial expression to come to the surface. "What do you mean, Alice?"

"Kerry," Alice said, "I've been praying on this and the Lord told me I had been spoiling you far too much and that for your own good, you need to start doing things for yourself."

"God dammit," Kerry thought to himself! "It was the same speech his mother had given him when he was twenty-five and had refused to get a job. Well, shit! Now he would have to get himself strong enough to get the hell out of here before she really started in on him."

But where could he go? The thought was frightening and made his mind basically shut down. He was asleep within seconds. That was his superpower as a child when his mother started in on him. He was so glad that bitch was dead!

CHAPTER 14
THE NEW YEAR – PLUS ONE HUNDRED FIFTY-SIX DAYS

Building C, Centers for Disease Control
Atlanta, GA
0545 Hours EDT

U.S. Army Special Forces Captain and A Team leader Charles "Cap" Schneider felt his eyes slam open with a brief feeling of disorientation. His memory kicked in quickly. He was in a highly secure building on the CDC campus northeast of downtown Atlanta, Georgia. Events of the past one hundred twenty days flowed through his mind quickly. The SF operation in Afghanistan to find a reported bio-laboratory. The firefight with JOTP terrorists and finding Miss Julie Carrithers locked in a medical examining room deep within the terrorist tunnel network.

His surprise to find Julie had survived and was recovering from the nano-technology enhanced Chinese virus. They had forced her to teach twenty terrorists the knowledge and rudimentary language skills they needed to travel throughout the world. She had not known it was to spread a deadly virus.

On his own initiative, with support from SOCOM, Cap had brought Julie out of Afghanistan to the CDC, along with the terrorist scientist's laptop computer. Though CDC researchers were dying from the virus, they were able to formulate a vaccine based upon research discovered on the recovered laptop and Julie's blood antibodies and completed a limited production run of 5,000 doses. Everyone still living, who was involved in virus research, was vaccinated.

It wasn't until nearly half of the vaccinated had died they determined two doses of the vaccine were required for 90% plus effectiveness. Captain Schneider felt fortunate to have survived the virus, with only a fever and a few skin blisters, after having had only one dose of the vaccine. They also told him his and Julie's natural immunity was probably superior to the vaccinated immunity. Fifteen hundred of the doses were sent to the President in Washington, DC. A delirious researcher had started a fire in the lab where production was being conducted destroying the production capability and worse, the single data server holding records for how the vaccine had been produced.

Cap heard the soft knock on his door before responding, "Come it."

Julie Carrithers walked into his room with a haunted expression on her face, and came directly to his bedside and buried her head on his shoulder before beginning to cry. This had become almost a morning routine. She was tortured and gang raped by the terrorists multiple times during her captivity before being thrown into a room with infected lab subjects to get the virus and die. Cap had been there to rescue her, so she desperately clung to him. When Cap learned his entire family had perished because of the virus, he treated her like his only daughter.

This morning, Julie's crying stopped sooner than previous bouts.

"Did you get any sleep last night, little one?" His voice was soothing and carried the affection he had developed for her.

"Uh, huh," she said in between sniffles. "And I woke up again with another message from God. Do you wanna hear it?"

Just like any doting father, Cap said, "Sure, sweetheart."

"Like, you know, um, her voice was sweet and full of love, and made my heart sing. She told me all the evil men that did those horrible things to me and everyone else were going to spend forever frozen in hell. You know, like Dante's Inferno? Their eyes frozen open, re-seeing and feeling all the terrible hurt they caused? And the ones who raped me, their dicks were all just slowly burning off, causing great agony, and then reappearing to burn off all over again. Over and over for all eternity." Julie smiled with inner satisfaction, thinking about it.

"And she told me I was the Chosen One who she sent back to save and redeem all the sinners in this world. Those she allowed to survive, anyway. Cap, do you think I am the Chosen One?"

Julie hesitantly looked up into his eyes.

"Sweetheart, I think God chose you to survive and help humanity recover from all of this." Framing his words carefully, he continued, "I don't think God is sending you out to dictate what people should do. Jesus was a teacher who passed his message on by his words and his example. That's what I think you're supposed to do. Lead people by example. And teach a different way for them to live their lives. Does that make sense?"

"Oh, yes," Julie almost shouted, jumping up from Cap's embrace with a new purpose and zeal.

Watching Julie hurry from his small room, Cap couldn't help but think she had missed his whole point. Like most enthusiastically zealous people, she had heard what she wanted to hear, whether they meant it that way or not.

Cap, dressed in his field uniform, walked out of his room fifteen minutes later, just in time to run into Ph.D. Professor Simpson, the senior researcher remaining alive at the CDC.

"You're just the man I'm looking for," said Doctor Simpson, bearing a hesitant smile.

"Have you got a minute, Captain?"

"Sure. What's up Doc?" Cap smiled at having used his best Bugs Bunny impression. Of course, it went right over Simpson's head.

"Yes, well, right. Ahem. The remaining survivors here, four doctors, including six aids, forty-five researchers, eight security personnel and twenty-five RNs (Registered Nurses), and six kitchen personnel, and two janitors left in this building came to me this morning with a bit of a crisis. The backup generators that have been giving us power since the virus struck are about to run out of fuel. It also seems the stores of food we have were contaminated by rats. The two aids were so upset they just sat down and cried and haven't moved since. What I need is someone to organize the people that are left here in this building and come up with a plan to survive as we try to replicate the vaccine. Oh, and Miss Carrithers has refused to give us any more blood to use in that attempt. Something about us being too stupid to make backup copies of everything as we went along so we can stop, quote, 'sucking her blood.' We need her blood to re-do the vaccine testing!"

Cap looked at Simpson for several seconds before responding, "A month ago I offered to do what you are asking regarding organization and both you and your people curtly informed me they didn't need help from 'the Military.' Frankly, I question whether you and your sniveling, whining people could effectively take direction. I do come from the Military and know very well how an effective chain of command and unit discipline works. Where are your people now and have you seen Miss Carrithers?"

A look of fear, mixed with respect, appeared on Simpson's face. "I think most of them are down in the cafeteria and I passed Miss Carrithers heading that way, but she wouldn't even speak to me."

"Okay, doctor, here's what I'm going to do. I'm going to gather a few things and come speak to you and everyone else in the cafeteria in thirty minutes. Anyone that's there can be included in what I have in mind. IF you people decide to follow my plan, anyone that isn't there or doesn't want to go along with the plan will be escorted to the door and expelled from this building. They can go it on their own."

"But, but, we haven't decided if it's even SAFE to unseal the doors yet. And ..."

"This isn't open for debate, doctor." Cap said this in a low, slow, gravelly voice. "If you and your people want to live, then be in the cafeteria in twenty-nine minutes."

Cap turned and walked back to his room. Inside, he pulled out the utility belt he had gotten from the security guardroom, with its older, but serviceable .38 caliber revolver to strap around his waist. It was a little uncomfortable, but was mostly there for show. He had also loaded the revolver with hollow-point ammunition and carefully loaded the ammunition loops on the belt for an impressive display of firepower, to the uninitiated. Cap readjusted the 10mm Glock 20 pistol in its shoulder holster underneath his desert camouflage uniform shirt. He then loaded up his go-bag that he had brought from Afghanistan. It had been a real bitch decontaminating it and the contents after arrival. With his go-bag over his shoulder and his operations notebook in one hand, he walked down the four flights of stairs to the main floor and the cafeteria.

In the cafeteria, Cap found the small group clustered around a frightened Julie, who was sitting in a chair with her arms wrapped around her knees. Several researchers were demanding she "participate" in the redevelopment of the vaccine. Cap's arrival caused instant silence, with all eyes turning to him. Julie jumped up from the chair and ran to him with tears running from her eyes.

Dropping his go-bag, Cap put a big arm around her shoulders and said, "It's okay, sweetheart." His eyes glared at everyone in the room.

All eyes in the room, however, were on the big .38 caliber revolver on his hip and belt brimming with bullets.

In a projecting, command voice, Cap said, "Listen up, everyone. I don't know or care what was just going on that caused you to surround and terrorize this young woman, but if I ever see it happen again, you will regret that you survived this plague. Is that clear?" He looked slowly around the room and, with a few exceptions, the crowd just averted their eyes.

Cap handed a pad to one of the security guards and ordered, "Please take down the names and titles of everyone here. You can start with me. United States Army Captain Charles Schneider, 7th Special Forces Group. For any of you that don't know what that means, I command a Special Forces A-Team of some of the smartest, most creative, and deadliest human beings on the planet. Our goal is not to kill people, but let me assure you we are very good at it when the need arises. Your senior man, Doctor Simpson, here, has asked me to take charge of seeing that you people can survive going forward. Rats have contaminated much of your food supplies. You have virtually no organization in place to further your continued ability to survive, such as food, clean water, electricity, and even security of this building."

One of the male nurses said, in a whiney voice, "Who made you king…"

"Silence!" Cap had not shouted the word, only used his command voice to issue the order. "Neither you nor anyone else will speak until I am through with what I have to say. Got it?"

With a stunned look and mouth gaping open, the man nodded his head.

"Now, I will continue. I will take command of this group only if the group decides that action is best for your overall survival. This will not be a democracy. This will operate under martial law with me in command. That means when you receive an order, you will do your best to fulfill that order without sniveling back-talk, moping around, or otherwise acting like recalcitrant children. If you do not want this to happen, I will grab up my bag here, gather a bag for Julie, and we will leave you all to fend for yourselves. But, let me warn you, look around. If

I'm not here to direct a united effort for everyone's survival, what happens when your electricity goes away in another day or two? The fuel is almost out for your backup generators. The rainwater collection system I set up on the roof is barely enough to cover basic needs, and we've been lucky with regular rains lately. Food? Security? Does anyone here know how to organize and manage each of those operations?"

"I will walk Julie to her room and gather what we'll need if you decide you don't want to sign on to my deal. And let me be clear, I will only stay if everyone that will remain in this building signs on. If anyone doesn't want to sign on, they are welcome to leave or, with the approval of the rest of the group, they will be expelled from this building. This is your call, people. I will be back for your answer in twenty minutes."

Cap took Julie's arm and walked out of the cafeteria.

In a soft, slightly frightened voice, Julie looked up at him and asked, "Cap, did you mean what you said about us leaving if they don't agree to your rules?"

"Julie honey," Cap said, "I will almost always say what I mean. Yes, I meant that. I'm sure there will be at least one or two that I will physically throw out of this building within the next couple of days if we stay."

Julie sheepishly said, "It just never occurred to me we might suddenly leave. But then, we do both have natural immunity and Mother God will protect me and, I presume you too. Is it safe out there?"

Cap smiled and chuckled. "I dare say it's a lot safer out there for us than in here. These eggheads have been cloistered and coddled their whole lives and don't really have a clue how to survive without all the protections and conveniences of modern life. And, the 'woke' idiots believe everyone else owes them deference. The world should be how they want it to be and should accept their own twisted view of reality. Well, Metro Atlanta used to have a population of over 6 million people. If five percent of those people have survived this virus, that's over 300,000 people wandering around in some degree of shell shock with no laws or government to keep them in line. That doesn't include the walking virus-infected that are probably out of their minds. Figure there will be complete anarchy outside this building. Do you know what that means?"

Julie shook her head no, with growing fear in her eyes.

"You should be afraid. By now, small groups of individuals led by essentially a gang leader will have begun efforts to pillage and take whatever they want. That's the first thing we're going to do here is work on securing this building."

Cap went around Julie's room and gathered up what he wanted her to carry if they left right away. When she tried to help, he politely but firmly asked her to take a seat and stay out of the way. Five minutes later, they were on their way back to the cafeteria.

When they walked into the cafeteria, the group was facing off against one of the four doctors and one researcher, a man and a younger woman in her early thirties, arguing.

Doctor Simpson looked at Cap and said, "These two don't seem to understand the situation and won't agree or leave."

Cap walked over to the two, towering over them with his 6 foot two-inch frame, and said, "So you're the only ones. Is that right?"

The woman stood up, with her hands on her hips and said, "You can't tell us what to do, you fucking Nazi!"

Cap's open hand smacked her across the face and knocked her several feet across the room to the floor. He looked at two of the remaining security people and said, "These two are hopeless and will get us all killed. Take them to the easiest door to unseal and throw them out."

Both guards said, "Yes Sir, Cap!" They then grabbed the man and drug the stunned woman along the floor toward the exit. When the man argued loudly, a security guard punched him in the stomach and drug him out of the cafeteria as well.

Everyone else in the room sat in stunned silence. The doors were heard opening and the sound of distant pleading voices cut off by the slamming door. Cap turned to address those gathered in the room.

"Those two," Cap began, "not only didn't comprehend how dangerous the world outside has become, they never would until this building was overrun and everyone in here either killed or raped and enslaved. For any of you babes in the woods who have delusions about what is or will soon happen outside, let me spell it out for you. Anarchy is the reality outside these walls. In laymen's terms, that means desperate people will take what they want and do what they want to with no restrictions on their conduct. There are no police officers or other authority to regulate the conduct of anyone. This is the Wild West on steroids. Survivors who have gotten hungry are venturing out and discovering that so long as they stay away from the sick and rotting dead, they can pillage stores and homes for what they need. We will need to do the same if we are to survive. It won't be long until those stores will run out and people get really hungry. There is very little food being produced. When you get hungry, you will naturally do whatever it takes to survive. Damn your fellow man or sympathetic feelings for the less fortunate."

The thoughtful nods of agreement from over half of those present encouraged Cap.

"I'm going to set up a command structure among us and will insist that you follow that chain of command from now on. It will become clear how this works fairly quickly. Let me say again, this is NOT a democracy. Once per week, we will have squad meetings where questions and opinions can be aired. From there, your squad leader will decide on each issue and, with my concurrence, address each issue. If you don't like it, suck it up buttercup and work hard enough for your squad that I can justify making you a squad leader. Performance is what matters. We will get through this, but for the foreseeable future, don't expect to get a lot of sleep or much relaxation."

Cap gestured for the security guard to hand him the list of personnel. After a quick glance at the list, he said, "Okay, the following personnel come with me to the kitchen for a briefing and the rest hang loose until contacted by your new squad leader in about 30 minutes. Let's start getting used to following orders right now. Hang loose means to stay in this area until you receive further instructions and not to wander off and do whatever you feel like doing. If we are to survive, people, we will ALL need to work together and work hard. If you decide you don't want to do that, there's the door, and if necessary, I will throw you out."

Walking into the kitchen, Cap was trailed by his seven squad leaders. He knew this would not be easy, as these people had not suffered nearly enough yet to understand their new reality.

CHAPTER 15
THE NEW YEAR – PLUS ONE HUNDRED SIXTY DAYS

Peter Worthington Residence
Outside of Cronin, Kentucky
1210 Hours EDT

Mike had just received a note from a young teenaged boy named Michael. He was a runner that delivered messages from the Military/Security Center in Fred Callahan's house. With its backup generator, the Callahan house now functioned as the communications center for Mike's security force and for Mike's slowly growing government.

The note was from Sean asking Mike to be available for consultation when he could get back to the neighborhood from Frankfort. Mike was about to catch a ride into Cronin when the note arrived.

Twenty minutes later, Sean walked into Mike's acting government office in Peter's home.

"Mike, thanks for being available. Thought this piece of information was worthy of your immediate attention. The Captain commanding your National Guard section in Frankfort received a hand-delivered note from a Full-bird Colonel (a rank one step higher than a Lieutenant Colonel) out of Fort Knox demanding he provide a status of all military assets available to him and to place his command under the authority of this Colonel, as the ranking military officer in Kentucky." Sean sighed and said, "And so it begins. My Captain did some checking and discovered this Colonel, if he's who he says he is, was the ranking Finance Officer at Fort Knox with no real command experience. He's only held staff positions during his entire U.S. Army career. How do you suggest I have our Captain respond?"

Mike said, "I once heard a very experienced leader and military officer say you should always gather the opinions of the most junior person present first, lest he be swayed by the opinions of his superiors. Sean, we both know who the most experienced person here is, but I'll ask you to just tell me. What do you think we should do?"

"Wanted to make sure we were thinking along the same lines, Mike. And, it really matters what you're thinking, but here's what I had in mind. Whatever the guy is from Fort Knox, or Fort Campbell, you will want to maintain both your total independence and your control over your military or security forces. You won't be able to do that with anyone else except for me and my team and the National Guard group we've assembled. Exactly what to tell this Full-bird Colonel, I don't know yet. Maybe something like, 'We are under the command of SOCOM and the duly appointed civilian leadership working closely with SOCOM. The SOCOM in-state Commander welcomes you into his command to further consolidate the Constitutional civilian control of the Commonwealth of Kentucky.' I'd say if the National Guard has given you their allegiance, they have given you authority as at least the Acting Governor. What do you think?"

"I like it," Mike said enthusiastically. "Although, didn't they give their allegiance to you? And, speaking of that, isn't this whole situation more something that should fall under a martial law or military situation?"

"Mike, let's get this straight. My higher command is no longer functioning. While we're on this topic, the TOP SECRET orders SOCOM received several months ago in the form of a Presidential Directive and, the whole reason I'm here with these SF Operators was to form an SF Battalion. Its purpose was to collect intelligence and provide support to the duly appointed government representatives during a time of expected anarchy. I have given my allegiance to you, so you're the Commander. History is full of lower-ranking officers and civilian leaders standing up to take the reins when needed. This is one of those times. Let's just go with that. Okay?"

"Damn," said Mike. "Nothing like spelling it out in capital letters. Okay, Sean. Just keep me on the straight and narrow. Oh, and history is also replete with upstart emperors rising quickly before their last trip to the gallows."

"Well, Mike. That's a big part of my job. Ensure that doesn't happen. We've got a lot of bridge and organization building to do if we're going to have any type of organized society instead of complete anarchy. Do you want me to respond to this Colonel or do you want to do so yourself?"

"I think I ought to do it," said Mike. "With my new title of Acting Regional Governor, I will recognize your authority under the Presidential Directive to command all military forces in Kentucky and this region, the specifics of which will remain unspecified. In fact, don't I, as Acting Governor, have the authority to promote you in rank? Can I make you a General?"

"I really don't know, Mike. Maybe we should bring in your brother-in-law into this. Didn't Marc say he was the acting Chief of Staff before being sent away by the President? That should give him some kind of authority."

Two hours later, Marc Baxter walked into the Great Room, which had been turned into a small conference room, to find Mike, Sean, Linda Sharpe, his sister Lauren, Fred Callahan, Lisa and Suzie, and Peter already seated.

"Glad you could join us, Marc," Mike said warmly. "Now that you're here, I can bring everyone up to speed on what's going on and hopefully come up with a solution." Taking a deep breath, Mike said, "Okay, we probably should have expected this, but it had not occurred to me. The National Guard group in Frankfort received a letter from someone claiming to be a surviving Colonel at Fort Knox. He wants the Captain in charge in Frankfort to submit to the Colonel's authority and provide to him a listing of all personnel and equipment available in Frankfort, to be absorbed into his new command at Fort Knox."

To Mike's surprise, everyone sat quietly, waiting for Mike to continue. "Does everyone catch the import of this demand and what he's obviously after?"

Marc smiled and said, "Mike. I'm pretty sure everyone here can see this is the beginnings of a military and political seizure of power by whoever this Colonel is. I'm also sure everyone's thinking that you've had a little while to think about it and we're all dying to know what you plan to do. Is that about it?" Marc looked around the room and either received knowing nods or one-word affirmative responses.

"Well, all right," said Mike hesitantly. "What I hoped to get were some thoughts and ideas on how best to handle the situation, and really, how I go about setting up an organized government that can justify doing what needs to be done. It's not like I want to be an Emperor or anything. I just don't want anarchy or some despot deciding to boss me and everyone else around."

"Honey," Lauren said, "you've already got the loyalty of everyone in the neighborhood and surrounding farms and in Cronin and even Frankfort."

Lauren suddenly coughed violently before excusing herself to walk into the kitchen for something to drink. Mike watched her go with some concern before returning to the question at hand.

Sean looked at Marc and said, "Heh, Marc. Aren't you still the acting Chief of Staff for the President? Does that give you any kind of authority from the White House? You know, like sole survivor type of stuff?"

Several conversations broke out at once to pursue this new idea.

"Hang on guys!" Mike had to raise his voice to be heard. When everyone had quieted, he asked, "Marc, what is your status? Do you know?"

"Now that's a good question," Mark said thoughtfully. "I really don't know."

Suzie surprised everyone by interjecting, "Marc, I have been researching the U.S. Constitution, at least before we lost power and the Internet. The U.S. Government has a program called Continuity of Government that, combined with the U.S. Constitution and its Amendments, sets out what happens if the President can no longer serve in his or her office. Everyone knows the line of succession goes from the President to the Vice President, then to the Speaker of the House of Representatives and then to the President Pro-Tem of the Senate. After that, it goes to the Secretary of State, Secretary of Treasury, Secretary of Defense, the Attorney General, then the rest of the Cabinet Secretaries. Succession is uncertain if none of those can step in, except..."

After a long pause, Mike said, "Except what, Suzie?"

"Well, because of the inaction of Congress, the previous President issued Presidential Directives giving a wide range of authority to the military during extreme emergencies, with emphasis on civilian control whenever there is a government to exert it. If the government either can't or won't exert control to assure citizens of their Constitutional rights, military commanders within the United States have authority to do so. I would think the current situation would qualify. The big thing in these military directives is for the military to support local and national civilian authorities, when possible. I think the Pentagon classified orders involved were reacting to situations where there was violent rioting and local authorities refused to do anything to protect the citizens."

Okay," said Mike, "so I have this straight. The civilian succession of power laws are real fuzzy after we eliminate the Cabinet members, but there's a secret military command-and-control system that kicks in if the civilians aren't around or don't do their jobs?"

"For your federal government, yes," said Suzie. "For the state government, you only go from the Governor to the Lieutenant Governor to the Attorney General. After that, there's no one specified by the Kentucky Constitution."

"Mike," said Marc, "it looks to me like you have a choice of either justifying filling the power gap by either civilian or military means. It makes more sense to me if you start from the local or regional route. A more problematic way to approach this might be for me, as Acting White House Chief of Staff, I appoint you as the Regional Governor. Didn't someone tell me that had fallen to Coyote Collins under the Fontaine Presidential Directive? Only problem is that puts me at the top of your chain of command and I'm neither suited nor do I want to be there. How about if you get appointed acting Governor of Kentucky, by, maybe, the National Guard Commander," Marc said, looking at Sean, "Sean then places all military resources at your disposal for the duration of this crisis? Or at least until you deem it appropriate to hold elections. You might even put a four or five-year deadline on holding elections. Thoughts anyone?"

Multiple discussions broke out among everyone present.

After over an hour of creative but serious discussion, Mike said, "All right, everyone. Let me see if I can sum up what we have. Basically, I'd like to take Suzie's amended suggestion and run with it. Sean, you're going to impose on your National Guard Captain to recognize me as the new acting Governor for the next five years. That is based on my insistence and your concurrence that we don't want to establish a purely military leadership with all the historical and third world problems that seem to naturally flow from that. Mine will be a civilian government, strongly supported by all available military resources. Now, when we have Kentucky fairly well-organized, we'll look at expanding regionally to take control of surrounding states, if, and only if, that seems to be a good idea. Let's crawl before we try to walk and then run. Does that sound right?"

"I agree and think Suzie's idea is the best approach," said Peter. "No offense, Marc, but I think Mike has a much better chance to get widespread support in this conservative state than to have to rely on legitimacy from a member of the past President's Cabinet."

Everyone expressed agreement. Any that held reservations or thought to go a different way wisely let things proceed for now.

"Okay then," Mike said. "Sean, Marc and Suzie, please stick around and help me with the wording of the letter to this Fort Knox Colonel? Anyone else is welcome to stay and contribute to that as well. Let's take a fifteen minute break before getting started. I want to check on something."

Mike looked at Lauren, who had quietly returned to the room, nursing a cup of tea.

"Sweetheart, can I see you in the other room for a minute?"

"Okay, Mike."

In Mike's office, Mike sat down next to Lauren on the couch and gently grabbed her hand. "Okay lady. What's going on? Are you feeling all right?"

Lauren took a deep breath before saying, "Mike, I didn't want to worry you, but no, I'm feeling pretty miserable. Doc and both Suzie and Lisa are worried I might have cancer growing in my lungs and spreading elsewhere. I'm guessing all that smoking I did when I was younger is finally catching up with me. That and the stress with everything that has happened."

Mike immediately reached over and gathered Lauren up in his arms. She would only stay there for a few seconds before pulling away from him. "Mike, we're doing everything we can for it and I do NOT want you to be taking any of this onto your shoulders."

Mike sat looking at Lauren with a feeling of helplessness, with tears welling up in his eyes.

"Now damn it Mike! I told you not to worry about this! We both believe a higher power is in control here, so let him do his job. Okay?" She leaned over and awkwardly tried to wrap Mike in her arms to comfort him.

After a few seconds, Lauren broke away from him, stood up, and said, "Please let this go and you go save us all." She then walked out of the room.

Mike sat quietly for a few minutes, feeling a wide range of emotions, before resolving himself to address this later in the evening. He then walked out and invited Sean, Marc, Suzie and Lisa in to discuss the letter.

***

Mike Broehm Residence
Outside of Cronin, Kentucky
2130 Hours EDT

Mike walked into his bedroom after failing to find Lauren anywhere else in the house. She was sitting up in bed reading, or at least pretending to do so by the light of an oil lantern.

"Hi, Honey," she said cheerfully. "I was wondering if you were going to get home at all tonight." She tried to present a twinkle in her eyes but was not quite able to make it.

"I was ready to drop everything and talk to you this afternoon, but got the distinct impression you didn't want to. Sweetheart, why didn't you TELL me?" Truth be told, he had wondered why she hadn't been even the least bit affectionate for the last couple of years, but particularly the last several months. He was kicking himself silently for not paying attention to his own wife's needs and especially not nailing down what was going on with her.

"Mike, there was nothing you could do about any of this anyway, and I know how much everyone else is depending on you. I swore Doc, Lisa and Suzie to secrecy about this condition."

"Condition?"

"Well, I didn't mention everything to you earlier. I took a trip into the town hospital with Doc, Lisa, Suzie and one of the SF guys. We were able to get the backup generator working and got both X-ray and an MRI done. The hospital was a mess, by the way. I don't know if that should be a priority to preserve it and protect it for our future use. Anyway, I have a large, four-inch diameter tumor in my lung and five smaller tumors spread throughout my abdomen. Lisa said that shows cancer spreading." Tears appeared in Lauren's eyes. "Honey, I believe God is in charge here. Lisa and Suzie are scouring the hospital records they found on treatment options, but I don't know there's anything we can do at this point."

Mike took her into his arms and just held her.

CHAPTER 16
THE NEW YEAR – PLUS ONE HUNDRED SIXTY-TWO DAYS

Non-Descript Warehouse
Outside of Frankfort, Kentucky
1215 Hours EDT

Blondi looked the boy up and down. He appeared to be around ten or twelve years old, but small for his age. He had a bad stutter and dragged his badly swollen foot when he walked. Tank had caught the boy trying to steal food from the warehouse and, after roughing him up a bit, was about to kill him when Blondi intervened. The boy's stuttering annoyed Tank mightily and his lame condition made Tank think he wasn't worth the trouble to feed or provide medical care. Blondi had bravely informed Tank he would take care of the boy and keep him away from Tank.

Blondi's appraising eye could tell that underneath the layers of grime, the boy was not unattractive, and probably had beautiful hair, if it was properly washed and cut.

Blondi was strongly gay and had not previously considered going for the younger generation, but he was also both extremely horny and very lonely. And he had just saved the boy's life, hadn't he?

"What's your name, boy?"

"B-b-b-b-b-Benny, s-s-sir." He was trying his best to be polite and brave, but amid all the death and then being so hungry all the time, he could barely stand up or keep his tears in check.

"Well Benny," Blondi said kindly, "my name is Blondi. If you think you can do what you're told, you may just have found a safe place where you can stay. But that old man, Tank, is the boss here, and he doesn't like you much. If you want to live and not be severely punished, you will want to stay away from him. Understand?"

"Y-y-yessir," Benny said with a sniffle, before shuffling over to Blondi and giving him a big hug.

"Damn, boy! You stink to high heaven! First, we'll get you cleaned up and get some clean clothes for you to wear. Then we'll see to your foot. What's wrong with it?"

"Goddam coyotes came after me and gnawed on it some."

"Well, shit!" Blondi said with disgust. "You're gonna have to be extra nice to me, boy, cause I'm got to ask Tank for some antibiotics for you. Well, hell!"

"You ever sleep in a hammock, Benny?

"No s-s-sir."

"Well, you'll get used to it. Only way to keep Tank from killing you. Follow me."

"Oh, yes s-s-sir!"

That night, as Blondi held Benny in his arms, he kept telling himself the boy would soon learn valuable skills that could, someday soon, help him cheat death once again. And he could tell the boy enjoyed being held by Blondi, since he fell asleep almost immediately.

***

Blondi woke the next morning to the sound of someone being spanked. It emanated from the tool cage a few feet away from where Blondi's hammock was strung up in the warehouse. A young girl's voice screeched with the sound of pain mixed with delight. Blondi heard Tank's heavy breathing as he continued to spank and pump away into the girl. After he had climaxed, Tank got up from the bed and walked out of the tool cage over to a bucket by the door and urinated. Blondi couldn't help but admire his deflating equipment.

"Blondi," Tank shouted, "I didn't hear you break-in that boy last night. Are you sick, boy?"

"No, Tank. I'll take care of that in my own sweet time." Blondi was thinking he hadn't decided if he really wanted to use the boy like that, but, of course, any port in the storm… "Now you remember, there are over a dozen men coming around noon to apply for the security positions. You know, you had me put fliers up?"

"Yeah, okay," Tank said. "What else is going on before that?"

"You need to look over the new people that came in the past couple of days."

"Yeah," Tank said wolfishly, "I've been busy working on skills for two of the girls. The little blonde has some real promise. You did a good job cleaning her up," he said with delight, thinking about her screams of protest mixed with just the right amount of pleasure. "Now what will I be lookin' at?"

"There's three more women, a young, grown man and a little girl, maybe eight or nine years old. None of them are connected to each other. The older woman claims to be an excellent cook while the other two women, in their late 20s, are shell-shocked at having lost families to the plague. Just like you told me, all three of the females have been stripped, collared and chained. The young man looks healthy and strong enough, only he's pretty disoriented himself. Not sure if he's even worth the trouble. I don't know what the fuck to do with the little girl."

"Hmm," said Tank. "All right. I'll take a look at 'em. Are they cleaned up yet?"

"Yes, Tank. I had all of them stripped and watched while they soaped up. They sure smell a lot better now and don't have any obvious diseases. You might want to remind Roberto that he's there to do what I tell him to. I wouldn't let him hump the women or the little girl without your say-so first. He wasn't very pleased and thought he could threaten me. Next time he does that, I'll kill him, like I've seen you do several times." Blondi patted the 9mm pistol nestled in an inside-the-pants holster.

"You keep it up, Blondi, and I'll make sure everyone knows not to fuck with you." Tank said this with genuine appreciation, recognizing Blondi as a competent lieutenant in his organization. "You can take the young'un, if you want him. I don't know how you people do that, but feel free to put a collar on him if you want."

Tank's deep chuckle at his own joke didn't even frighten Blondi anymore.

***

Tank looked over at the fourteen men standing below the makeshift podium made of wood boxes he had set up against the wall of the warehouse. He could see several of the men were armed, but he wasn't worried. Roberto and two other men he had recruited were standing off to the side with their shotguns and semi-automatic rifles to make sure nobody in the crowd got stupid. His new Chief Security lieutenant, Antonio Alverez, was floating around the perimeter somewhere to make sure their meeting wasn't disturbed.

Over a bottle of cheap scotch, Tank had learned Antonio had been an Army Ranger before being imprisoned and dishonorably discharged for rape and murder over in Afghanistan. So long as Tank gave him a girl to use and food, Tank was sure he would do what he was told to do.

"Okay, let's get this show on the road," Tank said in his booming voice. "If you want to join my organization and get access to food, housing and everything else that goes along with it, there are a few rules you'll need to follow. If you don't like it, in a few minutes you will have one chance to walk away and get out of this area entirely. No bullshit here, gents. I've run organizations in Eastern Kentucky and throughout the South for longer than most of you have been alive. One thing I don't put up with is bullshit, backstabbin', or disloyalty to me. Whatever woke crap you brought with you today, forget it, 'cause it will get you killed. Anybody got a problem with that or doing what you're told?"

There was a grumbling sound from the group before two men started walking away.

"Where the fuck are you two going?" Tank made the demand in his deepest, most dangerous voice.

One man turned and said, "We're just takin' your opportunity to walk away and leave your area. No harm, no foul." The man speaking causally pulled out a pistol and let his arm hang, pointing it at the ground. Four gunshots rang out in quick succession. The man holding the gun was killed instantly when his head partially exploded. The second man was knocked backwards by the blast of a 12-gauge shotgun.

Several of the men were crouched down and looking for cover. The rest were silent but watchful.

Softly, but with his deep voice carrying to everyone, Tank said, "That was unfortunate, but that's what being stupid and not following orders will get you. Any questions?" Nobody had any questions.

***

The Rhapsody
Port of Honolulu, Hawaii
1430 Hours Local Time

Cho sat at the desk in the Captain's quarters when he heard a knock on his door.

"Enter," Cho said.

The First Mate entered and said, "I have the update you requested, Captain Gao."

Cho motioned for him to take a seat on the couch in front of his desk.

"Captain," said the First Mate, "the Second Mate completed the refueling for this vessel and has also recruited an additional seventy-eight men and two dozen women from the port to add to our crew. We have fully provisioned the ship, thanks to the help of Mr. Chin and Mr. Kim, and we now have control of warehouses containing over a year's worth of provisions, near to the docks. Unfortunately, that does not include fresh fruits or vegetables. Two warehouses containing what used to be fresh, refrigerated produce contain only rotting remains now. There are enough canned and dried goods for more than a year. You probably noticed at the last meal, our kitchen crew has baked fresh bread. With another four days of training for the new crewmen and women, we will be ready to take this ship out for a short shakedown cruise around the island. Have you determined our next destination?"

Cho could tell the First Mate was both nervous and annoyed that Cho had not yet informed him of the next destination or any of his plans going forward. Cho, however, was working on plans to take control of the entire Hawaiian island chain, with its many resources. The military firepower alone would prove critical in his desire to create his own new Chinese dynasty. That desire demanded speed in asserting control early in the recovery. To wage an effective campaign to seize power, he had to have military resources and troops plus an infrastructure loyal to him. Much to consider and a great deal of work to be done. Chin and Kim were proving very useful in making this happen, but he also needed to find and identify some surviving military officers and experienced non-commissioned officers he could trust to move forward. And, of course, it would be very helpful if they were Chinese.

CHAPTER 17
THE NEW YEAR – PLUS ONE HUNDRED SIXTY-SEVEN DAYS

Fort Knox Army Military Pay Office
Fort Knox, Kentucky
1115 Hours EDT

Colonel Martin T. Briggs, a silver-haired, clean shaven man in his mid-50s, sat in his office carefully reading a letter from Acting Kentucky Governor Mike Broehm. He was fuming with frustration and barely contained rage. He had lost his wife and three children to the virus and did not want to put up with some political tin-hat clown. Such a man will not be allowed to get in his way to bringing order to the chaos he was sure was about to start.

"Sergeant!" Col. Briggs shouted through his open door.

A young Staff Sergeant poked his head into the door from his small candle-lit office.

"Yessir?"

"Come on in here, son," the colonel said in a normal tone of voice. "Have you ever heard of a man named Mike Broehm or a General Sean Callahan?"

"No Sir, have not heard of Boehm, but something about the name Callahan rings a bell. Yeah, I got it, sir. Isn't Callahan the Special Forces officer that lost a leg and was highly decorated for valor involved in some rescue mission in the Sandbox? Afghanistan, I think. He was a Major I think. Is that the one, Sir?"

"I don't know, but probably. Anyway, Broehm claims to be the Acting Governor of Kentucky and he has appointed, and apparently promoted Callahan as the military Commander for all military forces in Kentucky under some Pentagon classified order or other and supported by a TOP SECRET (TS) Presidential Directive. Do you know anything about any of that?"

"Well, Sir. If I recall correctly under all of our Continuity of Government training and TS orders, we do have the authority to enforce martial law in situations where the civilian government can't or won't enforce law and order. That's the authority you have been working under for the past two months, Sir. We are required to defer to and support the civilian government if there is an effective one in place. Concerning the state National Guard, I don't know how their system works, but the Governor is the boss of his state's National Guard, so a Governor could, with Congressional authority, appoint a General officer."

"Oh, and Sir, there was a bit of an incident at the Post gate when the letter was delivered," the Sergeant said.

"Continue, Sergeant," the Colonel ordered.

"Sir, you had directed the security detail working at the gate to take any military personnel and any equipment directly to your adjutant, Lieutenant Johnson, for debriefing and reassignment. A Master Sergeant dropped the letter off at the gate with Special Forces tabs on his shoulders in an Up-Armored Humvee. When he was directed to follow the gate guard to Lieutenant Johnson, the Sergeant laughed and informed the gate guard he was under orders from his Commander to drop the letter and return immediately. The gate guard could see several armed soldiers in the Humvee and decided to let the Master Sergeant go. He feared had he pressed the matter, a firefight would have broken out."

Col. Briggs envisioned a crusty SF Master Sergeant facing down a civilian security officer at the gate and wasn't surprised.

"Sergeant," the Colonel said with a sigh, "pass these new orders to the gate. The previous orders do not apply to anyone under the Command of LTC Callahan. Also, I will have a letter going out to Callahan early this afternoon. Arrange for delivery to the Kentucky Guard unit this afternoon when I have it ready."

"Yes Sir, Colonel!"

"Also, have Lieutenant Johnson report to me immediately."

"Yes, Sir!"

Thirty minutes later, the Colonel's Adjutant, twenty-five-year-old First Lieutenant Jason Johnson, knocked on the doorjamb before entering the Colonel's office and standing at attention, waiting to be recognized.

Col Briggs looked up and said, "At ease, Lieutenant. Have a seat. And read over this letter."

Lt. Johnson read the letter twice before looking up. "Colonel, if everything in this letter is accurate, it looks like this Broehm guy is maneuvering to take complete control of Kentucky, and maybe demand you place your command under Callahan. Is that how you see it, Sir?"

Col Briggs knew Johnson was an attorney who had his ROTC military commitment deferred until after law school. Why Johnson hadn't gone the JAG, or Judge Advocate General's Corp route, was unknown.

"Johnson, explain to me why a licensed attorney is in Military Intelligence and not JAG?"

Johnson handled the change of topic smoothly, having heard the question many times before. "Honestly, Sir going through law school, I wanted to go straight into the Army Reserve and there weren't any JAG billets available anywhere in Kentucky. My ROTC instructor in undergrad steered me toward intelligence, saying I seemed to be someone that would be good at it, so that seemed to be a good place to settle. I was on my two week active duty requirement here on Post when the virus struck. Of course, I've been here since that time."

"Well, in your legal opinion, Lieutenant, does Callahan have a more legitimate claim to command military forces in Kentucky than I do?"

"I don't think so, Sir. Though I'm not privy to the classified military orders or TS Presidential Directives, without verification they exist and how they apply to these totally unforeseen circumstances, I'd say you are the senior surviving military officer in Kentucky and have both the right and obligation to bring martial law and order to the state. I will note, however, that the Special Forces are uniquely trained to rebuild foreign governments and that training will make them particularly effective in this situation. They are also not particularly used to or happy with following orders outside of the Special Forces chain of command. They can, but don't like it. I had a couple of friends in both the Seals and Army

Special Ops groups. A tough, creative but independent bunch. I've heard the term 'irreverent' applied to them quite a bit."

"Hmm," said the Colonel, "I want you to deliver this letter to Lt. Colonel Callahan personally. I'll write it this afternoon, review it in the morning and you can deliver it tomorrow afternoon. Maybe even take a small convoy with MRAPS (Mine Resistant Ambush Protected armored vehicle) and some Up-Armored Humvees. If their damned SF Master Sergeant is going to show up in an armored vehicle and refuse my security gate's orders, they need to know it's not cool to mess with my authority."

"Do you really want me to go in with a show of force, Sir?"

"Okay, don't start shooting, but don't appear to back down, either. Are you up to this mission, Lieutenant?"

"Yes Sir. I'll take care of it, Sir." Lt. Johnson stood and saluted.

"Come by at 0900 hours in the morning, Lieutenant. My letter will be done then."

***

Mike Broehm Temporary Office Building
Outside of Cronin, Kentucky
0610 Hours EDT

Anna Roesch sat behind the beautiful blonde-oak desk in what was previously the small parlor located just off the entryway of a large, beautiful home. This was her first day in the new space and fourth day as Mike Broehm's new Executive Assistant. Truth be told, she was relieved to place the neighboring farmer in charge of her little farm, with all of its livestock, chickens, and responsibilities. Mike's office was a luxurious executive office located through the double doors behind Anna's desk. Mike's fledgling government sanitized and appropriated the home, two doors down from the Broehm residence as his new temporary office. Upstairs were six bedrooms that had been converted into four offices, leaving one spare bedroom and the Master Bedroom as-is. Lisa, Suzie, and Marc had offices upstairs, while Linda Sharpe had an office downstairs.

The house mesmerized Anna, having electricity and running well water, all courtesy of a whole-house propane generator. Mike had instructed that the air conditioning not be used, but instead they were to make-do with the ceiling fans in most rooms and a few floor fans, where necessary. Anna had forgotten how wonderful it was to have constant electric power. Her well-stocked office even had a working computer, printer, and a large copy machine with two dozen boxes of copy paper. And my God, she thought happily, to be able to flush the toilet without carrying up a 5-gallon bucket! New backups for each piece of equipment were stored in an adjacent storage room for use when anything stopped working. The SF guys had gotten into an office supply store to get the place set up. It even had a functioning kitchen with a working refrigerator!

When Mike entered the new office building at 6:30 a.m. it surprised him to find his lovely new executive assistant already seated at her desk. She was a mature and beautiful brunette in her early 50s with an eye-catching, well-rounded figure. To compliment the rest was a sharp wit, but an easy way about her that always seemed to be the calm in the storm. Fortunately, she was wearing a loose, high-neck smock, otherwise he had trouble keeping his eyes from wandering in appreciation of her lovely curves. For the past four days, she had handled the complete move from the office in Peter's house to the new, temporary office space. Mike expected, but dreaded the day when he would have to move his office to Frankfort.

"Good morning, madam! Care to take me on a tour?"

Her smile completely lit up the room, despite the summer storm clouds threatening outside. "Sure, Governor. Happy to."

"Now I don't want to hear that from you unless it's in a formal, appropriate setting. Okay? A simple Mike will do."

"Whatever you say, Govern..., er, I mean Mike." Her twinkling eyes immediately brought an unexpected chuckle from him.

With a big smile, Mike said, "You do like to push buttons, don't you, Miss Boesch?"

"Only with people I like. And, of course, only in the proper setting with no audience. Please step past my desk to these double doors to your new office." Opening the double pocket doors, she continued, "I'll give you a few minutes to absorb the whole thing. Mr. Roger Ferguson, God rest his soul, sure built a fabulous prepper house. You'll notice the windows are all pretty deep set? The walls are 24 inches of concrete. Each window has a concealed three-quarter inch thick steel shutter that slides into the side panel to create a bullet-proof seal. The doors are inch-thick steel that are perfectly balanced with spring hinges to make them easy to open and close. You will notice your office has a door in the back corner that goes to a hallway. Inside, you will find a back stairway going up to the second floor, as well as another steel door that connects to the kitchen."

Anna gave Mike another couple of minutes to look around in wonder. "Mike, how well did you know Roger?"

"Not particularly well, though I did like him. He spoke up to support what I was trying to do at each of the neighborhood meetings. Why?"

"When the cleanup crew tried to get inside, they found it impossible. Finally, they found an envelope inside of a zip-lock freezer bag on the table out by the pool in back. It had your name on it. Lisa opened it and found a high-security metal key to open the front and back door. It also had directions to a key box inside the house with multiple spare keys and keys to the rest of the house. Inside this building, she found both Roger and his wife's bodies lying on their bed in the master bedroom. On his desk, he had left a holographic will. Do you know what that is?" Mike shook his head no.

"A holographic will is like a regular will, but it is handwritten, dated and signed by the maker and is valid in the Commonwealth of Kentucky. Anyway, it's a legal document and Roger left his home and everything in it to you, Mike. Obviously he knew he and his wife were dying and his last act was to give you this home, with his stated intention that it should be your new office, and home, if you wanted it to be. When you asked me to become your executive assistant and find a good place for your new government temporary office, Lisa let me know about this place. I think she was waiting to surprise you with it."

"Wow," Mike said humbly.

"Oh, two other things," said Anna, "behind a two-inch thick steel door, at the foot of a concrete stairway to the basement, is a secure room not dissimilar to Peter's place. Nobody's been in there yet, but it's presumed to be a secure refuge and panic room type shelter in case of need. There's also a secret door under your back-stairway going downstairs into the basement to access it. If it's anything like the rest of the house, it should be quite something to see."

"And the second thing?" Mike asked, as his mind raced to keep up.

"Yes, the Master bedroom upstairs has been completely sanitized, and the mattress has been replaced by a new Tempurpedic® king-sized mattress from the bed store in Cronin. It also has a two-person hottub, a walkout shower and a complete new set of linens. I could only do all of this with the help of Lisa and her four-man cleanup crew. As a reward, each of them was allowed to shower and use the Jacuzzi yesterday afternoon before cleaning everything up to be ready for you this morning. I don't think any of them begrudge you for this. You, mister, certainly have an amazing way of making people love you."

"Now," Anna continued, "do you want to see everything I just described? Except for the basement, which you can do later. Your first appointment is not until 9:00 a.m. and shouldn't take much preparation. It'll be in the former living room, now a conference room, across the hall from my office."

After taking Mike on the grand tour, Anna ended in the kitchen. "By the way, how's Lauren doing today?" The concern and empathy in her voice was clear.

Mike signed and said, "Not well. It's probably not going to be very long now." Anna walked up to Mike and gave him a big hug. "God, I'm so sorry, Mike." She then turned and walked back to her office and desk with a heavy heart.

***

Alice's Home
North of Frankfort, Kentucky
0610 Hours EDT

Kerry walked away from Alice's house with a lot of regrets and some fear. Alice was sleeping soundly in her bedroom without the protection of her .38 caliber revolver, which was stuffed into his now-loose belt. He had also cleaned out her cupboard of all light-weight food that would fit in a pillowcase. She had found a water purification system somewhere, which now resided in the very nice backpack he found in her closet. The thought of feeling remorse for taking her things never occurred to him. After all, she owed all of this to him for having taught her so much about becoming more self-reliant. He had been her incentive to actually go outside of her house to forage, after all.

Kerry normally hated getting up at this hour of the morning, but it was the only time he could depend upon her being asleep. Hell, the woman must be part vampire the way she was up moving around all night, finally falling deep asleep just before dawn.

Once again, Kerry found himself on the road to Frankfort. Alice had told him it was about six miles down the road before he would start running into housing developments and a few stores. As he walked along, he saw a man coming the other direction wheeling a shopping cart, just like the bastard that had sliced his guts open. Only this wasn't that man but a younger, cleaner, more determined man, and his cart was loaded with baby formula and disposable diapers.

Kerry kept his hand on the butt of the revolver and stayed on the other side of the road before saying, "Hello friend. Can you suggest a place I can find people willing to help those of us that are down on their luck?"

The man's suspicious expression didn't change much. "Now you just stay on your side of the road, mister. But yes, you can go into downtown Frankfort, about five miles straight down this road, and you'll run into people that can direct you to the new Mayor of Frankfort. He helps people that need it, but you best be ready to work for it. The man isn't much about handouts but hand-ups. You'll have to work or you won't eat. Just warning you."

With that, the young man continued north on the road, while periodically glancing back to make sure Kerry wasn't following him.

Kerry muttered, "Guess that young feller ran into one too many lazy assed people who just wanted to take advantage of him." It never occurred to Kerry that he was another one of those types of people.

CHAPTER 18
THE NEW YEAR – PLUS ONE HUNDRED SIXTY EIGHT DAYS

Surveillance outpost along I-64
Outside the Outer Circle Freeway
Louisville, Kentucky
1030 Hours EDT

Hung and two of Linda's more reliable civilian security force men watched I-64 from a short ridgeline along the highway, 200 meters east of the Gene Snyder highway overpass over the Interstate. Their position allowed for an unobstructed view of the Interstate while also offering concealment.

"So what do you think, Hung?" The question came from the younger of the two other watchers. He was only eighteen years old. "They gonna just send a Humvee, or will they send something like a tank?"

Hung, who was relaxing with his back to a tree and eyes closed, said, "Hard to say. Depends on how arrogant this chair warming Colonel really is. We may have just sat out here all night and all morning for nothing if they decide to send their response using the Blue Grass Parkway instead of the Interstate. Then Bravo Team will get to report whatever they send. Fortunately, I'll hear it on the radio, regardless." Use of radios was one of many specialized skills intimately familiar to any SF team member.

"If I had to guess," Hung said, "I'd say they will have wanted to sleep on their answer overnight and will finish it and sent it out sometime later this morning. You two just make sure you have eyes and ears on that Interstate nonstop until we hear something. And if they do drive by, don't do anything stupid like get seen by their spotters. There's probably somebody that did a lot of patrols over in the Sandbox and knows what to look for. Got it?"

"Sure thing, Hung," both men said in unison.

Conversation dragged on for over an hour before Hung heard the distinctive growl of more than one MRAP armored vehicle rolling toward their position from the West. Hung took out his little green notebook and grabbed his pen out of a pocket as the column rolled by. Hung dutifully wrote: 1142 EDT MRAP, UP-ARMORED HV, MRAP, MRAP, MRAP, MRAP, 4-axel troop transport. He then transmitted the information over the secure net to both the Com room in the Callahan residence and to the Boone Center Radio Room in Frankfort.

Newly appointed Kentucky National Guard Commander General Sean Callahan received the typewritten radio communication, read it, and passed it around to his National Guard Battalion leader.

The Battalion leader turned to Sean and asked, "What are your orders, Sir?" No one present was under any delusions about the momentousness of this occasion.

"Execute Plan B." Plan B was designed to take advantage of the entry choke point between high fences to enter the Boone National Guard Center complex. The only realistic entry into the Center complex was through the armored and concrete barriers of the gate or across the adjacent airport runway from the civilian side of the airport. Two M1 Abrams tanks were stationed fifty meters behind the gates with Up-Armored Humvees with TOW anti-tank missile launchers attached to the roof to back up the tanks. Two other M1 Abrams tanks were parked and visible on the helicopter tarmac on the National Guard side of the airport, along with two Up-Armored Humvees with TOWS. Both groups were supported by four sandbag emplacements for SAW or M249 Squad Automatic Weapon belt-fed machine guns.

Forty minutes later, the Fort Knox column approached the main gate before coming to a complete stop. At a distance of seventy-five meters, the lead vehicle saw and recognized the Up-Armored Humvees and the two M1 Abrams tanks. Both tanks had started their engines, displaying their exhaust plume, as the column turned onto the driveway leading to the gate. The motionless standoff continued for nearly thirty minutes before the second vehicle in the column, the Up-Armored Humvee, pulled out of line and slowly approached the gated entrance, where an MP held up his hand, signaling them to stop.

The Army sergeant driving the Humvee opened his door and stepped out to speak to the MP. "Sergeant Maples, U.S. Army, out of Fort Knox. Who might you be, Sergeant?"

The MP replied, "Buck Sergeant Maples, I am First Sergeant Lopez, Army National Guard. What's your business here and why do you have several heavily armored vehicles coming up the driveway to this Center?"

Sergeant Maples was not prepared for the commanding presence of the six foot two inch Lopez. Upon seeing Maples stumble, Lt. Johnson exited the Humvee from the passenger side and approached the two sergeants.

Lt. Johnson barked the order, "At ease, Sergeants!"

Sergeant Lopez didn't move, with his M-4 rifle slung over his shoulder in the low-ready position. He cocked his head slightly with wry amusement at this young lieutenant busting on the scene "like his shit don't stink," thought the Sergeant.

"Sergeant, what's the holdup here?" Lt. Johnson's question was again barked out with authority. It was received like the bark of a small, annoying Chihuahua.

"My orders, Lieutenant, are to stop anyone from coming onto this Post without authorization. I'll ask you the same thing I asked your Buck Sergeant here. What are you doing bringing a heavily armed convoy up my driveway, uninvited?"

Lt. Johnson was becoming increasingly angry by the second. "What I'm doing here, Sergeant, is I am bringing a letter to your Commanding Officer from Colonel Martin T. Briggs, U.S. Army and Commander at Fort Knox. Now why are you delaying our passage and why the HELL are there tanks and armored vehicles blocking the way?"

Sergeant Lopez gave himself a five count before responding in a slow, deep voice. "Lieutenant, let me give you a piece of advice, free of charge, that I've given baby lieutenants repeatedly over the past twenty-five years in the Active Army and National Guard. Lose the attitude, 'cause it just makes you sound pompous and ridiculous. In this situation here, it could also get you and a lot of other good men killed. So grow up and start acting like the officer and gentleman you should be, by Act of Congress. Now, why don't we start over, shall we?"

After a deep, slow breath, Lt. Johnson said, "Sergeant, request permission to enter your post and hand deliver a letter from Full Bird Colonel Martin T. Briggs to your Commanding Officer."

"Lieutenant, please give me a few minutes to call this in and, after the proper authorization, I will provide transportation for you to our Headquarters building." Sergeant Lopez turned and walked back to one of the guard shacks at the entrance.

Five minutes later, Sergeant Lopez drove up to Lt. Johnson's Humvee in an Army pickup truck. The Lieutenant and three other soldiers, with weapons, exited the Humvee and walked toward the pickup truck.

"I'm sorry, Lieutenant, I only have authorization for you to enter the Post. If you insist on having your guard detail come with you, I will need to go back and get authorization. I should warn you, though, that my officer on duty was just leaving for lunch when he gave me your entry authorization." Sergeant Lopez waited patiently for Lt. Johnson's decision, as if he had all day.

"God dammit," muttered Lt. Johnson. "All right, fuck it!" Turning back to his three soldiers, he said, "You three stay here with the convoy. If I'm not back within 60 minutes, contact Fort Knox for instructions."

***

The route taken by Sergeant Lopez's truck showed virtually nothing to Lt. Johnson that was of any tactical value, except for the two tanks, four Humvees with TOWs and four machine gun emplacements. The Lieutenant was not knowledgeable enough, nor could he see well enough, to know if any of that equipment was in operational shape or was just for show. Five minutes later, the pickup truck pulled up in front of the National Guard Headquarters.

Lt. Johnson was escorted into the building by Sergeant Lopez, and another soldier he hadn't even known was sitting in the back seat. The first thing Lt. Johnson noticed was the building was well lit by LED fluorescent-type lighting and comfortably cooled by air conditioning.

Lt. Johnson asked, "You've got power throughout the Post?"

"Lieutenant, I've been instructed to refer questions you may have to the Post Commander." Sergeant Lopez's answer was not what Lt. Johnson wanted to hear, so he fired off a barrage of questions. He did not receive any response.

After turning down three different hallways and walking over a hundred meters, the Sergeant knocked on an unmarked door and opened it for the Lieutenant, beckoning him to enter.

Inside was a conference table with a Captain seated at the head and a Command Sergeant Major seated off to the side.

"Come in, Lieutenant. Have a seat. What is your name and assignment?"

Lt. Johnson was, once again, thrown completely off his game plan. "Uh, Sir, I, uh, I'm Lieutenant Johnson, US Army Reserve assigned to Ft. Knox and for the duration of this emergency, Adjutant to Colonel Briggs. I was ordered to bring a letter to a Lieutenant Colonel Callahan. Is he not available?"

"That's correct, son. He is not available. I am the Commander of this National Guard Post. And it's General Callahan. He has been promoted by the Acting Governor and assigned to command all military forces in the state."

"Uh, pardon me for interrupting you, Sir, but…"

"No need, son. Just don't interrupt me again. There will be an opportunity for your questions and even your observations in a few minutes. Let me fill you in on the situation here. Presumably at the direction of your Colonel, you have brought a heavily armed column of vehicles to my Post in what I can only interpret as a threatening show of force. Now with all the death and chaos that has happened over the past four months caused by power hungry people in positions of authority throughout the world, I find a young Lieutenant driving up to my Post, in my state, trying to intimidate me and this command. To quote my Command Sergeant Major over there, that shit won't fly here. Our new National Guard Commander is a highly decorated, field trained, professional soldier who enjoys the trust and admiration of every single man and woman in his command. We're taking the results of the shit show dumped on us all by those same power-hungry woke-assed communist leaders and we will re-build the country our Founding Fathers envisioned. You were probably never taught genuine history and instead you grew up thinking the United States was a terrible place lead by terrible people. I'm not going to re-educate you now, but to again quote the Command Sergeant Major, that is pure bullshit."

"Now, son. Please hand me the letter you brought, and I will see that General Callahan receives it. And I can assure you both General Callahan and Acting Governor Mike Broehm have all the legal and moral authority they need to hold the positions they have assumed. Now I am Captain Jeremy Dawson. The letter, please?"

Captain Dawson reached out his hand for the letter. Lt. Johnson reached into his portfolio and handed over the letter.

"Now, Lt. Johnson, do you have any questions you think I will answer or comments you would like to make?"

"Captain, I was going to ask about your strength here, equipment availability and whether you needed the kind of support Fort Knox could give you. Since you've figured out how to get power to your whole Post, your troops look healthy and well fed, and it is apparent that at least the personnel I have observed have a strong loyalty to your current chain of command, I will just request you to convey to Lieutenant Colonel, I mean General Callahan my Colonel's strong suggestion that you join with Fort Knox to combine resources. We expect a great deal of anarchy to break out as survivors of the virus come out of their shells in search of food and other materials."

"I'm happy to pass your message on. Anything else, Lieutenant?" Cpt. Dawson's question was congenial and reasonable.

"Not at this time, Captain."

The CSM walked to the door, opened it and handed the Lieutenant off to his waiting escort. As the Lieutenant walked out the door, Cpt. Dawson said, "Lieutenant?"

The Lieutenant turned with a questioning expression.

"Next time you stop by," said the Captain, "don't bring the show of force. There will be a new sign at the entrance to our driveway informing all that trespassers or any threats will be repulsed by force. Understand?"

"Yes, Sir."

The Captain, the Command Sergeant Major and Sean Callahan followed the truck carrying Lt. Johnson in a Humvee, at a distance, to the gate. They watched as the heavy MRAPS slowly and carefully backed out of the driveway and rolled away before returning to the conference room.

"Okay, gentlemen, and, of course, Command Sergeant Major," Sean said with a smile, let's take a few minutes and read this letter from Colonel Briggs.

FROM: Commander, U.S. Army Post Fort Knox

TO: Commander, U.S. Army National Guard Kentucky

This Command is in receipt of a letter from Mike Broehm, who claims to be the Acting Governor of Kentucky and cites authorities from unspecified TOP SECRET orders and a Presidential Directive placing them in command of all military forces in Kentucky. This Command does NOT recognize these authorities, in the absence of conclusive proof of their content and validity. Lieutenant Colonel Sean Callahan is forthwith Ordered to appear before U.S. Regular Army Colonel Martin T. Briggs within twenty-one days of delivery of this letter bearing a comprehensive listing of all personnel and equipment available to the Kentucky National Guard. Alternatively, LTC Callahan can bring conclusive proof of his claims, along with the personnel and equipment list ordered above. Our nation does not need anarchy nor do does it need a civil war. LTC Callahan will be provided appropriate quarters during his stay at Fort Knox, Kentucky.

Signed,

Colonel Martin T. Briggs

Commander, Fort Knox, Kentucky

"Well," Sean said thoughtfully, "that was interesting. Between that letter and listening to your conversation with the young Adjutant I think we're getting a decent picture of what we're dealing with. What are your thoughts, Command Sergeant Major?"

"Well General," the CSM said with a wry chuckle, "this piss-ant little Colonel seems to be full of himself. I imagine he's going to completely blow a gasket when his Lieutenant Adjutant gets back with his report. And, let me say, General, and you too, Captain, well played. Course you SF types have been handling tin-pot dictators and various foreign military officers for a lot of years."

Sean looked from the CSM to the Captain with a cocked questioning eyebrow.

The CSM said, "General, guess you didn't know the Captain here used to wear a Ranger tab. Had quite a rep down in the jungles of Central and South America in his youth."

Looking at the Captain, Sean asked, "Anything else I should know about your background, Captain?"

"No Sir," he said with a chuckle. "Only, maybe that I was enlisted during all the fun, to include malaria, down in Central America. I went to OCS (Officer Candidate School) when I got back home, then got my degree in business. I ran the Lowe's home improvement store before the virus hit and I lost my whole family and most of my friends."

"I'm sorry, Jeremy," Sean said. "Almost everyone is still hurting over all of this. Damn, man! You were truly masterful in the way you handled the Lieutenant. Just enough reason and fatherly advice mixed in with a tough, no-nonsense approach."

"Now," Sean continued, "can you both, plus Sergeant Lopez, take the rest of the afternoon and ride with me over to Mike's office and we can brief him?"

"General," said Captain Dawson, "aren't you in Command here?"

"Yes," said Sean, "I am in command of all military forces, but here's where I think our founding fathers were brilliant when they set up our Republic. If it's just two military commanders contending for control, they will probably fight it out with the best, or more likely the luckiest, taking the spoils. With civilian leadership and the legal support on our side, we have the best chance of avoiding that and still getting what we need. And I think Mike is the man to get that done."

CHAPTER 19
THE NEW YEAR – PLUS ONE HUNDRED SIXTY-EIGHT DAYS

Mike Broehm Temporary Office Building
Outside of Cronin, Kentucky
1330 Hours EDT

Mike had just returned to his new office building when he saw Sean and three other men in Army uniforms walking in the front door. He quickly walked in behind them and greeted Sean.

"Hi there, General!" Mike gave the greeting with enthusiasm. "What's the good word today?"

Sean stopped and said, "Good afternoon, Governor. Have you got a few minutes for us?"

"Sure," said Mike. "Anna, please hang the Do Not Disturb sign on the door and join us and take notes of what we say. Something tells me I'll need to refer to them in the future."

"Yes Sir," Anna said. "Would you gentlemen like water or tea? I don't think we have any coffee left."

"No thank you, Anna," said Mike. The other three also nodded no thanks.

"Come on in, gentlemen. I'm still trying to get used to my new office," Mike said as he entered through the sliding pocket double-doors.

After Sean had entered the room, Mike stopped Cpt. Dawson, the CSM, and Sergeant Lopez and shook each man's hand firmly while looking them directly in the eyes. He then said, "I'm Mike Broehm. Outside of this office use

'Governor', 'that guy Broehm,' 'the funny lookin' dude,' or even 'Mike.' Really, anything that's not profane. But, by ourselves in this office, please, just call me Mike."

Formal introductions were made by Sean with a brief description of each man and his background. Mike could tell Sean was impressed with each man, so he automatically felt the same way.

Mike introduced Anna as his Executive Assistant and Acting Chief of Staff. "If she comes to you with instructions, you can assume they are directly from me."

"Mike," said Sean, "here's the letter sent by Colonel Briggs."

Mike scanned it quickly without visible reaction, then asked Sean, "Please tell me exactly what happened."

Sean deferred the initial part of the story to Sergeant Lopez, then asked Cpt. Dawson to fill in the rest. Sean had asked each man to rehearse their portion of the story on their way from Frankfort, so each was concise in their descriptions to Mike.

Mike sat for a few seconds after Sean finished the story, then asked, "Command Sergeant Major, any comments or recommendations for me here?"

"Gov, I mean Mike," the CSM said, "I've dealt with several officers like this Colonel Briggs before. They are willing to crush their entire command just to get their own way and can't stand someone else being in charge. Guess that's why he was in Finance, since he probably either failed or recognized he'd never get his way among his combat oriented peers, and he knew he would never make General Officer. On the way, though, he could terrorize his non-combat trained subordinates in the pay office while swinging the powerful club of Paymaster at anyone daring to contest him. Not sure how this works in power politics, but on two occasions I've seen smart fellow officers push a guy like him to the point where he completely alienates all of his subordinates, followed by a mutiny. Here, the risk is it could push him into launching a civil war. What do you feel about that possibility?"

Mike thought about it for a few seconds before saying, "Just so you gentlemen know, I didn't want this job from the beginning. That being said, I believe strongly that we have a unique opportunity to rebuild this nation in the image of our forefather's vision and, with attention paid to our education system such as ensuring accurate history and the principles upon which our country is based, we can do it nearly as well and maybe even better. I'm also not God's gift or the Second Coming. What I am is just smart enough to know who I can trust and who's blowing smoke up my ass. I have also collected some incredible individuals to help me in this endeavor."

"In answer to your question, like our forefathers, I think this country and what it stands for is worth fighting for. I expect those of great intelligence and moral character that surround me will prevent me from doing anything too stupid. I would like to include each of you gentlemen in that group. Can I count on you?"

Mike's words, and their effect, were worthy of a speech leading troops into battle. They swept each man present up in Mike's vision and in a newfound belief that Mike would make it happen. Over the next hour, plans and an outline for contingencies were developed. Taking a diplomatic, but hard-nosed approach to Colonel Briggs and his expected pressure formed into a consensus. Firing upon fellow American soldiers was approved by Mike, with the caveat it should be a last resort. Any all-out assault by Fort Knox forces was to be met with harassing tactics and guerrilla strikes, then fall back. Sean had Mike's full authority to make those judgments. Sean would also send out scouts to watch for activity at Fort Knox and to gather intelligence.

"Mike," Cpt. Dawson, "two other things I need to mention. One of my soldiers told me his brother had found a flyer posted on a telephone pole on the North side of Frankfort advertising for a job with a new organization that promised food, security and a place to live for the security folks and their families. He went on up to learn more and did not return. When my Private went looking for him, he found a warehouse with armed patrols roving around its perimeter. His brother was nowhere to be seen. Also, the Private said he saw what looked like eight or ten naked women being led by a neck-collar and chain out of a building where they had apparently showered, toward the warehouse entrance. They looked like slaves being led to the auction block. One girl was black, while the rest were white from a young teenager to an older, gray-haired woman. What do you think we should do about it?"

"Take this information to Linda Sharpe, before you head back to Frankfort. I'd like her take on it and her recommendations. Looks like she may be about to be promoted to State Police Commissioner as well as all of her other duties." Mike could hear a soft groan from Sean, but ignored it. He knew Sean didn't think he got to see his fiancé enough as it was.

"Okay," said Cpt. Dawson, "how do I find her?"

"Ask your Commander," said Mike, "she's his fiancé. And the second thing?" Mike asked.

"Just so you know, we have a dozen helicopters, to include a two Blackhawks, two Apache attack helicopters and seven other utility choppers that are air worthy. There are four pilots to fly them, including our unit Flight Surgeon, with two additional crewmen, six service crewmen, and women to keep them operational. It might be worth your time to come out to our shop and get a close up look at what we have to fight with."

"Thank you, Captain," Mike said with appreciation. "I will plan on that day after tomorrow, if that works for you."

"Whatever you want, Governor. You're the boss." Captain Dawson made the statement with conviction.

***

Fort Knox Army Military Pay Office
Fort Knox, Kentucky
1500 Hours EDT

Lt. Johnson marched into Colonel Briggs' office and stood at attention in front of his desk. After making the Lieutenant wait for nearly two minutes, the Colonel glanced up and said, "At ease, Lieutenant. Report."

The lieutenant continued to stand at attention, looking straight ahead, and said, "Sir, I delivered your letter to Captain Jeremy Dawson, Commander of the Frankfort Post of the Kentucky National Guard. Captain Dawson promised to convey the letter to General, I mean Lieutenant Colonel Callahan immediately. The implication was that Callahan was not present on the Post, Sir!"

With eyes boring into the Lieutenant, the Colonel said, "All right, Lieutenant, at ease and sit down. Now." After he sat down, the Colonel continued, "Obviously, things did not go as we expected. Start from the beginning and tell me, in detail, what happened."

Lt. Johnson gave a precise report of everything that had occurred, to include the insubordination of Sergeant Lopez.

"So," the Colonel said with growing anger, "they greeted your show of force at the gate with two main battle tanks, several armored vehicles with TOWs, machine-gun nests and both a Sergeant and Captain with an attitude. Does that about sum it up?"

"Sir," said the Lieutenant, "the entire post appeared to have functioning electric power and had organized an unknown, but significant number of survivors. They did not allow me to see much of the Post nor what defenses were present besides at the main gate."

The Colonel rose to his feet, walked deliberately to an open shelving unit against the wall and lifted a snow globe, and began tossing it casually into the air. "Do you know what this is, Lieutenant? It's a snow globe given to me by my daughter, against the wishes of my ex-wife, for Christmas the last year she was in Middle School. I haven't seen her in over ten years, but when I checked, it appears she was taken by the virus."

He continued to toss the globe slowly in his right hand. Suddenly, he wound up and smashed the snow globe against the wall by the door frame. Pieces of glass, plastic, and a splash of water scattered off the wall.

"Goddamn it, man! How dare they defy me!" The Colonel's rage was nearly out of control. "I gave you one simple order, and you screwed it up royally! Come here, Lieutenant."

The Colonel motioned to the large conference table by the window. "Do you see this map of the Frankfort National Guard Post by the airport? Notice anything obvious? There's an airport runway, smooth and flat as can be, and suitable to easily support tanks or other heavy equipment that is just like a beckoning driveway right into the heart of that Post! Okay, here's what I want you to do. I want you to make sure we have a functioning helicopter at OUR airport and take a flight over and verify what defenses they have on the other side of the landing strip, then I want you to have an attack plan developed, material, vehicles and equipment prepared and a battle plan ready for five days from now. Any problems with that? Oh, and you should include at least two attack helicopters to provide air support to the operation."

Seeing the Lieutenant's hesitation, the Colonel said, "Problem with any of that, Lieutenant?"

"Well, Sir. Just so that you are aware, the Kentucky National Guard also has helicopters and likely Stinger anti-aircraft missiles at that Post. If they know we're coming, Sir, it could be very messy and possibly make an attack costly and ineffective."

"You put the plan together, Lieutenant, and get at least one flyover with photographs to support it. Be ready to brief me on the plan at 1800 Hours local in three days. The flyover should happen sometime tomorrow. Am I clear, Lieutenant?"

"Sir, yes Sir," said the Lieutenant, saluting.

***

Building C, Centers for Disease Control
Atlanta, GA
1530 Hours EDT

Captain Schneider sat at the table in the cafeteria's corner, looking at the steaming cup of coffee delivered to him by the kitchen worker. He had told the woman delivering it to take a big sip from the cup two minutes earlier after noticing the woman was shaking when she put the cup down on the table. The woman had run screaming from his table to disappear back into the kitchen. He then stood up, picked up the cup, and walked into the kitchen. The woman and two other kitchen workers were crouching down behind a metal table with terror in their eyes.

"All right," Cap said softly. "You're going to tell me who doctored or gave you the cup to serve to me. Right now. Don't think about it. Just tell me."

The woman fell on the floor into a fetal position, crying hysterically. Cap looked at the male crouching behind the table. "If you want to live," Cap said simply, "you will tell me who did this."

In a gasping, frightened voice, the man said, "It wasn't me, Sir, please!"

Caps stare bored into him. "Tell me who it was. Right now." His eyes gave the man nowhere to go or any other alternative.

"It was Doctor Bergstrum," the man blurted out. "Oh, my God! Now he's going to kill me!"

"No, he won't," Cap said calmly, "But, if you have lied to me, I will." Cap turned and walked out of the kitchen.

Marching down the hallway, Cap saw Dr. Bergstrum retreating toward his office. When he got to his office, he slammed and locked the door. Cap broke open the glass pane to the fire hose and grabbed the firefighter's ax, then swung it at the glass window of Bergstrum's office door, shattering the glass. Through the window Cap could see Bergstrum crouching behind his desk, feverishly opening drawers. Cap reached through the window and unlocked the door before walking in with a purpose.

"You goddam Nazi! I won't give you the satisfaction," said the hysterical doctor. He had grabbed a scalpel from his desk drawer and held it menacingly for a moment, then turned it on himself, slashing his own throat. "Go to Hell, You…" His words faded as the blood pumping from his throat stopped going to his brain and he collapsed across his desk.

Cap took a deep breath before exiting the office and walking quickly to Julie's room, where he found her reading casually at her small desk. "Julie, honey, has anyone come to see you in the last hour?"

Julie had a surprised, skeptical look on her face before answering, "Only that weird little scientist, Doctor Smellman. About forty-five minutes ago, he knocked on my door and offered me a cup of hot coffee. You know I don't drink caffeine, so I thanked him for his kind gesture and declined. He seemed real disappointed. Do you think he likes me or something?"

"No, Julie, come with me. Now." Cap turned and walked out of her room toward the small laboratory Ph.D. scientist Victor Smellman called his work home. Along the way, Cap passed Dr. Simpson and motioned for him to follow, quietly. Cap walked quietly down the hallway until he reached Smellman's laboratory door, where Cap and the other two stopped to listen. Inside there were three or four people arguing quietly, but intensely. A few words could be deciphered, such as, "What if it doesn't work?" and "That silly bitch doesn't drink caffeine. I didn't know what to say or do!" Then Cap heard, "We have got to get the two of them dead. Bergstrum should be able to take care of that damned soldier, then it should be pretty easy to overpower the weird little bitch."

Cap looked at Simpson and mouthed the question, "You heard?"

Dr. Simpson lowered his head and sadly shook it in the affirmative. Julie's face was aghast with uncomprehending amazement.

Cap promptly kicked in the door and discovered Smellman and three others standing only a few feet away from the door around a table. Cap raised his 10 mm automatic and quickly fired four shots, hitting two of the men in the forehead and the other two in the chest. Both Julie and Dr. Simpson were frozen in fear and macabre fascination at seeing four people executed before their eyes. The two men that were shot in the chest lay gasping and quivering on the floor. Cap knew where his bullets had gone, so he turned toward the door, leading Simpson and Julie outside into the hallway, closing the door behind him.

In the hallway, Cap stopped Julie and Simpson and said, "They'll be dead in another two minutes. No need to watch. So that you know, Simpson, Bergstrum, Smellman and his cronies threatened one of the kitchen ladies into taking a poison-laced cup of coffee to me, warning her not to let any of it touch her exposed skin. They did this in the presence of two other kitchen workers, who were also threatened. The male kitchen worker told me it was Dr. Bergstrum that had told them to bring the poisoned coffee to me and threatened to kill them if they did not, or if they could not keep their mouths shut. What you just heard through the door was Smellman's and his cronies' confession to the conspiracy to murder both me and Julie. In a time of Martial Law, there is no other sane option for handling this situation. People like that will kill whomever they like, including you, doctor."

Standing in the hallway, Simpson was just understanding the dangers and reality of his current circumstances. He had been around long enough and had been managing these very people long enough to see the truth in Cap's assessment. It reinforced his initial inclination to follow Cap's lead.

"Simpson," Cap said quietly, "gather everyone you can find. Let's have another short meeting in the cafeteria. Rumor control is one of the more challenging parts of command, and I want everyone to hear exactly what happened here and why. And so you're not blindsided, I will want your squad to go back to Smellman's lab and take care of bagging up and disposing of the bodies and cleaning up the mess in the lab. Do you have one of the janitors on your squad?"

"Yes, I do." Simpson said it with some relief.

"Okay, that's good. Here's a leadership 101 tip. Pull your janitor off to the side and tell him you want him to advise your squad on what to do to clean everything up correctly, with your supervision, but NOT to do any of the actual cleaning himself. Take this opportunity to let the entire squad get their hands dirty and working together on a messy task. It wouldn't hurt for you to pitch in on a couple of small cleaning things just to show them you don't think you're above doing these things yourself. Anybody that won't do what you tell them to do, you can send them to see me."

Cap saw the understanding in Simpson's eyes and upgraded his assessment of the man.

"All right, then. Cafeteria in fifty-five minutes. Julie, please come with me." Cap then walked away to his new office.

CHAPTER 20
THE NEW YEAR – PLUS ONE HUNDRED SIXTY NINE DAYS

Surveillance outpost along I-64
Outside the Outer Circle Freeway
Louisville, Kentucky
0545 Hours EDT

The SF Operator with his civilian observer started when they heard the low-flying Blackhawk helicopter roar above Interstate 64 from West to East at 300 feet above the roadway. Daylight was just breaking and both men could clearly see a soldier sitting in the open doorway of the chopper on this balmy, sunny morning. The Operator immediately fired up his radio to advise the Comunications Center outside of Cronin and the Boone National Guard Center to expect the chopper in fifteen or twenty minutes. The operator knew the chopper was traveling at around 120 miles per hour and was about 30 miles away from the base in Frankfort.

***

Boone National Guard Center
Frankfort, Kentucky
0550 Hours EDT

The sound of the air-raid siren echoed across the base and airport. Men and a few women scrambled out of their bunks, grabbed their rifles, and, partially dressed, went directly to their assigned positions. Over the next ten minutes, word spread that a Blackhawk helicopter was likely inbound from Fort Knox at 300 feet above ground level. The generator fired up in the portable control tower set up on the tarmac near several parked Blackhawk and other types of helicopters. The generator activated the portable radar stations set up on the perimeter of the airfield. Three minutes later, an incoming bogey was spotted four miles to the Southwest, closing fast. On the emergency frequency, the sole surviving trained air traffic controller broadcast, "Aircraft incoming to KFFT, Frankfort, Kentucky airfield. Identify yourself."

The demand was repeated twice more before a pilot responded, "Frankfort Control tower, this is Blackhawk 03223C, inbound to your airport for a flyover and landing. Where's a good place to set her down this morning?"

Thinking quickly, the controller keyed the microphone and said, "Blackhawk 03223 Charlie, identify your base location and your intentions. Also, be advised the military side of the airport is closed to all unauthorized traffic. Do not, I say again, do not land on the military side of this airfield. You may land on the civilian side of the field by the Field Base Operators building if you like. Transport will be provided to the other side of the field."

While the Blackhawk took three leisurely circles around the entire airport, including the Boone National Guard Center, the controller repeatedly demanded he identify his home base and his intentions. With Captain Dawson standing next to him, the Controller ordered, "03223 Charlie you WILL identify your home base and your intentions immediately or you will be fired upon. Do I make myself clear?"

The radio speaker activated with, "Frankfort Control, we are departing the area to the North."

The controller responded, "Blackhawk, say your home base and intentions."

There was no response, and the Blackhawk disappeared to the North at low altitude.

The Captain walked over to Sergeant Lopez, who was in charge of security for the facility, and said, "Sergeant, next time let's make sure there are several men with armed Stinger missiles readily at hand, just in case they're needed. Okay?"

"Yessir, Commander," the Sergeant responded with enthusiasm. "It'll be a good wake-up call for the younger guys that we're now in a war zone, just like over in the sandbox."

***

Non-Descript Warehouse
Outside of Frankfort, Kentucky
0620 Hours EDT

Tank holstered his .357 Magnum revolver after having executed a man from his security force. The man had, without permission, raped and beaten a fourteen-year-old girl that was wearing a collar and chain. When Blondi had caught him, he threatened to cut Blondi's tongue out if any word of what happened got out. Tank had Antonio and Roberto roust the man out of his bunk early that morning in the warehouse, tying him up with ratchet straps before he was fully awake. They then took him behind the warehouse where Tank had previously dug a large pit with a Commonwealth of Kentucky piece of heavy equipment. Neither Roberto nor Antonio cared much for the man, particularly since Blondi had just described what the man had done to brutalize the girl. Tank had shown his disgust after hearing Blondi's rendition by first slapping him across the face, knocking him down at the edge of the pit, then drawing his .357 Magnum revolver and blowing away part of the man's head. Tank then used his booted foot to roll the body into the pit.

"Roberto," Tank said. "Fire up the front-end loader and put a couple feet of dirt over this fool. Nobody spoils one of my girls and threatens Blondi without my say-so. Make sure that word gets passed around."

"Sure, Tank," Roberto said congenially. "We'll make sure everybody here knows the rules."

Roberto began walking toward the equipment when suddenly a helicopter roared overhead as it quickly flew past, only 300 feet above the ground. Tank instinctively crouched down while Roberto and Antonio both dove for the nearby cover of the warehouse wall. Blondi just stood gawking in the direction the helicopter had disappeared.

"Where the fuck did that come from?" Tank bellowed the question as the noise had temporarily affected his hearing.

"Ahh," said Antonio, "so it's true what the two compadres that you hired yesterday told me. The National Guard base at the Frankfort airport has been showing signs of life. This must be a helicopter from that base."

"Well, hell," said Tank. "Just what I don't need is any soldier boys sticking their noses into our business out here. Antonio, why don't you have one of the boys take a bicycle ride over toward that base and look to see what's going on there? It can't be more than six or eight miles. Get one of 'em that's savvy with doing that sort of thing and maybe have him take food and water to spend the night and then another day. Let me know what he finds tomorrow evening." "Okey-dokey, Tank. I know just the one to do it. Me! I'll bring you back what you need by tomorrow evening."

Antonio was gliding away quickly before Tank responded. It always surprised Tank how smoothly and effortlessly the man moved. Almost like he hovered across the ground instead of walked like everyone else.

Tank turned to Blondi and said, "What do you know about the National Guard people over by the airport?"

"Hell, Tank," Blondi said defensively, "all I know is the political people never considered them to be hardly worth noticing. You know, since the State Police were the ones responsible for protecting their shiny little asses, they considered the military pukes to be only a drain on what would otherwise be additional discretionary funds. I'm sorry, I'm just not much help on that front."

"Antonio should be able to get us something by tomorrow afternoon or evening," Tank said thoughtfully. "I just don't want any surprises coming from there. We got a nice thing going here, but it may not be the best thing to be so close to the Army. I just remembered there's another warehouse a ways North and East, just outside of Cynthiana. That could be a good place to move our operations if I decide to. Take Roberto and three of his most trustworthy men to go over there and set up operations. By tomorrow, I want to load up trucks and take part of the stuff in this warehouse and most of our people, as well as the girls."

To himself, Tank thought, "Maybe I should groom one of these guys to run the operation here, while moving myself a ways to the Northeast. Yeah, think I'll look into that."

***

Lt. Johnson had climbed aboard the Blackhawk helicopter just as the sun rose on the Eastern horizon. The beauty of the morning was tarnished by the loud hum of the twin-turbo engines as the chopper readied for departure. The lieutenant sat in the open doorway, tethered to a safety line. After having ridden in a few Vietnam era Huey helicopters, it still amazed him at how powerful the twin-turbo engines were in comparison.

Without satellite based GPS, which worked only sporadically, the pilot had followed the Interstate directly to the Frankfort airport, using the VFR or Visual Flight Rules chart (map) on his iPad as a backup. He did not see the camouflaged observation point overlooking I-64 just outside of the outer circle freeway, only a few minutes into the flight. The Lieutenant's helmet microphone was hooked into both the aircraft intercom system and its radio system. He had given orders to use the encrypted radio system to maintain communications with the tower at the Fort Knox Post airport. Because of their low altitude and the radio system being limited to "line of sight," they lost contact with Fort Knox fifteen minutes after takeoff. That was a good detail to know and report.

About ten minutes out from Frankfort, the pilot advised the lieutenant to expect some type of contact soon. Sure enough, his headset activated about four miles from the Frankfort airport with, "Aircraft incoming to KFFT, Frankfort, Kentucky airfield. Identify yourself." The Lieutenant ordered the pilot to remain silent for the first two times the message was repeated, before telling the pilot to respond only with the aircraft type and tail number.

The controller advised the military side was closed and demanded to know their home base and intentions. Lt. Johnson told the pilot to take a few slow circles around the airport and base to allow the cameras to capture everything that was exposed to view from the air.

When the controller threatened to fire upon them the Lt. Johnson said, "Okay, pilot, let's depart to the North. Shall we?"

"Yes, Sir," said the nervous pilot. "You never know about the Guard guys and their itchy trigger fingers."

The pilot flew about thirty kilometers North of the airport to get out of range of their presumed portable radars before turning straight West, then eventually South, flying over Shelbyville, Kentucky to I-64. Increasing altitude to two thousand feet above the ground, they were able to report their location and estimated time of arrival at Fort Knox tower.

***

Fort Knox Army Airport
Fort Knox, Kentucky
0930 Hours EDT

Forty-five minutes after landing at Fort Knox airport, the lieutenant marched into Colonel Briggs' office and stood at attention, waiting to be recognized.

The Colonel was impatient, so he immediately ordered the lieutenant, "At Ease, Lieutenant. And sit down, then report."

"Sir, in a nutshell, they were waiting for us when we flew over. Even though it was barely 0630 in the morning. They had a controller contact us on the emergency channel, about four miles out, demanding we identify ourselves and our intentions. My pilot believed they had activated their remote field radar system and were seeing us on their screen. After they repeated the demand several times, I had the pilot identify us as a Blackhawk, give only our tail number and say we were coming in for a landing. The tower immediately informed us the military portion of the airport was closed to unauthorized traffic and we should land on the civilian side. They would send a vehicle to transport me or us. They then demanded to know our home base and our intentions. We ignored them for nearly three slow circles over the area to take photographs. They then informed us to respond or they would shoot at us. Sir, I saw several machine-gun nests and machine guns on top of their four tanks and armored vehicles tracking us. I did not see any man-launched anti-aircraft missiles, but believe they probably have those available."

After a deep breath, Lt. Johnson said, "I finally had the pilot respond to the controller that we were departing to the North. Having obtained all the intelligence I felt was possible, we departed before some National Guard soldier got, as my pilot said, an itchy trigger finger. I will need to review the photographs and video taken, but there were three machine-gun nests along the road accessing the civilian side of the field and two additional M-1 Abrams tanks and two armored vehicles protecting that side from uncontested access."

"All right, Lieutenant," the Colonel said slowly, "give me your gut feeling. Could we successfully attack this base and win?"

The lieutenant paused before saying, "Sir, if we attacked them, they would put up a hell of a fight. Until I get the Battle Plan developed and go over it with some very combat experienced senior NCOs (Non-commissioned officers or Sergeants), I can't give you an accurate assessment."

"Do that, Lieutenant," the Colonel said. "My original timeline stays in place for your briefing, subject to change, of course."

"Yes, Sir!" The lieutenant saluted and departed the room.

CHAPTER 21
THE NEW YEAR – PLUS ONE HUNDRED SIXTY-NINE DAYS

Mike Broehm Temporary Office Building
Outside of Cronin, Kentucky
1215 Hours EDT

Mike sat in his office reading an updated report on information gathered from the team sent to Cronin and the surrounding area. They were performing a count of survivors and to get a status of how the individuals were surviving. He heard someone come into the front door of the building and quickly determined it was Sean and Linda talking to Anna.

"Mike was waiting to see you, Sean," Anna said. "Who's your friend?"

Sean said, "This is Lieutenant Scott Ferrell. Anna, I presume you will sit in on this meeting, anyway? Shall we go on in?"

Anna poked her head into Mike's office and said, "Governor, I mean Mike, Sean, Linda, and Lieutenant Scott Ferrell are here to see you."

"Please bring them in, Anna," Mike said. "And if you don't mind, please invite Lisa and Suzie to join us. Will you?"

After Mike was introduced to Lt. Ferrell and everyone was seated around Mike's small conference table, Mike asked Sean, "What's the latest, Sean?"

"Mike," said Sean, "you're aware of the Blackhawk helicopter that buzzed the National Guard Center in Frankfort. At 0545 this morning our OP, or observation post, just East of Louisville, radioed notice that a Blackhawk was flying low and fast, Eastbound, over I-64. Boone National Guard Center was awakened to emergency sirens and immediately took up defensive positions around the Base and the airport. About twenty minutes later, the Blackhawk was seen approaching on their field radar. They attempted contact over the emergency channel for a full minute before the chopper finally responded with their Blackhawk designation and tail number only. When asked their intentions, they advised they were inbound for a slow-circle around the airport followed by landing. They directed him to the civilian side and ordered the pilot to identify his home base and his intentions. He did not respond, so after watching him take two slow low-level circles around the base and airport, the air traffic controller demanded he reply or he would be fired upon. The Blackhawk turned to the North and announced he was departing the area. Radar lost him about ten nautical miles north of Frankfort. Radar picked him up again north and a little east of Shelbyville at 3,000 feet, which is about 2,000 feet above the ground."

"Say what?" asked Mike.

"They usually give altitudes for aircraft using altitude above sea level, unless specifically noting it is AGL or above the ground level," said Sean.

"So," Mike said, "I understand you and Captain Dawson are pretty sure that was Adjutant Lieutenant Johnson sitting in the doorway of the Blackhawk?"

Mike glanced at Lisa and Suzie and received nods, showing they were up to speed with the situation.

"Yes, Mike," Sean said, "I saw the high-speed digital photographs taken by two of the intelligence people in his command. Johnson was wearing a helmet with microphone in front of his mouth, but jawline and pencil-line set of lips were pretty distinctive."

"Okay," Mike replied, "so we're confident it was a Fort Knox chopper. Do you think they were doing a reconnaissance of the Headquarters to prepare for an attack?"

"Mike," Said Sean, "first, let me ask Lieutenant Ferrell give you a bit of his own background."

"Thank you, Sir," said the Lieutenant. "Governor, a little less than three months ago, I was part of an Apache attack helicopter unit out of Fort Campbell. It's the home of the 101st Airborne Division and the Post that straddles the Kentucky/Tennessee border between Hopkinsville, in Western Kentucky and Clarksville, Tennessee. I was flying the gunner's seat of my Apache on a two-bird live-fire training mission to Fort Knox. Our training mission had barely begun when it was called off because of a combination of weather and the virus. With weather building over most of Western Kentucky, we diverted to KFFT Frankfort airport. Right after we set down, they ordered us to stand down in Frankfort and wait for further orders. Like I said, it was just as the virus was sweeping the country. We stayed the first few nights at the airport guarding our fully armed birds, then everyone got sick. I just got a bad case of the flu, but the other Apache 2-man crew and my Pilot-In-Command all died from the virus. Every one of them had small children at home–if they survived."

Mike could see the tears building in the Lieutenant's eyes.

Lt. Ferrell continued, "Anyway, after another couple of weeks living on survival rations kept in the birds and scrounging for food and water in the National Guard hanger at KFFT, I had mostly recovered. The base appeared deserted, so I hiked across the runway and over to the main road, US 60 I think, where I found an abandoned gas/mini-mart full of useful supplies. I also met a guy scrounging like me, who lived nearby. He let me know of a house down from him that had been empty for a while, so I just sort of moved in and hunkered down. About a month ago, I could hear vehicle activity coming from the base and airport, so I walked over. When I met Captain Dawson and Colonel, I mean General Callahan, let's just say I joined up."

"Governor," the Lieutenant said, "the two Apache attack helicopters can be ready for action, with full combat loads, in about fifteen minutes. Unfortunately, we don't have any additional munitions to reload when this load is expended. I can fly either of them, but really needed a primary pilot to be an effective fighting unit. Then a couple of weeks ago, the National Guard air wing Medical Officer or Flight Surgeon, Major Ron Shouse, showed up at the base on a motorcycle, of all things. He had somehow wrangled a check-out in an Apache about a year ago. I guess adventure training like that is another one of those carrots the Army dangles in front of people with valuable skills they want to recruit. Medical doctors don't, or at least didn't, seem to be motivated to waste time practicing medicine for the military. Anyway, he had gone into some hidey-hole out in the country with his family when the virus struck and kept himself and his family alive. It took only one meeting with General Callahan to convince him what you and we are doing is worth joining. Sir, it really means a lot to all of us that nobody is ordered to join, like what that Colonel over in Fort Knox is pushing. Like everyone else in your new military, I am a willing volunteer."

"We're happy to have you, Scott," said Mike warmly. "Now, what can you tell me about that Blackhawk?"

"Well," said the Lieutenant, "it was an older model, but well maintained and its engines sounded pretty good and the pilot seemed to know what he was doing. I only saw one pilot and no co-pilot. It was conducting an ordinary low-level surveillance mission of the base and surrounding area. I saw what looked like all four cameras operating. It's a high probability they sent it specifically to see how our base defenses were laid out and how vulnerable we are to both an air and ground attack."

Mike momentarily frowned, then said, "Lieutenant, do you know if Fort Knox has any attack helicopters?"

"No Sir, they don't," the lieutenant said, "only a couple of Blackhawks and some fixedwing assets. The only close attack helicopter resources are at Fort Campbell. With the General's permission, I reached out by military radio systems a couple of weeks ago trying to contact anyone at Fort Campbell, without success."

"Okay, thank you," said Mike.

Mike looked at Sean and the Lieutenant. "I get the feeling you trained soldiers are pretty prepared for whatever this Colonel Briggs might send your way. Am I correct?"

Sean said, "Yes, and no, Mike. Yes, my SF Master Sergeant and Jeremy Dawson have completed an analysis of the defensibility of the base in Frankfort and its airport. They identified several vulnerabilities and are working toward addressing each of them. We have a skeleton tank crew for each of our four Abrams tanks and just over 120 rounds of high explosive shells for their main guns. There are only two-man crews capable of operating six of our ten Up-Armored Humvees, with four having the TOW missile systems on them. We have only twenty TOW missiles. We've got enough munitions for a quick fight, Mike, but it just occurred to me we should reach out to the Blue Grass Army Depot outside of Richmond. I think it is likely they will have about everything we would need regarding munitions, including even some things needed to reload the Apaches."

"Sean," Mike asked. "If Fort Knox sends over a strike force, will you use the available Apache? And Scott, are you willing to shoot down their Blackhawk if you receive the order or are fired upon?"

Lieutenant Ferrell didn't hesitate. "Yes, Governor, if my Commander gives the order, they have already crossed that line. Might I suggest, Sir that I be given instruction and the authority to radio them over the emergency frequency first, with a warning? They probably have nothing that's a genuine threat to me unless they get really close, and then it still won't be much of a threat."

Mike looked again at Sean. "It's your call, Commander. I'd feel better issuing a warning before blowing a helicopter out of the sky, but I think it's your judgment whether delaying might put any of our people in peril."

Sean nodded. "Scott, let's just plan on issuing them a warning as soon as you can establish contact. After that, if they keep coming, then it's on them."

"Yessir," said the Lieutenant.

CHAPTER 22
THE NEW YEAR – PLUS ONE HUNDRED SEVENTY-ONE DAYS

A Non-Descript Warehouse
Outside of Frankfort, Kentucky
0725 Hours EDT

Former SF Lieutenant Linda Sharpe lay quietly motionless next to her SF Staff Sergeant, both in personally assembled ghillie suits. She had been surveying the initial activities around the warehouse below when she heard one single click over her radio communications system. Two other SF operators had staged about seventy-five meters west of her position. When both teams had arrived three hours earlier, they could only examine the immediate area using their NVGs or night vision goggles and thermal imaging goggles. Her Sergeant had found and identified what looked like a regular observation post twenty meters to the west of the position she ultimately set up.

Straining her ears, Linda heard the nearly silent rustling of someone walking to the observation point, pause there to urinate, and then walk on down the hill toward the warehouse. In the morning sunlight, the man came into Linda's field of view as he started down the hill. A quick glance to her Sergeant resulted in his raising one finger, showing the man had been alone.

Ten minutes after the presumed security guard entered the area of the warehouse, a small shed door was unlocked and opened by the security guard, who then entered the shed. A few moments later, he came out of the shed, leading a thin chain attached to the collar of an older, naked woman, closely followed by nine other naked women and girls chained to each other in a line. They led the group to a twenty-foot square cinderblock building where earlier they had seen four men delivering 5-gallon buckets of water. The women led into the building were brought back out by their guards twenty minutes later with wet skin and hair before being taken to a nearby area with picnic tables set up. There, each was given a bowl with some kind of soup or hot cereal in it and allowed to sit and eat.

Linda quelled her initial instinct to shoot and kill all the guards and rescue the women. She began to develop a plan for the raid on the compound, which would probably occur around dawn, as soon as the next day. A quiet conversation with her Sergeant, and agreement was reached to pull out and return to their security office back at the neighborhood around noon. They took photographs of everything and everyone, including a large, older, grizzled graybeard that had to stand at least six foot three. The way everyone acted around him, Linda believed he was likely the boss.

***

Fort Knox Army Military Pay Office
Fort Knox, Kentucky
1800 Hours EDT

Lt. Johnson knocked on the Commander's door and marched into his office and stood at attention to be recognized.

"At ease and sit down, Lieutenant. What do you have for me?"

"Sir," said the Lieutenant, "I have been able to collect a half a dozen NCOs with combat experience to lead a strike force of about 200 men. Only a third of these men have ever served in combat. This group amounts to about ten percent of the 2,000 soldiers we have available on this Post, which should leave enough personnel to keep this Post functioning and secure. Over half of these men were recruits in basic training when the virus struck. There are two older-model Abrams M1 tanks with experienced drivers, but only one tank crew has any gunnery experience. We filled the rest of the tank crew out with recruits. Along with the tanks, I have fifteen Up-Armored Humvees, as well as the two of the

MRAPS that drove over with me to Frankfort the last time. Only three of the Up-Armored Humvees have crew members that can actually use their weapons systems, be it roof-mounted TOWs, surface-to-air missiles or machine guns. Everyone has been to the range with their M-4 rifles enough to be relatively proficient."

"So what you're telling me, Lieutenant," the Colonel said with disgust, "we don't have an effective fighting force and I should just pack my tent and sing 'kum by yah,' is that it?"

"No Sir," Lt. Johnson said, "I haven't finished my presentation yet, Sir. We do not YET have a fighting force that could reasonably be sent anywhere and win a fight. But, with training, and this is a training Post, Sir, we can have a fighting force that could whip those arrogant National Guard pukes into compliance and joining under your leadership. It's just going to take a couple of months to do that."

The Lieutenant had successfully calmed the Colonel's anger. "All right, Lieutenant, I will want weekly reports on how you're progressing. I also expect you to continue to recruit survivors to join our Post. Also, make sure you continue to reach out for any organization down at Ft. Campbell. In fact, plan on an exploratory chopper flight down there in the next week to see for yourself what they have going. I can't believe there's nobody running things with all the assets they have down there." After a moment's pause, Col. Briggs said, "No wait, Lieutenant. Belay that last order. Let's let sleeping dogs lie down there. Just what I need if some senior Colonel or someone should decide Fort Knox should be under his command!"

***

Mike Broehm Temporary Office Building
Outside of Cronin, Kentucky
1900 Hours EDT

There were seven people sitting around the larger conference table across the hall from Mike Broehm's office. Notably, Mike was not present. Sean Callahan headed up the meeting.

"Anna," said Sean, "do you know everyone here?"

Anna had had already looked around, noting Linda, her SF Staff Sergeant, Sean, Hung, a man in his late 50s or early 60s and a slender Army Major. "I'm Anna Boesch, Mike's assistant and Acting Chief of staff. I do know everybody except for these two gentlemen. What are your names and positions?"

The older gentleman said, "I'm George Kessler. I used to be vice-Mayor of Frankfort and have begun organizing survivors in town. I've been communicating with Captain Dawson and he asked me if I could help with something, but didn't give me any details."

The second man said, "I'm Ron Shouse. I used to be an Ear, Nose and Throat surgeon and was the medical authority for the flight wing of the National Guard in Frankfort. Now, I'm not sure exactly what I am, except for a survivor of the virus and an admirer of Mike Broehm. I'm not sure why I'm here either, but suspect the General here will fill us in."

"Thank you, gentlemen," Anna said, "Sean?"

"Linda, "it's your show. Do your thing."

"Yes, sir, general sir!" Linda said with exaggerated exuberance. "And we can discuss that later!"

Chuckles sounded among the group. Before Linda could continue, Sean looked at her, smiled and said, "Yes, dear is sufficient. For those that don't know, Linda's my fiancé." Amused enlightment blossomed on several faces.

Linda turned on the big-screen TV and plugged a thumb drive into a box connected by wire. Up popped a clear video of a line of naked, chained and collared women being led into the cinderblock building. "During a surveillance of a warehouse six to eight miles north of Frankfort, this is what we saw. Yes, after watching for most of this morning, I can confirm this is exactly what it appears. Someone or some group has captured and enslave fellow survivors. This would be a perfect case for the FBI or the Kentucky State Police. Of course, there are no law enforcement organizations now, so at Mike's direction, I am operating under a state of Martial Law. I want to take tomorrow to gather an arrest team and we will raid this compound at 0630 the day after tomorrow. I will want three teams totaling fifteen armed military people, led by myself, the Staff Sergeant and Hung, to conduct the initial assault, taking out any gun-toting combatants and bringing the rest to prone, spread-eagle positions in the open area. These bastards are to be considered enemy combatants. Non-compliance to your orders will be met by a lethal bullet, unless there are extenuating circumstances. I want every one of our people to get through this unscathed. There are no acceptable losses on our side. Does everyone understand?"

Linda looked around and received quick nods from everyone at the table, including Anna, who was just caught up in the moment.

Linda said, "Okay, team leaders, you will meet with me after we're done here and we'll get specific on staging and the operation. Questions for now?"

"Yes, madam," said George, "can you tell me why I am here?"

Sean instantly responded, "I'm sorry, Mr. Mayor, that's my fault. When Linda's team takes control of this compound, there are going to be combatant prisoners, but more importantly, there will be victims that will need housing and all kinds of care that the military is ill-suited to provide. Will you be able to provide help in that regard?"

"Hm," said George, "I see what you mean. The steps I and a couple of my surviving people have started will definitely need to be increased. How soon will this raid happen? Does it have to be the day after tomorrow, or could it possibly be delayed for another couple of days?"

"I see what you mean, however the longer we wait, the more chances the victims can come to harm or even be moved somewhere else," said Sean. Looking at Linda, he said, "Linda, I know time is of the essence, considering what is happening to those people. What are your thoughts?"

"I just have a feeling that speed is important here. I know it will be tougher for you, Mayor, but the price for delaying beyond the day after tomorrow just seems too high. If it were up to me, I would prefer to go in first thing in the morning." Linda's resignation only showed the fire she felt inside.

Sean then asked, "Linda, Hung and Ron, do you folks have any feeling for when or if this knucklehead at Fort Knox will actually stage a military attack of the Frankfort National Guard Base?"

Knowing the protocol for these types of questions, Hung said, "Sir, Fort Knox can't possibly have any kind of efficient fighting force in place. Like the rest of the world, they've got to be slowly climbing out of shell shock from the virus and all the changes in the world. Even if Briggs were some kind of Julius Caesar, he would need some time, like more than weeks, but probably months, to put something like that together. Presuming the Lieutenant here is correct regarding the lack of offensive air power, any type of ground attack would be like the Keystone Cops going up against a hung-over 82nd Airborne."

The resulting laughter from all present was spontaneous.

"Sean said, "Linda, honey? Your thoughts?"

"I have to agree with Hung," she said. "Just like we've been doing, they would have to cobble together a fighting force, equipment and ammunition to even attempt it. And, there's the very real question of whether the men would even be willing to fight fellow American soldiers for some dingbat Colonel. The description of the Adjutant didn't sound like the Colonel would be a very popular leader. In fact, that gives me an idea. Will talk to you about it later."

"Okay," Sean said. "Major, you're up."

"It seems to me you have some very perceptive people, General," Ron said. "I agree with everything they've said and would guess we're dramatically ahead of virtually everyone else in the military world in reorganizing. If Linda is thinking along the same line I am, some intelligence work will be a nice force-multiplier as well."

Linda smiled and nodded her head.

"Okay folks," Sean said. If there's nothing else for this evening, those organizational meetings for the upcoming raid can begin in the morning."

Linda looked at Hung and said, "Hung, please hang around after the meeting. Would you?"

Ten minutes after the meeting broke up, Linda asked Hung, "Who do you think would be the best two recruiters we have to go to Fort Knox for a week or two and develop some inside sources?"

After giving it thought for a few seconds, Hung said, "I think Smitty, you know, Tommy Smith, and maybe Joel Fleishman might be your best bet to go with him. I've known both of them for a long time and though there are a couple of the others that recruit better overseas, these two will fit in with the usual soldier crowd just fine. Also, I think Smitty and Fleishman were both posted to Knox in the past."

"Okay, thanks," said Linda, "please have them come see me at my office first thing in the morning."

"Will do, Ma'am," Hung said.

CHAPTER 23
THE NEW YEAR – PLUS ONE HUNDRED SEVENTY-ONE DAYS

Hung/Lisa Residence
Outside of Cronin, KY
2210 Hours EDT

Hung lay on his back breathing heavily, the bedsheet partially covering the lower half of his body when Lisa returned from the bathroom and, with a grand flourish, pulled the sheet out of the way. Hung could only gape in amazement, watching this cross between an angel and Aphrodite, the Greek Goddess of Love, kneeling on the bed completely au naturale in the candlelight. They had made love twice already that evening and she wanted to admire his physique as much as he reveled in admiring hers.

"My love, dear sweet Lisa, where did you learn to do those things?" Hung asked in complete innocence and love, and immediately regretted it as the cloud of insult momentarily crossed her perfect face and eyes.

"Oh, my God, did I offend you? I'm so sorry!"

Suddenly, she was on top of him again, rocking her hips over his lap until she felt him grow into her. Over ten minutes later, they both lay, gently touching each other, gasping for air.

"My dear Huntsman," Lisa said in a dreamy, loving voice. "Don't ever be afraid of where I have learned something that brings you pleasure. You must promise to never repeat what I am about to tell you. Okay?"

Hung nodded, wordlessly.

"You know some of the background of my best friend in the world, besides you, of course? Well, for several years she received the best training possible in how to please men. Whether she lived or died depended on her mastering everything they taught, plus more than that, she added to her repertoire by superior deduction. Most of it didn't just come out of books, either. I know you're more experienced than I and so I will ask her for some suggestions every once in a while, to make sure you don't get bored with me."

"Dear God, my love! I could never get bored with you!" Hung's voice was adamant, but he, too, realized life is full of change and even the best ice cream or ribeye steak needs variety once in a while. "And you must promise me something in return. If you ever get bored with me, I want you to tell me and either I will or you can go ask your bestie for ways to change that. I know it's tough to keep up with your brain, but your body will also always fascinate me and I hope you can see I am an excellent student in certain areas! Like this gorgeous, standing, succulent nipple right here. What to do?"

Hung then demonstrated exactly what she hadn't even known she wanted him to do.

***

The Rhapsody
Port of Honolulu, Hawaii
1130 Hours Local Time

Cho sat at his desk in the Captain's cabin when his door quietly opened and a crewman walked in quickly toward Cho. The man had a glazed look in his eye and held a large knife in his left hand. Cho got up quickly, reaching for the pistol in his desk drawer when the man launched himself, knife extended across the desk. Cho just had time to lift his leg in a defensive maneuver to intercept the knife point headed for his heart. The knife sank deeply into his upper left thigh and stuck. Cho punched the man hard in the throat, causing him to release the knife. When the man gagged, clutching his throat, Cho grabbed a handful of his hair and slammed his face onto the desk, knocking him unconscious. Cho then sat down carefully before calling Kim and then the sick bay.

Kim arrived a few minutes before the Nurse Practitioner and took the unconscious crewman into Cho's spacious sleeping chamber where he handcuffed and duck taped the man to a metal chair.

When the Nurse Practitioner arrived, she carried a medical bag with all the tools and bandages for a knife wound. Surveying the knife sticking into out of his upper thigh, she said,

"Okay, now. So you tripped and somehow stabbed this fourteen inch dagger into your own leg. Is that right?" Her words dripped with sweet sarcasm.

"No, Madam," Cho said gruffly, "a crewman didn't like the medical treatment he received from sick bay and came to kill me in frustration. Please tell me specifically, how will you be treating this? And yes, it must be done here and not in sick bay." Cho's response caught the NP by surprise, though it brought a slight smile to her face.

"Until I remove the knife, I can't be sure there are no arterial cuts, but based on where it is, that is unlikely. After removing the knife, I will need to first swab the wound with antiseptic, followed by installing a few sutures inside the wound canal, then stapling up the exterior wound before applying the dressing. I recommend a general anesthetic to let you sleep away the whole process, since the pain will be excruciating." She had already prepared a syringe with the anesthetic.

"No," Cho said simply. "Just use a local anesthetic and do what you have to do."

The NP's eyebrows raised questioningly, then said, "I will not insert the inside sutures without the general anesthetic. Any normal human would buck off the table. I can do the rest, but even with the local, it's going to hurt. A lot. You sure you want me to do that?" At his nod, she could only respond, "Men" under her breath. Giving the local numbing agent fifteen minutes to work, she quickly withdrew the knife and began to skillfully clean out the wound with an antiseptic patch. It impressed her to see his level of control, not to flex his leg muscle. Instead, he tensed the rest of his body to the point cords stood out in his arms and neck.

Watching the NP apply the four staples to close the wound, Cho didn't miss the irony that he was being stapled up by a Nurse Practitioner named Marla Stapleton.

"Now you are aware, Captain Gao, that as I said previously, there should be some internal sutures closing the inner portion of the puncture," Miss Stapleton said sternly. "I could have applied them had you allowed me to put you mildly under sedation, but frankly, I don't like to inflict that amount of pain and try to work without the sedative and you refused it. So here we are. The wound is closed and the bandage should stay in place for at least seventy-two hours before you come down to Sick Bay, where I will change it. Avoid flexing the muscle in that leg as much as possible because each time you do, you move the puncture channel a little. You will tear loose every place that is trying to heal back together. Do you want some pain killer? I can go from aspirin to Tylenol to Advil, all the way up to the opiates: morphine, and oxycodone, which you have already refused. None? Men!"

When Stapleton closed the door on her way out, Cho called out, "Kim!"

Kim opened the door to his sleeping chamber and Cho saw the now conscious attacker struggling in the chair with duct tape over his mouth. "This Pilipino named Sergio, from the housekeeping staff, doesn't want to talk to me, so I recommend we cut off toes, one at a time, until he decides to fully confess."

"No, Kim," said Cho, "I learned something from the Bulgarians a few years ago that was more effective and a lot less bloody." Cho walked carefully over to the man in the chair with a stout wooden walking stick. "Kim, take off his shoes."

When the struggling man's feet were bare, Cho swung the end of the walking stick down onto the man's right foot, breaking several of his bones. The man tried to scream but was quelled significantly by the duct tape over his mouth.

"Now, Sergio," said Cho, "inflicting paid through the feet can go on indefinitely without causing death." Cho wacked his other foot with the same amount of force, breaking several bones. "This will literally go on for hours, or even days, until you tell me everyone that was involved in convincing you to risk your life to kill me. The question is, how much can or should you endure to protect everyone else that is responsible? Whatever they promised to you, well, you will never see it."

Cho wacked each foot again, every thirty seconds for two minutes before continuing. "When you're ready to stop suffering for the others, just nod your head and the pain will stop." Sergio nodded his head furiously, resulting in Kim ripping the duct tape off his mouth.

"Capitan," Sergio said gasping, "there is nobody that sent me. I just went crazy with drugs! Please believe me!"

Cho shook his head back and forth disappointedly. "Kim, please come get me from my office when Sergio has decided to stop lying to us. Will you?"

"Yes Sir, Captain," Kim said, while applying more duct tape to Sergio's mouth.

Cho hobbled out of the room to his office, where he brought out a bottle of fine singlemalt Scotch Whiskey from a cabinet and poured it into a tumbler half full. He then laid down, with his back propped up on the leather couch, and took several powerful pulls from the glass. He woke some time later, hearing Kim gently say, "Captain, Captain, I think he's ready now."

Cho took the almost-empty glass from the coffee table and drained it before beckoning Kim to continue.

"Captain, at first he identified five other men on the ship that he said were part of this conspiracy. Under questioning, I was able to determine there were only three others, including that doctor that was face-planted by the First Mate. This doctor was the ringleader. Sergio could give specific details about what the good doctor and the other two said and did, while the last two, I think, were just enemies of Sergio's."

"You are confident of all of this, Kim?" Cho asked while examining Kim's entire body, as well as his face.

"Yes, Sir, Captain. As confident as I can be."

"Hmm," said Cho. "I want you to go arrest the Doctor and the other two. Two hours from now, I will announce their crime of mutiny and attempted murder and execute them off the side of the main deck. There is to be no official announcement, but anyone that is around is welcome to observe. Questions?"

"No, Sir, Captain!"

Two hours later, standing on the main deck, Cho was not a happy man. He did not want to execute three of his crewmen and the only ship's Doctor for the attempted mutiny, and the wound on his bandaged leg throbbed incessantly. Kim had just confirmed to him that besides Sergio, two others had confessed to the plot, under interrogation, blaming the Doctor for recruiting them. The Doctor confessed after only five minutes of intense interrogation, blaming it all on that "monster" Captain Gao. When Cho finished proclaiming the charges and his findings of guilt, he limped calmly to the four men, kneeling on a ramp hanging over the open sea with weights tied to their legs and fired one round from his 9 mm pistol into the back of each man's head, causing their body to pitch overboard into the water. Word spread quickly around the ship.

A few minutes later, Cho was seated in his office sipping from his glass of Scotch.

Kim walked into the Captain's office. "Captain? I just asked that damned NP about your condition and she wouldn't tell me anything. I haven't had time to ask you, so I have a request. You going to be all right?"

Kim had looked the part of a concerned friend/subordinate and even sounded the part, but Cho wasn't completely sure. He could usually tell if people were being truthful with him, but on two occasions, he had actually been wrong and nearly ended up dead. His gut did send him a good vibe about Kim, however. Much more so than Ho Chin.

"Good. I am glad to hear that Nurse Stapleton can keep her mouth shut. And she doesn't flash her breasts around for attention, either." Cho had to admit he had admired the nurse's shapely figure and appreciated that she was competent and confident enough not to use those assets to get anyone's attention. "Not for anyone else, but it's a stab wound going in my thigh about four centimeters. She wanted to put in internal stitches, but wouldn't do it unless I allowed her to sedate me. Said something about not wanting to hear anyone screaming and thrashing about after inflicting that amount of pain, without sedation. She then gave me four staples plus bandages to close up the wound. How is the rest of the crew reacting to this mutiny attempt?"

"You are reasonably well-liked, Captain," Kim said matter-of-factly. "I overheard the First Mate talking to someone confidentially in his cabin and he expressed admiration how you managed to survive the attack and your immediate and proper reactions to it. He was prior Navy. They're all glad the attackers are no longer on the ship and most approve of how they were removed. I think a majority are realizing this is a new world now and are believing you can best assure their survival and maybe even their place in rebuilding it."

"Good," said Cho. "I am told by the First Mate that we are ready for a shakedown cruise around the islands. Is this correct?"

"Yes, Captain," Said Kim. "The First Mate informed me you had directed him to plan for a two-day voyage, with stops at the three most populous islands, after Oahu. Is this correct, Sir?"

"Yes. Have you prepared the three teams to drop off at those islands to recruit for our new Hawaiian government?"

"I have, Captain," said Kim. "I have also instructed the teams sent to each military base to have meetings scheduled over the next two weeks with whomever is determined to be in charge at those bases. Those could be tricky, Sir. There are many rumors being started that you are not of Taiwanese decent as we have said, but are, in fact, from the People's Republic of China that is responsible for release of the virus on the world. Since the American President made that accusation in her last address to the country before communications stopped, it is a powerful message."

Cho thought ruefully about his own part in getting the virus to the terrorist group in Afghanistan with the intent of spreading it to the rest of the world. Damn Chairman Song! It was under Song's orders the virus operation was developed and released. But, it was through the totally unexpected cleverness and abilities of the uneducated terrorist leader of the Jihadists of the Prophet (JOTP), that the virus was stolen from the MSS team that was sent to infect the terrorist martyrs. The JOTP leader had captured Cho, killed the MSS team and stolen the virus only to have his own scientists manipulate the Chinese virus, through nano-technology, making the Chinese-developed vaccine useless and the virus even more virulent. If Cho were a Godfearing Christian man, he would be crushed under a tremendous burden of guilt. He was not and had the psychological makeup of someone that took everything as it came and lived without regrets.

"Kim, put out a whisper campaign attacking anyone that says such a thing as being racist and uninformed," Cho said. "Then spread the message that Hawaii will quickly rebuild its infrastructure and regain its place as the bridge between East and West, all under American Founding Fathers principles. Patriotism and hard work will become the slogans from now on. What do you think?"

"If properly delivered," Kim said thoughtfully, "and you have a few strategically placed speeches and appearances, you will be able to seize the powers of the Governor of Hawaii, especially if you're able to gain the support of the remaining military. That, of course, is critical."

"Agreed," said Cho. "Now send in the First Mate and we can set sail within the hour."

"Yes, Sir, Captain," said Kim, intentionally avoiding the seagoing terminology of, "Aye, Aye, Captain."

CHAPTER 24
THE NEW YEAR – PLUS ONE HUNDRED SEVENTY-TWO DAYS

Marc and Suzie's Residence
Outside of Cronin, KY
0615 Hours EDT

Suzie woke with a start from a light sleep. She didn't know if she would ever wake up without the feeling of intense fight-or-flight apprehension she had experienced since her first day at Charm School. It was annoying that with all the wonderful, new events in her life that she should begin each day reliving that awful place. There, she was given a choice of either learning to be a master manipulator of men, or they would kill her. She spent the first two weeks being raped multiple times each day, while they forced her to thank her rapist. Her demeanor had to show that she desired, and even exalted, at the opportunity being given to her. She learned quickly that she had three extraordinary talents in her favor. First, she was much brighter mentally than those at the school, having a prodigious memory and extremely quick wit. Second, she had the innate ability to tell whenever someone was lying to her, to the point she could sense what most people, men in particular, were thinking. Third, she could compartmentalize things in her life, allowing her to seal-off emotions while being able to access and learn from any experience. These skills made her capable of being an incredibly adept intelligence weapon targeted toward the husband of the American President. Horrific as that entire experience was, it had brought her to America, into contact with her best friend and the man she with whom she wanted to spend the rest of her life. Was it Karma? Fate? She didn't know and did not consider the issue important to her at that time.

Suzie then looked across the bed at the dark, curly-haired man, who would soon be her husband. When she first saw him almost one hundred days earlier, he was bald, with pale white skin and had the spindly, emaciated frame of a man who had worked twenty hours per day in an office with no sunlight and no exercise. Only his dark eyes showed the intense intelligence and character inside of him. Once he had a few days to recover, he seemed to revel in pitching in to help build anything or do any physical labor outside. His soft and slightly puffy and pale face had become chiseled and his shoulders, legs and butt had developed muscle quickly. Once they were together, any concerns she had about his being able to physically keep up with her had been dispelled. Getting out of the Washington, D.C. pressure cooker turned him into a different man.

"Hello there," Marc said with his best little-boy grin wrapped around a testosterone-driven desire as he admired the most beautiful woman he had ever seen. It was morning, after all. "I want you. Now and always. Are you okay with that?"

The sheet had already fallen down from her bare breasts, drawing his lustful eyes, so she slid it down the rest of the way before taking his hand to pull him onto her. "Put up or shut up, big boy," she said mischievously. "Is that how you say it?"

"No, this is," Marc said with a smile, while climbing aboard.

Sometime later, laying with her head on his chest and teasing his chest hairs with her fingers, Suzie said, "Do you think Mike liked my ideas on his appointing Judge-Executives for twenty different counties in Kentucky?" Before the virus, there were 120 counties in Kentucky and had been attempts for over a century to merge them down to a more reasonable number. No county government, however, had wanted to lose their own county seat or control of their infrastructure. After the virus, Suzie felt it was the best opportunity to do so.

"Sweetheart," said Marc, "the idea makes plenty of sense, but I don't know how ready everyone is to start instituting fundamental changes after all the trauma experienced. But, if the change is to be made, doing it now will be a lot easier than after governments are in place."

"My incredibly adept lover," Suzie said sweetly, while stroking him just right, "have you given any more thought to Mike's request for you to take over as his Chief of Staff? Anna is great as his Secretary and Personal Assistant, but she really isn't qualified or suited to being his Chief of Staff. She's too nice!"

Marc sighed, "He does definitely need the help, but dammit, I just got out of that position and I really never want to get into it again!" He tried to turn over, but she hung onto him in a very persuasive way.

"Three things I think you should consider," Suzie said in her most sensual voice. "First, Mike is not anything like Katherine Fontaine. He doesn't even want power. He just wants to do what is right for those he cares about. Second, this isn't Washington, D.C. and it will be a long time, probably not in our lifetimes, before the power centers will develop to challenge the sanity Mike wants to bring to us. And, finally, you didn't have me in Washington, D.C. Baby, you're stuck with me and I will always have your back. Nobody will ever, ever threaten you, or they won't be around very long."

Marc momentarily felt a chill run down his back as he contemplated exactly what she meant. There was no doubt in his mind that she would eliminate anyone she felt threatened his safety.

With an enormous sigh, Marc said, "Okay, the love of my life. I'll talk to Mike about it this morning."

Suzie let out a whoop of delight, smothered him with kisses and teased him into another passionate round of lovemaking.

***

Mike Broehm Temporary Office Building
Outside of Cronin, Kentucky
0900 Hours EDT

Mike walked into his office building to find Marc Baxter talking to Anna at her desk.

"Good morning, you two," Mike said affably. "Are you conspiring to fix all of my problems today or just add to them?" Mike said this in a joking manner, but there was quite a bit of sincerity as well.

"Good morning, Mike," Marc said, "I would accuse you of talking to Suzie, but since she works for you, I guess that goes without saying. Besides, since I love talking to her, there's the presumption that everyone should feel the same way. Am I right?"

"Wellllll," said Mike, "I'm not sure anybody else is going to enjoy being around her the way that you obviously do, but your point is well taken. She's a fascinating young woman. Now that we have that out of the way, did she have any suggestions for you and how you might consider spending your time?"

"Yes, she did, but I won't get into THOSE details, but she also suggested," Marc continued, "I reconsider doing what you spoke to me about yesterday. I have an offer for you. Yes, I can function as your Chief of Staff if, and only if, you agree that I have an open door to you, anytime or any place, plus I can quit any time I want to, and finally, I get Lisa to be my administrative assistant."

Marc stopped talking, almost holding his breath, and just looked at Mike.

"Done. With a caveat. Lisa's got to be available for consulting in medical and biology matters. Will that work for you?"

The firm handshake and brotherly hug sealed it.

Turning to Anna, Mike said, "Would you work on finding Lisa's replacement for me? I can't just lose a staff member and not replace her."

"Sure, Mike," said Anna with a smile, "I do the difficult at once, but the impossible might take a little bit longer. I think some French author wrote that a couple or three centuries ago."

"Thank you, my dear," said Mike. "As usual, you continue to make me look good despite myself!"

Just then, Mike's nine-year-old runner, Kevin, burst into the office and said breathlessly,

"Mr. Mike. Doc sent me. Come quick. Your house. Oh, and Mr. Marc, too!" Kevin had tears streaming down his face.

Mike glanced briefly at Marc, and both men rose and jogged toward Mike's house. Entering his front door, Mike saw Lauren laying in the living room on the couch, hooked up to an IV bag on a pole, with sunlight streaming through the window. Mrs. Baker, who had been caring for Lauren as her health declined, got up, walked by Mike, squeezing his arm, and walked out. Doc stood next to her, beckoning Mike and Marc to come forward. "Mike," said Doc, "I'm sorry, but it won't be long now. I've got her on the morphine drip, so she isn't in any pain. At this point, it's in God's hands. I know you both are people of strong faith, so I think you know what to do from here. I'll be in the other room." Doc walked toward the kitchen.

Mike and Marc each took one of Lauren's hands and wept.

Forty-five minutes later, Mike called out, "Doc?"

Doc came in and listened to Lauren's heart with his stethoscope before bowing and slowly shaking his head. "Mike, you two take as long as you want. I'll be in the kitchen when you've had enough time say your goodbyes. Then, why don't both of you come see me in the kitchen? There are four guys waiting outside in the hallway to handle moving her to a secure place."

Mike had been saying his goodbyes to Lauren for the past several days, so he was ready after only ten minutes. When he rose to bring Marc into the kitchen, the four SF Operators came in to move her body.

"Gentlemen," Doc said, "With all the death and everything else that's happened over the past few months, we've all had to deal with loss like never in history. We know people are fairly predictable, but individually different in how we process grief. Whatever you're feeling right now is completely normal. Everyone, in varying degrees, goes through the Seven Stages of Grief. Disbelief and shock, Denial, Guilt and Pain, Bargaining, Anger, Depression, and Acceptance. Time will heal most of it, but it's never going to be pleasant. I encourage you to let yourself feel and learn to cope with the loss."

"And Mike," Doc said softly, "everything happening right now has competent people managing it. I'm sure they'll keep you up to speed on what's happening, but don't feel your input is absolutely necessary right now. You know and trust Sean, Linda, Anna and everyone else to manage things, so either let it all go for as long as you think you need to, or jump right in— but not today, or maybe not even tomorrow."

Mike said, "Thank you, Doc. You're right about all of that. I can't speak for Marc, but over the past few days and nights, I've been sharing memories and saying goodbye to Lauren and could see that it was coming soon. Yeah, it hurts, but it isn't the end for her spirit nor for mine. Her journey is continuing on another plain. That's all. And yes, I'm going to miss her. And Doc? Thank you for handling everything so well here."

Doc nodded humbly to Mike, feeling his loss, but also his centered sense of power and faith.

Mike looked at Marc and said, "I'm going for a nice, long walk. Probably sit down by the lake for a little while if anyone needs me. Then I'll go back to my office and probably crash in the Master bedroom there tonight. Are you going to be okay, Marc? Will Suzie be home when you get there?"

"Marc nodded his head as his tears seemed to suddenly explode down his face."

"Good," said Mike as he, Doc and Marc walked out Mike's back kitchen door.

After several hours numbly watching the fish come up for insects on the smooth lake surface, Mike noticed it was getting dark, so he shook his head and walked back toward his new office. He opened the door to find Anna waiting for him in the conference room/living room. She didn't say a word, only came and gave him a quick hug before leaving him to his grief.

****

Non-Descript Warehouse
North of Frankfort, Kentucky
1530 Hours EDT

Antonio approached Tank just inside the warehouse as he was instructing several of his guys what to take and put on the truck. "Tank?" Antonio asked respectfully. "Speak to you privately?"

Tank motioned him to step outside of the large roll-up doors where the loading was taking place and walked around the corner of the warehouse. "Okay, Antonio, what's up?"

"Tank," said Antonio, "I just returned from the airport in Frankfort and don't like what I saw. There were several team members instructing small groups of National Guard soldiers in movement and tactics."

"Wait, what are 'team members?'" Tank asked curiously.

Antonio said, "They are Special Forces Operators, you know, like Greenie Beanies, I mean Green Berets?"

"Oh," said Tank, "is that the first time you have seen them?"

"Yes, Tank. And I also saw a short training flight of an Apache attack helicopter that looked to be fully loaded with weapons. Like air-to-air missiles, air-to-ground missiles, and multiple high-rate-of-fire machine guns. Trust me, that's one big bird of prey dealing out death from the air."

"If they are going to attack us," said Tank, "when would you say they will probably strike?"

"My guess, is they could come just after dawn, as soon as tomorrow, or the next day."

Tank held up one finger to show Antonio to wait. Finally, he said, "Okay, here's what we're gonna do. I want you to take six of the ugliest and least desirable women and put them in their shed and have five of the worst guards to run security on this whole compound. You'll need to stay around to make sure they do what they should be doing. In fact, you might even suggest they should try out the girls to break 'em in or something. You know, distract them about why everyone else has gone. We'll be taking everyone else and everything else we can carry out by truck over towards Cynthiana to the new location. Also, the five you pick should probably be the ones with the least idea where we are going. You might also mention, kinda casual-like, that I expect if they find anyone trying to intrude on our operation here, they should shoot first and get the background information later. Capiche?"

Antonio's smile was getting larger, clearly being familiar with the Italian word for understand. "And I should maybe have a truck hidden away a couple miles from here and fade into the woods during any type of attack, or preferably before the attack, and make my way in your direction in a couple days after things here settle down?"

"That's why I like you, son. You think like I do! Be thinking of any of the girls you might want for yourself and she'll be waiting for you when you get there. I'm going to be loaded up and out of here within the next hour. And don't go getting yourself killed or captured. Sounds like some of these guys coming our way are pretty good."

"You got it, Tank. I'll see you in a couple of days." Antonio smiled at the thought. "And you pull the pretty little blonde with the narrow hips and big tits aside for me. She just looks fun."

Tank shrugged. "Whatever floats your boat, my friend. You'll have earned her!"

CHAPTER 25
THE NEW YEAR – PLUS ONE HUNDRED SEVENTY-THREE DAYS

Non-Descript Warehouse
North of Frankfort, Kentucky
0500 Hours EDT

Squad leaders for each of the assault squads met with Captain Dawson, Sean, Linda, Doc and Major Shouse at the National Guard armory before rolling out to the staging area five miles away. Sean and Linda were there to observe only.

"Gentlemen," said Captain Dawson, "We have new intel on this morning's operation. Snipers settled in place yesterday afternoon and observed a mostly deserted camp. There are half a dozen women there and a handful of up to six guards, but that's it. After consultation with General Callahan, our planned storming of the compound has been modified. Assault Squads One and Two will roll up to the warehouse in four of the Up-Armored Humvees. I will be in the lead assault vehicle. When we encounter the guards, we will order them to lay down their arms and prone-out on the ground. Anyone that refuses will be shot, but here's the change. Shoot for shoulders or legs. We want prisoners for intel. Of course, if one or more are that stupid, they die before any of our people or the hostages are injured. Assault Squad Two will immediately go to the blockhouse where the female hostages are being held. That building is to be secured by Assault Squad Two until all six guards are detained. Assault Squads Three and Four will remain back 100 yards down the road as a quick reaction force. Questions?"

One of the SF Squad leaders asked, "Sir, are there still only two snipers in an over-watch position?"

Cpt. Dawson smiled, "Thank you, Sergeant. Besides the two snipers, Major Shouse and his Apache will provide over-watch as well, just outside of where those on the ground can hear them. Are you ready to go, Major?" Major Shouse nodded. "All right, leave and get overhead as soon as possible. You've got infrared and thermal targeting optics available? Good. Let us know what you see as soon as you're overhead. Has everyone done their radio checks? Anyone have questions? Okay, sunrise is at 0613, so we will depart this post at 0615. Make sure your people are fully briefed on the changes."

Over the secure radio net, the two snipers on each side of the warehouse could hear the Apache announce being on station high over the area. "Freedom Group One, Birdman, is on station overhead. Be advised there are three heat signatures of figures overlooking the warehouse, two on the North side and one on the South side."

"Birdman, this is Over-Watch One one-hundred twenty meters to the South of the warehouse. How close together are the two signatures to the North?"

"Over-Watch One, the two thermal signatures are about forty-five meters apart. The figure to the West appears to be out in the open and the one to the East is partially concealed from me under a pine tree. Both appear to have long guns."

"Birdman, this is Group Leader," Captain Dawson said over the radio. "Have OverWatch Two to the North flash you three times with his infrared flashlight."

"Roger, Group Leader. Standby." Major Shouse ordered Over-Watch Two to flash his infrared flashlight toward the sky three times. Moments later, the flashes were observed from the figure out in the open. "Over-Watch One and Group Leader, I have confirmation flashes from the figure to the West, on the ground and out in the open."

"Birdman from Group Leader, are you confident of eliminating the threat without collateral damage?"

"Group Leader from Birdman, my Lieutenant is completely confident of being able to eliminate the target threat with a short, ten-round burst from the 30 mm canon. Collateral damage under these conditions will be limited to less than five feet."

"Roger that, Birdman," said Captain Dawson. "We will roll up on the other side of the warehouse. Should you detect any threatening movement, to be interpreted broadly, you have authorization to eliminate the threat. Do you copy?"

"Copy that, Group Leader. Birdman standing by."

Major Shouse keyed his intercom button. "Lieutenant, you copy all of that?"

"Yes, Sir, Major," said Jeremy Johnson. "My eyes will be pretty focused on this other sniper, so, if you don't mind, Sir, please keep a watch out for any other threats?"

"Will do, son," said the Major.

Both men in the helicopter observed the vehicles of Assault Squads One and Two approach the warehouse. One lone figure detached its self from the side of the warehouse and held up his hand to the vehicles. With the machine gunner on the roof of the first vehicle training his belt-fed weapon on the guard, the guard carefully placed his shotgun on the ground, took three steps to the side and lay down spread-eagle on the ground. A few moments later, four other guards exited the warehouse, unarmed with hands up and joined their buddy on the ground.

"Major," said the Lieutenant, "our bad sniper just sighted his rifle on our bird."

"Fire," said Major Shouse.

A ten-round burst made the bird shudder as it sent the high-explosive rounds toward the unknown sniper. Through the magnified view finder, the man's body was torn to shreds by four of the ten exploding rounds, followed by the pine tree falling onto what was left.

"Group Leader, we have eliminated sniper threat," said Major Shouse.

"Copy that, Birdman. Continue to surveil the area for any other potential threats."

***

Boone National Guard Center

Frankfort, Kentucky

1500 Hours EDT

Sitting around the conference table was most of the Assault Group, going through an after-action debriefing conducted by Captain Dawson. "Staff Sergeant, what did you see and find regarding the dead enemy sniper?"

"Captain," said the Staff Sergeant, "the guy must have been a professional. I did not know when he arrived and set up under that tree and I'm pretty observant about those types of things. He wasn't wearing a ghillie suit, but he did have on a worn camo uniform with a Ranger tab on the shoulder. I had seen him giving instructions to the guards early yesterday evening before he disappeared. His wallet said he was Antonio Alvarez from Fort Lewis, Washington. There was a photocopy of his dishonorable discharge in his wallet as well. That struck me as very odd, that anyone would carry around a document like that."

The Captain next turned to Sergeant Lopez, who was in charge of handling and interrogation of the prisoners. "What did you find out from the prisoners, Sergeant? And by the way, masterful how you announced to your security team guarding the five prisoners about the elimination of Alverez by the Apache. I could see them almost instantly relax, knowing he was dead. Did that help in the interrogation?"

Sergeant Lopez smiled and said, "Yes, Sir, it did. Three of the five were quick to sing about the entire operation, which is being run by a guy named 'Tank Monahan.'"

"Hmm," said the Captain, "that's the same name as the man supposedly responsible for the assassination of the Kentucky Governor a few months back, just before the virus struck. Anyway, go on."

"Tank had contracted with Coyote Collins, Regional Governor appointed by the President's administration, to supply secure warehouses to store confiscated food and other supplies gathered by Tank's contract goons. After the virus began to clear, Tank showed up at the warehouse and has been building his own arbitrary fiefdom and criminal enterprise financed by the goods seized on behalf of the U.S. government before everything fell apart. Tank apparently thought when the Fort Knox helicopter buzzed the airport in Frankfort a few days ago and happened to fly right over their warehouse operation, it was a National Guard chopper based in Frankfort. They sent Antonio to Frankfort to scout things out yesterday and observed our preparations for today's assault. Tank began a quick plan to move away from our base to another warehouse he set up somewhere to the Northeast of here. Plans sped up yesterday after Antonio's report, so they loaded everything and most of the slaves on trucks and moved to their new location. They left the six girls and five guards behind to make us believe they were the complete operation. They ordered the guards to shoot first if anyone tried to mess with their security duties. Last night, Antonio gave each of the five guards their choice of the remaining girls to do with as they wished. Only the two that wouldn't talk took him up on it. The girls confirmed that."

Everyone at the briefing was showing barely contained rage.

"Captain," said Sergeant Lopez, "The three guards that talked also told the story of how Tank had Antonio and another chief underboss named Roberto shot and killed two of the men who tried to walk away from the whole operation during their initial hiring meeting. Basically, guards knew they were either going to go along and do what they were told, or be killed. Regarding the girls, I've already turned them over to the Frankfort Mayor, who is arranging for their care and attempting to find any surviving family members. Sir, what do you want to do with the five guards?"

The Captain looked to Sean Callahan with eyebrows raised.

"Captain," Sean said, "I spoke to Mike about this already. We will handle this as strictly a Martial Law situation in hostile territory with no support available in the form of jails or jail personnel. I suggest you bring the five, one at a time, before a three-Judge panel, appointed by you. The panel can determine guilt or innocence and make judgments regarding punishment from letting him go, forfeiture of anything he owns, to corporal punishment, all the way up to execution. This is a harsh world and, like the rest of you, I look forward to having a criminal justice system with more options than we have today. I would expect the panel to dispense their judgment this afternoon. Do you have any questions, Captain?"

The Captain measured General Callahan for a few moments before responding, "No, Sir, General."

Captain Dawson turned to the Special Forces Staff Sergeant and Sergeant Lopez. "Lopez, go find another one of the National Guard Sergeants, brief him on what has happened and give him the good news that I have selected him to sit on the three-Judge panel, along with myself and the Staff Sergeant here. Court will convene in one hour in the drill hall and will be open for observation by anyone that is not currently assigned. Let's set a precedent for how justice will be carried out."

***

Mike Broehm Temporary Office Building
Outside of Cronin, Kentucky
2000 Hours EDT

Walking into Mike's conference room, Sean and Linda were surprised to see both Mike and Marc Baxter sitting at the conference table, along with Anna.

"Mike," said Sean, "I'm so sorry about Lauren."

Lauren's funeral had been conducted just after noon. At Mike's insistence, it was an informal affair at the gravesite in a new graveyard in a corner of the neighborhood park. Mike and Marc spent less than five minutes, each commending Lauren's spirit to God's hands before they invited everyone present to the nearby pavilion for a wake-style meal and celebration of life. Several tables were set up, covered with food and desserts made by ladies and a few men living in the neighborhood. They had cooked or baked most of the food on gas or wood grills. After only an hour, everything was winding down and everyone drifted away to handle the new normal chores of living.

"Thank you, Sean," said Mike. "The funeral was short and sweet, followed by an hour of stories before everyone had something calling for their attention. Thank you for asking your SF buddies that were not tied up in your operation to help take care of the burial. Front-end loaders sure make digging a grave a lot easier. Also, and thanks to you Linda, for coming back early and briefing me on the operation. I look forward to getting more details now. But, first I suggest you have a seat and eat some of this barbecue chicken and other things left from the wake. It's really good! I just had another helping myself."

While eating and toasting a bottle of wine to Lauren and a successful operation, Mike received the details of the day's military operation. "Sean, what did the Tribunal do with the five captured security guards?"

"The three that talked to Sergeant Lopez and provided the most information about Tank's activities, etc. were basically acquitted because of being in Tank's organization. We learned Tank had already had two guys killed for trying to walk away from the whole setup during their initial orientation meeting. So basically the guards and everyone else working for Tank were under a 'do what you're told or die," situation. They didn't get their guns back, but they were allowed to leave with their stuff and all the food and water they could carry."

"And the other two?" Mike asked quietly.

Sean took a breath and said, "Those two had beaten, raped and otherwise abused two of the girls the night before, at the invitation of Antonio. They were executed by a firing squad, Mike, within minutes of their having been found guilty. Captain Dawson is a very competent commander and ran a fair, but thorough Court Martial tribunal."

Mike nodded. "Now when you said Tank, is this the same guy that paid to have the Governor killed?"

"Yes, Mike," said Sean, "that's the one. He's apparently teamed up with a gay guy named Blondi, who kinda acts as his lieutenant. Oh, and you'll love this. One of the guards said he had talked to Blondi and learned Blondi and Tank had survived the virus in a prepper's basement with another guy they both knew named Kerry. Kerry was such a slimy asshole that Tank choked him out several times while going stir-crazy in the basement with him. Captain Dawson was fairly confident Blondi was the political analyst from the Lexington newspaper and that Kerry was our very own Kerry DuBois. That little fucker appears to have lived through this! Forgive my French, which is not appropriate for a General Officer, but what the hell, that's what he is, a little fucker."

Mike was incredulous. "Kerry DuBois survived?"

"The guard said Blondi told him they had left Kerry in the survival bunker/basement after Tank choked him out the last time. Blondi said he deserved it. Blondi then described Tank as someone that could give him a chance to stay alive so Blondi's committed to him. So, Kerry survived, at least until then. I get the impression Kerry is like a cockroach, you know, kinda hard to kill?"

Mike chuckled, "Yes, that description fits Kerry to a 'T'. Back to Tank. Were you able to find out where he and his group moved?"

"Unfortunately, no," said Sean. "Antonio, hmm, I didn't mention him yet, did I?"

"No," said Mike.

"Before the initial assault vehicles rolled up to the warehouse, the infrared and thermal optics available on the Apache helicopter spotted three snipers about a hundred meters from the warehouse. Only problem was we only had two snipers out. The third was a little less than fifty meters away from one of our guys, who didn't even know he was there. The chopper kept a close eye on the interloper before seeing him raise a scoped rifle, pointing it directly at the chopper. A quick ten round burst of 30 mm high explosive rounds tore him to shreds. A closer look identified him as the boss of the remaining guards named Antonio, who also was a former Army Ranger that had received a dishonorable discharge from the U.S. Army after conviction of murder and rape in Afghanistan. He was definitely a bad guy and was identified as one of Tank's hit men. Our presumption was that he was going to watch his men get killed or arrested by us and fade into the woods until he could make his way to where Tank moved his operations. Count one for the good guys. He won't be adding his expertise to Tank's group anymore."

Sean uttered a sigh of resignation before saying, "Unfortunately for us, he was the only one remaining in this area that could identify where Tank went."

"Sean, or anyone else?" Mike asked. "Do we have any idea when or if Fort Knox will try to attack you, me, or anyone else in our area?"

Linda said, "No, Mike we don't. I have sent two Operators to gather intelligence at Fort Knox and determine that. They arrived yesterday in the Elizabethtown area and I expect to hear from them within the next two weeks, though they are scheduled to report every 72 hours. In this type of undercover operation, those are not hard deadlines. Fortunately, they have the latest encrypted radio gear and, when they can get to the hidden radios, they'll be able to provide a lot of information. I'll make sure you and everyone that needs to know will be advised pronto."

"Okay," said Mike. "You still have observers in position to see if anyone is coming this way from Fort Knox?"

"Yes, and no, Mike," said Sean. "We have an observation point on each of the two most likely routes to Frankfort from Fort Knox, but if there's any suspicion we're watching, it's possible to use back roads and avoid detection. That's why Linda got her covert operation entering Fort Knox to find out not only what's happening, but what's going to happen. Fortunately, we don't think Colonel Briggs is the type of man who will conceive of layers of intelligence or the various tripwires we have in place. His Adjutant/Lieutenant is more likely to think of those things, which is why we sent in the covert operators. I picked both men to blend in and gather intelligence without raising any eyebrows."

"Thank you both," said Mike. "Please keep me advised. I think I've had about as much fun as I can stand for today, so will bid each of you a good evening. Anna? Will you be here in the morning at usual time?"

"Yes, Mike," she said.

Anna's heart was about to break knowing the sorrow and tension Mike was enduring. She kept telling herself she should remain aloof and be available for whatever Mike might need, while not, by her caring presence, cause him any additional problems. Lauren's death was not unexpected, but had just happened. It had been a very long time since she had met and admired a man as much as she did Mike. And being totally honest with herself, she had never met a man like Mike. She would give up her life for him, anytime, anywhere.

CHAPTER 26
THE NEW YEAR – PLUS ONE HUNDRED SEVENTY-NINE DAYS

Non-Descript Warehouse
Outside of Cynthiana, Kentucky
0630 Hours EDT

Blondi awoke in his usual hammock hanging between two medium-sized trees nearby the warehouse. Tank had filled the warehouse with useful food, water, and other materials such as blankets and towels. Blondi's hammock had gained a waterproof rain tarp to shield it from most rain, but it was the addition of mosquito netting that he appreciated the most. Benny was snuggled in his arms in the hammock and didn't wake up right away. Blondi could tell that little Benny wasn't really interested in him physically. Benny wasn't, nor would he ever be, gay, but he was willing to do whatever Blondi told him to do, knowing he owed his life to Blondi. So Blondi chose not to use little Benny as a lover, but just as a little cuddle buddy and gopher/assistant. That was enough until Blondi could find someone more suitable.

This was the first full week since Tank had moved him up to the new warehouse outside of Cynthiana. There were several buildings in the warehouse complex, a number of which had available generators providing electricity and even pumps for well water. Tank's community now numbered over forty armed guards, twenty laborers and sixteen housekeepers, and twenty-two girls with their leather collars. Their chains were removed, but each was aware they could be reattached quickly if they didn't do exactly as they were told. Tank had allowed these girls to wear simple white shifts to cover their bodies, at least until he ordered them to strip to see what they had to offer. Naked, they were just too distracting for the men in his camp and drew too much negative attention from any other observers. Roberto had organized things pretty well and even found sources for gasoline, vehicles and food. Of the sixteen housekeepers, four of the older women were excellent cooks, including one who had run a commercial kitchen in Cynthiana. Initially, it had been a challenge for Blondi to find propane to provide fuel for the half-dozen camp stoves set up in their makeshift kitchen. They solved the problem when one of the security foragers found a propane tank-truck parked at a gas depot on the outskirts of Cynthiana.

Two hours later, Roberto had grabbed breakfast from the camp-stove kitchen under the awning and sat patiently near the warehouse door waiting for Tank to make an appearance. When he finally walked out of the warehouse, he was shirtless and looked pretty ragged, with wild hair sticking straight up on his head and his bare chest partially covered by his growing gray beard. He walked to the water barrel that collected rainwater at the corner of the building and dunked his entire head into it. Roberto made a mental note not to drink from that rain barrel anymore.

"Tank?" Roberto spoke to Tank softly when his boss approached the awning. "I have something for you when you have time."

Everyone in camp knew not to talk to or otherwise disturb Tank before he had his first drink of the day, be it coffee or whiskey, or both. When Tank's blurry eyes focused and recognized Roberto, he bit off the savage comment he was about to make, grunted, and walked on past him to get his coffee. He added a three-ounce shot of whiskey to his coffee cup from a bottle that had protruded from the hip pocket of his jeans. The jeans had a size 44 waist and commensurately sized back pockets. Taking a powerful pull from the coffee cup, Tank turned and walked back to where Roberto was sitting and straddled a nearby chair backwards.

"Okay, Roberto," Tank said in his gravelly voice, "what's up?"

"Tank, yesterday afternoon I sent one of my young men on a crotch-rocket..."

"A what?" Tank interrupted him.

"A crotch-rocket is a smaller sized motorcycle that looks like a racing bike or a motocross-style racing bike. Anyway, I sent him to check out the old warehouse we just left and to play stupid if he was stopped by anyone in that area. Antonio has failed to return as he promised. The scout returned a few minutes ago. There were two Army soldiers camped beside their Humvee by the old warehouse. Our guy asked where he might find food and maybe some work, as he had a small child sleeping back at his farmhouse that survived the sickness. The soldiers suggested he go into Frankfort where an acting Mayor was organizing help for people. He then offered an unopened whiskey bottle in trade for some of the food the soldiers had heated over a camp stove. They accepted it. Next thing you know, the soldiers were drinking the whiskey and telling my guy about a very bad group of men who had enslaved women and girls before the National Guard came to rescue them. All the evil men gave up without a fight after the military helicopter blew their boss to pieces with explosive cannon fire. They then executed at least two of the guards and let the rest go, for some reason. These soldiers believed a large number of the bad guys had escaped before they raided the place and were somewhere off to the northeast. The National Guard was going to go look for them when they had time, but organizing state government seemed to be the focus right now."

"So," Tank said, "you think Antonio was literally blown away by the cannon fire? And two of the remaining guards were executed?"

"I don't know, but Antonio was the only one left that could be considered a boss."

"Hmm," said Tank. "Those military fuckers aren't messing around. Let's keep a nice, low profile here and try to avoid killin' or even annoying the local folks. Also, I've got another warehouse up around Maysville, on the Ohio River. Think I should develop that location as well and maybe not have any of the collared girls around to catch unwanted attention. Yeah, that's what I'll do. Get me two of your trustworthy guys and we'll send 'em up there to check it out. "

***

Mike Broehm Temporary Office Building
Outside of Cronin, Kentucky
0900 Hours EDT

Mike had called a meeting of his closest advisors, including Marc, Lisa, Suzie, Anna, Linda, Sean, Peter, Elizabeth, Scott Shelby, and Acting Mayor George Kessler. When all were seated with a glass of ice water, Mike opened the meeting.

"Thanks to everyone for coming on short notice," Mike said. "I thought now might be a good time to round up the more important events and moves we're making to bring organization back to our lives. Linda, did you have a chance to put together a thumbnail of what's been happening on the Security front?"

"Yes, Mike, I did. And George and Scott, I've only met you gentlemen once, so here's the fifteen second background for me. Former U.S. Army Special Forces A-Team leader and First Lieutenant Linda Sharpe. On a mission to Afghanistan myself, and another female SF operator were captured by the terrorist organization that ultimately spread this terrible Chinese virus around the world. Anyway, I was rescued by the most incredible man and second most incredible leader I've ever met and we're to be married in about seven days." She smiled quickly at her husband-to-be. "Mike, who is heading up this meeting and is the most incredible leader I've ever known, asked me to take over first, the security for our neighborhood, and then head up the effort to organize and provide police protections for survivors in Kentucky."

Linda continued, "A couple of weeks ago, the Kentucky National Guard in Frankfort was informed of some type of criminal enterprise had enslaved women and some men at a location a few miles north of Frankfort. This criminal group had also murdered several people. It was determined that until I can organize a bona fide police force, we will have to operate under Martial Law, just like the Special Forces trained me to do in foreign countries. That will be the framework we are working on for the immediate future. Six days ago we raided the criminal compound, killing one and capturing five enemy guards and freeing six brutalized women, which I believe were turned over to Mayor Kessler's care." Linda received an affirmative nod from George.

"We also learned from the captured guards the organization was being run by a man named Tank Monahan. He's the guy that hired the assassin to kill the previous Governor of Kentucky and reportedly has a lengthy criminal and prison record. He's a big, sixty-four-year-old, grizzled looking mountain man who likes to build Mafia-style operations. Under the federally appointed Regional Governor Coyote Collins, he had contracted to supply secure storage facilities for all the food, water and other materials the government was collecting for redistribution to those that needed it. He was then contracted to provide the thugs that were sent out to appropriate those materials, using government script as payment. I've got a former Kentucky State Police Detective and the National Guard trying to sanitize Coyote Collin's Frankfort office space so we can search it for documentation of where Tank's secure warehouses are located. Collin's office had at least three virus victims die there, making it a major hazardous material site. This guy Tank is a very bad man and is known to run with Mickey Blondiac, known as Blondi and Kerry DuBois, a nasty little narcissist from this very neighborhood. Blondi wrote a political column in the Lexington paper before the virus. Kerry worked in the Kentucky Transportation Cabinet as a mid-level manager. "

"Gentlemen," said Linda, "I know this is a bunch of information without providing a lot of background detail. With Anna's help, I had a one page list of bullet points concerning what I just said." Linda handed out the one-page list to everyone. "What I didn't go over was the military situation, the economic situation, or the government reorganization ideas. Someone else will address those, I presume, Mike?"

Mike said, "Yes. Thank you, Linda. Excellent job as always. Did you have anything else?"

"No," Linda said, giving Mike a courteous smile.

"Okay," said Mike, "Next I'll ask Peter and Scott to fill us in on how our new bank is doing."

Scott Shelby stood up and walked to a white-board and removed its cloth cover. On it was a series of numbers and two empty boxes. "Here is a listing of the assets the bank currently has, most of which were provided by Peter in the form of long-term-storage food and some other materials. For these things, we have given Peter this many credits." Scott pointed at the '10,000' written on the board. "We are using that as the baseline for determining value of …"

Peter stood up and said, "Excuse me, Scott. Let's avoid going into the weeds too deeply. Mind if I take over?"

Scott chuckled at himself and said, "Doing it again, was I?"

Peter said, "I think if I give the Reader's Digest version, that'll be sufficient. Scott has on his chart some of the basic assets of our bank, upon which we base the credits we have available to operate. How this works is the bank gives credits to, say, a cattle farmer taking paper ownership of his cows while the farmer continues to take care of the cows. Everyone can go to the bank and get paper credits and use them like currency used to be used, if they give the bank title to something they own. When it all shakes out, and it's working already, people can begin to build businesses, sell property, and we have started our own little economy here in Central Kentucky. In fact, the owner of the local Peddler's Mall survived the virus and has opened his Mall up for operation, functioning as a cooperative. The bottom line is commerce is happening semi-efficiently. Everyone here is now receiving a salary in credits with which they can buy food, produce and other things at the Mall or anywhere else, for that matter."

"Thanks, Peter," said Mike. "Not bad for less than four months into this whole thing. On another topic, since Marc became my Chief of Staff a few days ago, he has been working, along with Suzie and Lisa, on our new government. Marc, the floor is yours."

"Thanks, Mike," said Marc. "What Mike has decided on is that we work on a five-year plan. For the next five years, Mike will appoint people to take over several governmental positions of authority, with the plan being to have elections in five years for at least some of these Posts. Suzie proposed we take this opportunity to drastically reduce the number of counties in Kentucky from one hundred-twenty to twenty. That number is definitely a subject for discussion, especially as we run out of refined fuels for vehicles and travel becomes more of a problem. I don't think anyone sees any fuel refining starting up anytime soon, especially here in Kentucky. The question was really whether to go with twenty counties or thirty. Presuming the 95% plus mortality rate is accurate, or even close, we went with twenty. So Mike will need to appoint twenty honest men, with organizational skills, to be Judge-Executives for each of those counties. George, would you consider being the first?"

George was stunned, but after thinking about it quickly, he decided he liked what Mike and his group were doing and readily agreed.

"Good," said Marc. "Now that we have a bank and a government treasury, we can start paying you from that. You'll have five years to get your county organized and I will ask you to sit on the committee that I will form in Frankfort to re-draw the county lines. You may want to be thinking about where the new county lines are for the new Franklin County."

Marc continued, "The next government issue we looked at is in both the government arena, and Linda's security/law enforcement arena. For now, as we mentioned earlier, we will operate on a Martial Law footing. Mike and everyone else I have talked to about this agrees we will want to convert that to a State Police as soon as possible. We think six months from now, or let's just say the New Year, is a suitable target to get something like that up and running. If it takes longer, so be it. Under Mike's emergency authority, we will supplement with the Military as long as we need to. I'm thinking one of the first things they'll need to address is the expected counterfeiting of our new bank's currency. I'm told that may make an appearance within the next couple of months." Marc looked at Peter, who nodded cautiously, while Scott Shelby looked a little troubled.

"Okay," said Mike, "General, what can you tell us about the military and any threats you see?"

With reticence, Sean chuckled softly, "Mike, I'm still getting used to that title. Maybe I should start calling you Gov'na all the time. What do you think?"

The look on Mike's face brought a hearty laugh out of everyone. "Don't you dare, GENERAL," Mike said with emphasis.

When the laughter settled down, Sean said, "Not to be discussed outside of this group, Linda has sent some people to Fort Knox to gather intelligence about this Colonel Briggs' intentions toward us. Our team just sent their first report. Fort Knox is currently in an all-out effort to train and organize an assault force for action against us here in Frankfort. Besides a few tanks, MRAPS and Up-Armored Humvees, they have found a couple of guys capable of operating drone surveillance birds. I mean the small ones, with four helicopter type rotors and cameras, just like we were using in the Sandbox at the small unit level. Without weapons aboard. We may have some defenses against that, but I won't go into it here. They also have a C-130 transport plane, several four-seat single engine scouting planes and six Blackhawk helicopters, but only crews available to fly one of the Blackhawks and one of the four-seater single-engine planes. The report also said there are several combat seasoned NCOs conducting training of the new recruits and have begun working on an Operations Plan to attack and seize the Frankfort base. There will be more intel to follow. Mike, under the current circumstances, if there were to be an attack conducted here, with no completely unexpected variables, it would end in a slaughter akin to the 'Charge of the Light Brigade.'"

"Let's make sure we keep our intel sources operating in this and figure out a way to avoid killing American soldiers doing their misplaced duty at the demand of a lunatic Colonel." Mike made the statement with heavy resolve. "Sounds like we should be smart enough to do that with the intel, soldiers and equipment we have. That being said, if it comes down to losing ANY of our people or the death of those soldiers, I will morn their passing. Understand?"

"Yes Sir, Mike," Sean said with conviction.

Mike continued, "Has there been any contact with Fort Campbell, by us, or Fort Knox?"

"No," Sean said, "our attempts to reach anyone there have been unsuccessful. We don't know if Fort Knox has even tried, but under the circumstances, it's likely the Colonel wouldn't want to chance learning of a superior officer surviving there to take command."

"One more question for Sean and Linda, but also the group here," Mike said. "Does anyone have contact with someone that is monitoring or communicating over HAM radio? I just thought of that as one way to hear about what else, unconfirmed, of course, is happening around the country and the world. Sean?"

"Mike, my radio guys monitor the entire spectrum of radio bands. Initially, after the virus struck, there were quite a few broadcasters giving a play-by-play of what they were seeing and, frankly, suffering. That number has dropped off to only a handful, mostly due to non-availability of power. With the virus clearing from the air over the past several weeks, I would expect there to be more in the coming weeks. I can direct my guy on radio duty to make an effort to monitor those broadcasts. I see what you mean about its potential value."

"Great work, everybody," said Mike. "Let's keep it up, and try to avoid any crises for four days from now. Someone, or I should say someones have a rather important day coming then."

Linda smiled and said, "Thank you, Governor. And thank you in advance for officiating our nuptials."

CHAPTER 27
THE NEW YEAR – PLUS ONE HUNDRED EIGHTY-THREE DAYS

Sean and Linda's Residence
Outside of Cronin, Kentucky
0600 Hours EDT

Sean woke up in his bed feeling something was very wrong. He looked over and discovered Linda wasn't in the bed beside him before instantly realizing she had intentionally stayed over at Marc and Suzie's house the night before. It was his wedding day, and he was both excited and frightened. It seemed to take him twice as long to swing out of bed, strap on his prosthetic leg, and get dressed. He decided he didn't like it when she was gone. Not at all. The wedding wasn't until 5:00 p.m. that afternoon in the neighborhood pavilion, but he wasn't motivated to do anything. With a deep breath and iron determination, he rose and walked over to the Com and Security Office in his parent's house. Since the secure radio equipment was located there, he had offered his parents to get them moved into a vacant, nearby home. His mother wouldn't hear of it. She had become attached to the SF operators coming and going in her house, taking great pleasure in seeing they were well fed and had clean clothes. This was all because of his dad, Fred Callahan, having set up their house with an all-house propane generator many years earlier.

Walking into the backdoor of the kitchen, his mom greeted Sean, bearing what she lovingly described as her "shit-eating grin." She loved the slang used in Kentucky. "Soooo, son. Did you sleep well? Did you eat all the oysters I carefully thawed and cooked for you last evening? Have you been working out every day? You stopped wearing those 'tighty-whities' I hear awful stories about, haven't you? I want grandchildren and you, buster, need to do your part! Now that I think of it, why haven't you two been making babies already? I know you know how…" Her smile probed his eyes, which he averted.

Sean had grown up seeing first-hand how blunt and sarcastic his mom could be when it came to sex and the human body. In her culture, it was something freely discussed and therefore fair game for teasing.

"No mom," Sean said smiling, "I'm still waiting for Linda to teach me. Maybe tonight? Who knows?" He had learned his shit-eating-grin from the best!

"General," said the radio operator as he walked through the door. "Captain Dawson needs you in Frankfort right away."

Sean stood, received the toasted bagel his mother thrust into his hand, and walked out to his vehicle.

***

Boone National Guard Center
Frankfort, Kentucky
0700 Hours EDT

Captain Jeremy Dawson was waiting for Sean in the Commander's office, along with a Staff Sergeant. "General, I'm sorry to bother you today, but I thought you might want to know this right away. One of your guys at Fort Knox just radioed advising of an armed drone flight planned for this afternoon to target our headquarters building, including the very room I met Lieutenant Johnson in when he came here the first time. According to the Staff Sergeant here, their drone can only carry one Hellfire missile and will be targeted to take out part of this very building. It can fly up to 35,000 feet above sea level, but will probably come in at under 10,000 feet. It has to fly that high to be within line-of-sight so that they have radio control of the drone. That's all we have at the moment, General."

"What's the status of your Stinger surface-to-air missiles?" Sean asked in a calm voice, seeing the level of excitement being experienced by Dawson.

"Sir, we have thirty missiles, all of which are checked out and deployable." Seeing Sean's reaction, Dawson calmed himself as well. "It will require a larger sized surveillance/attack drone to carry one, so it should be visible on our field radars."

Sean asked, "Did our source have a definite time of launch?"

"No General," said the Captain. "Just in the afternoon."

"Recommendations, Captain?" Sean asked quietly.

"General, let me defer to the Staff Sergeant here."

"Staff Sergeant Brown, General. I worked on drones extensively in the Sandbox and this one sounds like it's probably a Reaper drone with a high-explosive, laser guided Hellfire missile that is incredibly efficient and accurate for any mission. What me and the guys always figured is if we could paint the Reaper with radar, we can launch a Stinger at anything at or below 12,000 feet from the launcher. Sir, I think the Apache also has something that can take out the drone as well. What I would do is set up a picket of four Humvee launched Stingers, ten miles apart across the most likely route the drone will take. When it is acquired by the field radar, send the data to the Humvees and shoot the son-of-a-bitch down. Sir. If we miss, the Apache can try a missile or, as a last resort, its 30 mm cannon against the Hellfire missile and then the drone."

Sean paused for consideration, then turned to Captain Dawson. "Jeremy, make it happen."

"Yes sir, General."

Forty-five minutes later, the four up-armored Humvees with Stinger mounts were deployed twenty miles to the west, in a line approximately ten miles apart. The Apache helicopter was on standby for launch on a two- minute warning. Captain Dawson had also ordered the evacuation of the Headquarters building, moving his temporary office to an unused office within the helicopter hanger by the runway.

Once set up in the hangar, Captain Dawson looked at Sean for any further instruction.

Getting none, he said, "And now we wait."

"Jeremy," Sean said, "consider sending out a line of five or six Stinger MANPADS (Man Portable Air Defense System) to a distance of a couple of miles from the base, in case the Hellfire missile was to be launched."

"Right away, General," said Captain Dawson. "Should have thought of that myself."

Sean then walked out of the office, carrying a handheld radio for direct contact with Captain Dawson, and went to the National Guard Radio Room. He contacted the SF radio room in Sean's parent's home and asked to speak to Mike. Five minutes later, he briefed Mike on the situation.

"Sean," said Mike, "this really doesn't sound right to me. It's hard for me to believe they would send out an untested drone, with a valuable Hellfire missile, to take out the command of the National Guard when their own assault force is dramatically lacking in the ability to fight. Could this be a ruse to flush out anyone within their ranks that's giving up intel on what they're doing?"

Sean swore under his breath. After signing off with Mike, he walked over to Captain Dawson and relayed Mike's suspicions.

Dawson responded, "Well, shit! That either means we have a spy in our own ranks, or more likely, they sent someone over to this area to keep an eye on us."

Dawson walked over to the radio room and asked the communications Sergeant, "Sarge, where's the new guy your guys hired from over in Fayette County? You know, from the SECRET site?"

"Sir that would be Whittaker. He's due in for a shift here in a couple of minutes. In fact that's him walking across the hanger floor now. Heh, Whittaker," shouted the communications Sergeant. "Come on over here, pronto!"

Whittaker walked into the communications room, saw Captain Dawson and the General and said, "Uh, oh. Am I in some kind of trouble?"

"No, son," said Sean, "I'm General Callahan, Commander of military forces in Kentucky. Do or did you work on some highly classified communications gear?"

"Well, General, I would say I can neither confirm nor deny that accusation, but something tells me that either those classifications don't matter anymore or that wouldn't matter to you, regardless."

Sean chuckled wryly, "Now that's an accurate assessment. I'm with the 7th Special Forces Group and I have a feeling I have personally used some of the communications gear you made available to my unit. Would that be correct?"

"Yes, General," Whittaker said simply.

"Okay, then. What I'm looking for is intercept and triangulation equipment. Myself and my team have used that to great effect around the world and wonder if you'd know where I could find usable equipment of that sort?"

"Now General," said Whittaker, "I don't know where any of that 'classified' equipment might be accessed, at least not without going to a certain classified facility and somehow getting through the existing locks and security systems there, but I might know where to find something that kinda works the same way but is made of parts available, online, at a RadioShack type store, before they went out of business, of course."

"Hmm," said Sean, "tell me more."

"Well," said Whittaker, "with a little help from a couple of radio-savvy people, the three of us could set up a triangulation and identify the location of any radio transmission, encrypted or not. We could also get a recording if it isn't encrypted. Are we worried someone is surveilling us and reporting back to someone?"

Sean asked, "How long would it take to get this in place? And yes, I want to root out any surveillance that might be happening of this operation."

Whittaker seemed to do the math in his head, before saying, "By the time I get the equipment and position it a couple of miles in three locations around the field, I'd say two to three hours. Also, General, they might use the laser to bounce off of satellites, but with everything shutting down, I wasn't able to contact any satellites with my equipment at home, so I doubt they can either. Therefore, they'll have to be using our ground-based systems."

"Please see that it is done as soon as possible," Sean said.

Looking at Dawson, Sean said, "Captain, will you see this man has everything he needs to get set up ASAP?"

"Yes Sir," said the Captain, who gave the order to another Sergeant that had just walked in with a message. Both the Sergeant and Whittaker departed the hanger.

"And Captain," continued Sean, "The next time you hear from the Operators, let's send them the immediate recall code. I've got a feeling they may be doing the same thing we're about to, and I want to get our men out. They may have been burned by sending this most recent message to us. Oh, and what do you think about leaving the Stinger emplacements where they are for the time being? At least until our guys get out."

"Sir," said the Captain, "I will plan on leaving our Stingers out in the field until at least our guys can get out and back here. After that, I think it's prudent to bring the Stingers in to take up a smaller number of stations around the perimeter of this field."

"Copy that, Captain," said Sean, "and would you concur it appears the threat of imminent drone attack is likely bogus?"

"Yes General, I think they have played a smart intel game on us," the Captain said thoughtfully. "We're definitely going to up our game to stay ahead of them from now on. I'll have our guys knock it around once we address all the immediate actions, and come up with ideas for collecting on their intentions. General, I don't see any reason for you to stay and interrupt your plans for the day. Seems to me you might have more important things to do."

"Yes Jeremy, I think I will go on back. You know where to find me. Thanks!"

***

Fort Knox Post Commander's Office
Fort Knox, Kentucky
1430 Hours EDT

Lt. Johnson marched into Colonel Briggs' new office, snapped to attention. The Colonel let the Lieutenant stand there for several seconds before looking up from his desk. "At ease, Lieutenant. Have a seat and report."

"Sir," said Johnson, "I told you about the intel operation suggested by my Intel Sergeant to identify whether we have any leaks here at the Post?"

"I seem to recall approving your sending a couple of experienced snipers to the vicinity of the Frankfort airport to observe and report, yes. I don't recall it being an intel operation. Tell me again, with details."

"Yesterday, one experienced sniper, along with his observer, were sent to observe and report activities coming into and out of the Frankfort National Guard Center. Starting last night, I had my Intel Sergeant start a rumor within the group training up as an assault force that we were going to send a fully functional attack drone to fire a Hellfire missile into the National Guard Headquarters building this afternoon. We do, in fact, have an attack drone with two Hellfire missiles available in a hanger over at the airport, but it isn't currently operational. My goal was two-fold, Sir. First, I wanted to see if there was an immediate reaction to the rumor in Frankfort, which would show they have sent spies over here. Second, I wanted my Intel Sergeant to observe and report if there were any members of our assault force that would object to hostile action against fellow American troops. I think we need to know where their loyalties lie before we consider any type of military assault."

The Colonel had sat back in his chair, contemplating what the Lieutenant said. "Lieutenant, I am quite impressed with your thinking. I have to admit that I wasn't listening carefully when you briefed me on this operation before. Both of your objectives seem to be important and very well thought-out."

"There's more, Sir," said the Lieutenant. "At 0800 this morning, they reported a group of Humvees bearing some type of weapon system covered in a tarp on their roofs departed the Boone Center main gate. Thirty minutes later, five regular Humvees departed the same gate. The first Humvees may have had Stinger racks on their roofs, but we don't have any confirmation of that. All of this movement could be a sign the rumor has reached the National Guard base, but confidence in that assessment is, at best, fifty percent."

The Colonel seized on the Lieutenant's report with enthusiasm. "Excellent, Lieutenant! Now how do we figure out if those bastards have penetrated our Post, or are gaining their intelligence from some other means?"

"I'm relying a lot on my Intel Sergeant, Sir," the Lieutenant said. "He seems to think the best way of going about this is what we're already doing. He has two of his people mingling with our troops, looking for anyone asking too many questions. Our signals people have begun monitoring all the electronic activity in or around our Post and have busted into two houses where HAM operators had radios transmitting, without locating anything suspicious."

The Lieutenant continued, "Also, the training battalion making up our assault force will reach an operational level within 30 days. My NCOs keep telling me it will take several months before they will be ready for actual combat, but I think they come from the school of overpreparedness. Especially if we can get that drone with its Hellfire missiles to be fully functional. I have two qualified technicians working on that now."

The Colonel's face really brightened up at this latest news. "Yes! Make it happen, Lieutenant. And have your Sergeant draw up the papers. You have just been promoted to Captain! Consider it a battlefield promotion!"

CHAPTER 28
THE NEW YEAR – PLUS ONE HUNDRED EIGHTY-THREE DAYS

Mike Broehm Temporary Office Building
Outside of Cronin, Kentucky
1500 Hours EDT

Sean entered Mike's conference room to find Mike, Marc, Linda, Lisa, Suzie, and Anna already seated and waiting for him. All looked relatively relaxed and even had a slightly festive feel about them.

"You all look pretty happy, considering everything," Sean said with mild trepidation.

Looking at Linda, he said, "Honey, what do you know that I don't?"

Suzie giggled a little and said, "That is good that he can read you that well, Linda. He will make a very good husband." Her comment caused everyone at the table to smile and chuckle, causing Sean to become even more perplexed.

"Honey," Linda said, "It's okay to see you on our wedding day, so long as I'm not yet in my dress. And yes, we do know something that you don't and it's intel that is known nowhere outside of this room, except among the SF operators. When contact was made with one Operator over at Fort Knox to recall them, he said their recall wasn't necessary. I made that call, sweetheart. Seems one of their sources is the Intel Sergeant working for Lieutenant Johnson. He had spread the rumor among the Fort Knox assault battalion about the drone and Hellfire missile, on orders from Johnson, and hadn't been able to contact our guys. Johnson's entire operation involving spreading the rumor was to see if they had any leaks within the battalion and to assess battalion members for their loyalty to Colonel Briggs. They also sent a sniper/observer team to Frankfort to monitor comings and goings at the National Guard base. We have them located, thanks to your new friend, Mr. Whittaker. We're waiting for you to decide what we want to do with them once you've heard a few options. Also, they have no technical capability to locate or intercept our guy's signals. The equipment our guys use is the latest available and is very difficult for anyone to detect, much less intercept and locate. And, most importantly, I see no reason plans for 1700 today can't happen!"

Sean had been following each of Linda's revelations with fascination. "Okay," he said, "I agree the operators can stay on station for now. Incredible job, by the way. I will also make sure I live up to the high bar that Suzie has set for me going forward. And Mike, thank you for pointing out what should have been obvious to us experienced military folks. We're obviously losing our edge and this was perfect for increasing our focus. Now, what decisions need to be made before I go home and change?"

Linda said, "Honey, I recommend we let the sniper/observer team alone for at least another twenty-four hours. Let's let everyone think about the various options and decide tomorrow afternoon. If that's okay with you, we're done here for today. Correct?" Linda surveyed the room and received smiles of agreement all around.

Mike said, "Get out of here, General. I will see you at 1700 hours sharp!"

∗∗∗

Mike waited at the pedestal just in front of the fireplace in the covered pavilion as the wedding march played on a boom box. A gorgeous LT walked slowly up the aisle in a white, lace trimmed wedding gown on the arm of Fred Callahan as Sean waited patiently at the front in his black suit with a brilliant white shirt and black tie. The pavilion was packed to overflowing with mismatched folding chairs and camp chairs that spilled out into the grass on either side. The music stopped when Fred placed Linda's hand into Sean's and they turned to face Mike.

With a big smile, Mike said, "Folks, thank you for sharing this wonderful bright spot in our new history of the neighborhood. This is my first try at this, but both the bride and groom have assured me it is impossible for me to screw it up, so here we go. I know we've all been to weddings where the officiator droned on and on about boring but heart-felt platitudes. That will not happen here. We're here to celebrate the union of Sean and Linda, not listen to me speak. They have both been literally around the world several times over, so I think I'm more interested in what they have to say to each other than anything I have to say. So I'll start by asking Sean, 'what would you like to say to Linda?'"

Without missing a beat, Sean said, "Linda, I offer you my love, my life and my sacred honor. You have been there for me in my darkest times and have shared my joys and triumphs over these past few months. You are my everything and I will spend the rest of my life trying to repay you for the wonders you bring into my life."

Mike said, "Okay Linda, what would you like to say to Sean?"

Like Sean, she didn't miss a beat. "Sean, I have admired you from the first time I met you. I didn't realize the depth of my love for you until you saved my life on that day in Afghanistan. I hate you lost your leg, but you have shown me nothing but gratitude for returning the love and passion I so much enjoy giving to you. You, too, are my-everything, and I will also spend the rest of my life repaying you for the wonders you bring into my life."

Mike said, "Sean, please take Linda's hand. Do you, Sean, take Linda, to have and to hold, for richer or poorer, till death do you part?"

Sean said, "I do."

Mike then said, "Do you Linda take Sean…"

Suddenly, there was the sound of a rifle shot as one of the SF Operators fired from the edge of the crowd. Everyone had gone to the ground, except for Mike and both Linda and Sean, who had drawn their .45 caliber Glock pistols from concealed holsters before going into a defensive crouch. The SF Operator lowered his rifle and said, "Sorry, LT, Sean, a zombie down by the creek. All clear now, so long as no one goes over that way. We're upwind."

Both Sean and Linda holstered their pistols. Linda looked at Mike, turned to Sean and said, "Yes," and pulled herself into Sean's embrace for a passionate kiss.

Mike quickly followed with, "By the power vested in me by all of you, I pronounce you two man and wife! Everyone, may I present to you, Sean and Linda Callahan!"

Despite the unpleasant distraction, the crowd erupted into a loud cheer. Both Fred and Penny Callahan were the proudest people there.

With difficulty, Mike was able to get everyone to quiet, then said, "There is food and drink on the tables off to the side there and please be sure to load up and enjoy. Sergeant, will you take two guys and ensure that was the only zombie and stake out the limits of a safe zone?"

The after-wedding party only lasted about thirty minutes, but as the first wedding after all the death, they deemed it to be a resounding success.

Later that evening, Sean and Linda lay panting in bed after finishing the obligatory consummation of the marriage. Both agreed they would have to work a lot harder to improve on their game from that first example.

***

Mike Broehm Temporary Office Building
Outside of Cronin, Kentucky
2330 Hours EDT

While lying in the spare bedroom of Mike's new office, Anna heard a key unlock the front door of the office building. The generator in the building had been turned off for the night, but she could just see the faint glow of candlelight coming from the front hallway and up the stairwell. Quietly, she reached for the 9 mm pistol on her nightstand and was thankful for the tritium glow-in-the-dark night sights on the pistol. Downstairs, she could just hear someone in the kitchen putting ice cubes into a glass and then shuffle to the leather couch in the conference room and sit down with a deep sigh.

Anna had stripped down to just a large t-shirt before crawling into bed. Quietly, she crept down the stairs with her pistol in one hand and her hand gently touching the handrail for balance. At the bottom of the stairs, she could clearly see a glow of candlelight coming from just around the doorway. A quick peek revealed Mike sitting on the couch with a drink in his hand and his head back, staring at the ceiling.

Thinking quickly, Anna stepped back from the doorway and said in a normal voice, "Mike? Is that you?"

There was a pause, then Mike got up from the couch and said, "Oh, Anna, I'm sorry. I didn't mean to startle you. I forgot you said you were spending the night here."

Anna came through the doorway with her pistol pointed at the floor and smiled at the startled Acting Governor. "No problem, Mike! I'm used to meeting handsome men sneaking into my house at midnight. Although usually, I know they're coming and they don't stop for a drink before joining me." The twinkle from the candlelight was dancing in her eyes.

Anna glanced at the drink in his hand and asked, "What're you having?"

"The cheapest tolerable sipping bourbon I could find."

"That's an awful lot of bourbon in your glass," she said. "Looks like you could use some help." With that, she marched over to Mike, took the glass from his hand, and poured a long, slow gulp into her mouth. "There, this way you won't be hung over in the morning."

Her smile brought a bright smile from Mike in return. She could feel the burn of the alcohol and its immediate absorption from her empty stomach into her bloodstream. God, he was a handsome man, she thought.

Mike took her hand and led her toward the couch, where she stopped and set the glass and her gun on the coffee table and pushed Mike into a sitting position on the couch. Anna then found herself swinging one leg over and straddling his lap, causing her long t-shirt to ride up a bit and the V-neck to drop scandalously to display more than just her cleavage in the candlelight, while her hands reached out and clasped behind his neck. She didn't know if it was the alcohol, or circumstances, or all of the above. She suddenly felt herself pressing her body hard into his, while looking into his burning eyes. "Mike, your pain these last few days has been tearing me up. Do you know that, big guy? I just want to take your face in my hands, kiss you and let you know it's all going to be all right."

Mike moved his hands from her bare derriere (how did they get there?!?), to reach for her face to kiss her gently, then with ever-increasing passion. Suddenly his hand found her more than ample breast, then erect nipples, as they ground against his stomach through his thin shirt. With one motion, he stood up, scooped her up in his arms, and carried her up the stairs to the Master bedroom. She awoke five hours later to the first graying light of dawn, with his head buried between her bare breasts, feeling the most contented she could ever remember.

An hour later, both Anna and Mike were both out of the shower and at their desks, working on the long list of things to be accomplished that day when first Linda Sharpe and then Marc Baxter arrived to start their day.

Mike looked at the same group at his conference table that had sat there twenty hours ago, including Marc, Sean, Linda, Lisa, Suzie, and Anna. All looked somewhat refreshed and rejuvenated, except, of course, for Sean and Linda.

"Okay," said Mike, "I hope everyone has given thought to what we should do about the sniper/observer outside the gates of our National Guard base. Let me get the opinions of the nonmilitary first. Lisa?"

"Heh everyone," said Lisa, "with the least experience of anyone here, including Anna," she smiled at Anna, nodding her head, "I can just say I don't think it's a good idea to just let them stay and keep doing what they're doing. Sorry, that's all I can say about that."

Mike nodded and said, "Anna?"

"I don't like the idea of that observation post being there and think any military base has the right to evict anyone spying on them." Anna said this with conviction. "How to do that? I defer to those with more experience."

Mike next looked at Suzie. "Suzie?"

"In Communist China, they would be immediately killed or hauled away to a prison cell for long-term interrogation. Even though this is America with a Constitution and Bill of Rights, a sovereign nation has every right to defend itself. I would say seize them with a show of overwhelming force, interrogate them and send them back to Fort Knox with very little information and no immediate excuse to consider it an 'insurrection,' justifying military retaliation."

Mike said, "Linda?"

"Mike," Linda said, "Suzie's right about this having the potential to send this Colonel Briggs off the edge. Let's capture and detain them long enough to ask many questions and return them to Fort Knox without their weapons and a demand to cease and desist."

Mike nodded, and then said, "Sean?"

Sean said, "Yes, let's send Up-Armored Humvees with a dozen troops to arrest and detain them. I'll have the Command Sergeant Major and Sergeant Lopez interrogate them before having an Up-Armored Humvee deliver them back to Fort Knox. They should be detained early this afternoon."

Mike nodded his agreement before saying, "Okay, Sean. See that happens and let me know how it goes and what the two soldiers have to say."

***

Boone National Guard Center
Frankfort, Kentucky
1500 Hours EDT

The Command Sergeant Major (CSM) sat in front of the Sniper, a Buck Sergeant across the table in the conference room. The Sniper was duck taped to the arm of the rolling office chair and had been literally rolled into the conference room. A very large Corporal stood behind the Sniper ensuring his good behavior.

The CSM said, "Okay Buck Sergeant Ross. I'm Command Sergeant Major Thompson, U.S. Army National Guard, and this scrawny little feller next to me is First Sergeant Lopez, also with the U.S. Army National Guard. In case you didn't notice, we've both been around the Army, both active and Reserve/National Guard since before you were born. Now son, what I want you to do is tell us who you are working for and what the hell you were doing spying on my Post? And let me save you the breath of bleating out your name, rank and serial number. I know who you are and that you are assigned to Fort Knox and I frankly don't give a shit about your serial number. Now, son, can we have a conversation or does this meeting have to go another direction?"

Sergeant Ross just sat silently, glaring at the CSM.

"Okay," said the CSM, "let's try this. First, we're both soldiers in the employ of the United States Military. When this damned Chinese virus hit, it has literally fucked the entire world, including the USA. In the aftermath of that, it's time to pick up the pieces. Do you even know who your commander is? This Colonel Briggs? Have you met him, son? Right now, we are commanded by General Sean

Callahan. He just received the Silver Star for Valor for action in Afghanistan several months back and was a Company Commander in the 7th Special Forces Group. He was here in Kentucky recovering from injuries sustained over in the Sandbox, as well as on highly classified orders from both the President and the Pentagon to prepare for society to collapse. You remember how bad things were before the virus hit?"

Both the CSM and Sergeant Lopez could see they had Ross' attention. "Under Continuity of Government protocols AND a Presidential Order from the last President, we in the military have the duty and authority to step in and support civilian government or even take over if the civilians can't maintain order. General Callahan is operating under those orders. More importantly, he has placed himself and the Kentucky National Guard under the Acting Governor, Mike Broehm, who Callahan knows personally and vouches for completely. That's pretty high praise for someone in the Special Forces Community. Our research has identified your Colonel Briggs as a non-combat starched pants kinda officer that sees an opportunity to build his own kingdom. Every wonder why he hasn't gotten your Post together with Fort Campbell? Give you a dollar to a dime it's because he knows his Bird Colonel rank won't likely give him the Command."

"Now," continued the CSM, "every man-jack of us in Frankfort was given a choice to either join back up with General Callahan as Commanding General with the National Guard or become civilians again and make our own way. He promised each one of us to take care of us and ours as part of the deal. Were you given a choice? I doubt it. Mike Broehm wants to rebuild Kentucky and see the country rebuilt under the principles of our Founding Fathers and the U.S. Constitution. Have you heard anything over at Knox except all that woke shit and 'do as you're ordered?' Now you're probably wondering what we're going to do with you. Later this afternoon, we will load you and your observer into an Up-Armored Humvee and drive you both unharmed, back and drop you off at the gates of Fort Knox. You can tell them we were told about your observation post by a sympathetic civilian that wondered what you were doing spying on our Center. We kept your weapons and radios because you were spying on our base. You were returned to Fort Knox because we're not at war with any American, or anyone else. However, we will do what it takes to protect and defend the U.S.

Constitution and our legitimate government. In fact, Mike has promised there will be elections five years from now as we continue efforts to bring back a normal government and life to Kentucky."

"Finally," said the CSM, "they sent me to talk to you 'cause they know I don't do bullshit. All of that being said, is there anything you can tell me that could be useful in preventing any more stupid actions from coming out of Fort Knox?"

Sergeant Ross sat and thought about what the CSM had just said. He had been in the Army long enough to usually weed the bullshit from the real stuff and felt strongly the CSM was giving him nothing but real stuff. "Okay, Command Sergeant Major."

Getting a nod and a motion from the CSM, the Corporal to cut off the duct tape and freed his arms. "I appreciate your telling me all of that and giving me a lot to think about. A lot of us have started to do a lot of thinking, but that's all I will say about that. Besides that, I don't think I should say anything else at this time, except to say I don't think I'm at war with you or anyone, but I am a U.S. Army soldier who took an oath. That oath, however, allows me to not do anything I think violates the Constitution. I'll leave it at that."

"Thank you, son," said the CSM. "Under these circumstances, you've done all you can do, and you did the right thing without stepping over any lines. Now, please step outside with the Corporal and wait patiently for your ride back to Fort Knox. You have my word everything I told you, including your free ride back home, is absolutely true."

The CSM gathered himself to interview the Sniper's Observer. Thirty minutes later, the Observer left with duct tape cut off and walking under his own power, having had a similar interview. Both men were returned to a point 100 meters from the gates at Fort Knox, as promised.

CHAPTER 29
THE NEW YEAR – PLUS ONE HUNDRED EIGHTY-FOUR DAYS

Fort Knox Post Commander's Office
Fort Knox, Kentucky
2200 Hours EDT

Newly promoted Captain Johnson found himself and his Intel Sergeant, MSG James O'Malley, standing in front of Colonel Briggs' desk at attention, waiting to be recognized. Johnson was finding it incredibly annoying that the Colonel felt the need to make his own Adjutant kowtow to him this way in an unnecessary display of his authority. None of these thoughts were indicated in any way in his demeanor. After waiting at attention for over two minutes, the Colonel looked up and said, "At ease, Captain and Master Sergeant. Please sit down."

"Colonel," said the Adjutant, "Master Sergeant O'Malley has just finished debriefing our Sniper/Observer team, and I wanted you to hear the raw intelligence directly. Sergeant?"

"Yes Sir, Captain," said O'Malley. "This afternoon at approximately 1400 hours the Snipers were in an observation post outside of the Frankfort National Guard base when they were suddenly surrounded by three up-armored Humvees with roof mounted machine guns. Both the Sniper and Observer were captured, searched, detained, and taken to the National Guard Headquarters building for questioning. Their questioning, and by their description it was not an interrogation, was conducted by Command Sergeant Major Thompson of the

National Guard. Both the Sniper and Observer were given similar information by the CSM, who informed them of the same information you received from the National Guard previously relating to the authority of both Acting Governor Mike Broehm and General Sean Callahan. The CSM emphasized every Guardsman was given a choice of whether to reenlist with the Guard, under Callahan's command or go about their way. Callahan also promised to take care of each Guardsman or woman and their families from now on. Another point of emphasis was that under both the Presidential Order and Continuity of Government, the military was directed to support existing civilian government, whenever possible. A final point of emphasis was Broehm's intention to rebuild the government in Kentucky under the framework of the U.S. Constitution and without all the quote 'woke shit,' close quote. He also promised elections in five years and didn't want to have a war with anyone, but especially with fellow American soldiers. The CSM ended with the declaration that he and all the National Guardsmen under their command would fight to protect both their Command and their Governor."

The Adjutant asked O'Malley, "How were the Sniper and Observer treated?"

O'Malley responded, "Well, Sir, that's what caused my earlier description calling their conversation with the CSM an interview and not an interrogation. The only question they were asked was to share any information they thought would help prevent any hostilities with Fort Knox. They were told up-front that they would be unharmed and be provided transportation back to Fort Knox with only their weapons and radios being seized. Both of our guys declined to provide any information to them."

Colonel Briggs, who had been slowly building his anger and rage, took this opportunity to explode. "How DARE those arrogant bastards arrest and detain MY soldiers! And seize their weapons and radios!?! God dammit man, that's inexcusable! Captain, how soon will the Assault Battalion be ready for action?"

The Adjutant, showing no emotion, said, "We can be ready in three weeks, Sir, but obviously the longer we delay the higher our level of readiness will be."

"I will come to the training area daily to observe and want daily reports from you on the readiness and planning status for our assault. Those traitors will NOT be allowed to defy my authority! Will the drone be ready for action in three weeks?" The Colonel was fuming with anger.

"Sir, the technicians are planning a test flight in one week," said the Adjutant slowly, with hesitation.

"Okay. Daily updates, Captain. Do you hear me? Dismissed, Gentlemen!"

"Sir, yes sir," said the Adjutant and MSG. Both men rose and marched out of the Colonel's office.

***

O'Malley followed the Adjutant to his office, located down the hall from the Commander's office as directed, and closed the door before taking a seat.

The Adjutant said, "Well MSG, any comments on what just happened?"

O'Malley moved uncomfortably in his chair before looking into the Adjutant's eyes and diplomatically saying, "Sir, it would appear the Colonel is quite adamant about initiating military conflict with General Callahan and the National Guard."

"That's LTC Callahan, Sergeant," said the Adjutant. "An Acting Governor does not have the authority to promote anyone to the level of General Officer without the Advice and Consent of the Congress, and that's not possible with no Congress in place."

O'Malley sat without responding.

"O'Malley," said the Adjutant, "I need to know you're in full support of our command structure at this Post. You've told me there is quite a bit of hesitation among the ranks at the prospect of bringing these traitors into line. Where do you stand?"

With the Adjutant's eyes boring into his, O'Malley replied, "I vowed to support and defend the Constitution of the United States against all enemies, foreign and domestic, Captain. As a duly sworn soldier of the United States Army, I support my chain of command."

The Adjutant, being a trained attorney, immediately noticed the slippery nature of the Master Sergeant's response, but upon further thought, he decided it was the best answer he was going to get. He needed the man and his support to successfully conduct the assault and crush the traitors, challenging the duly appointed regular Army authority. And who knows, a lot can happen in a battle.

The Colonel would demand to be at least observing the conduct of the raid on Frankfort. He also felt his ace in the hole was the drone with the two Hellfire missiles that would take out the Guard's leadership and maybe Mike Broehm as well. He had sent two of his most trusted subordinates over to the vicinity of Cronin in civilian clothes to identify where Broehm's office was.

"O'Malley," said the Adjutant, "I want you to get me some intelligence on where the Guard leadership offices are within their Headquarters building. Also, see if you can find out where Broehm lives and where his office is. Use whatever resources you need to do that. Okay? Any questions?"

O'Malley looked at the Adjutant carefully and said, "No Sir." He then rose and departed the office.

The MSG walked over to his office to check messages before sitting down behind his closed door. In this new, woke military it had been all he could do to keep his mouth shut at all the lunacy. Never in his twenty-nine years of service had he ever found himself in a spot such as this. He took his oath very seriously, and it had never been tested. Until now. The only problem was there did not appear to be a right answer. What the Colonel and Lieutenant, now Captain, were trying to do was clearly insane. Killing fellow Americans with a reasonably legitimate claim to civilian leadership control? Worse, taking patriotic and lucky survivors of this virus into a battle they wouldn't win and all for the ego of one Colonel with no combat experience? Was he looking at this all wrong? He certainly believed he had more of the facts than did the Colonel or his Adjutant. He had done his best to relay those facts in the most way accurate possible, and they had basically ignored him.

On the other hand, thought O'Malley, he had been talking to a very bright and persuasive SF Operator that gave a logical and reasonable overview of what was really happening here. The man hadn't come right out and told him who he was, but O'Malley had been around intelligence long enough to know. The act of even talking to the man could be viewed as treason and the antithesis of honoring his oath. But was it? Under the Constitution, and according to all of his training, he was entitled to refuse any order that violated that same Constitution. If he refused the Adjutant's orders, he would be arrested and sent immediately to lock-up and hundreds of soldiers and many of his few remaining friends would likely die, for nothing. If he helped the enemy of his Colonel and Adjutant, he could save the lives of a lot of good men. Is this the same conflict that faced Benedict Arnold? What is the "Right" thing to do?

Throughout his career, O'Malley had never had problems making decisions. When he began talking to the SF Operator, it felt like the right thing to do. He rationalized it as working with the legitimate U.S. Army Command and not an arrogant, potentially power-mad Colonel. After seeing the Colonel's meltdown a few minutes earlier, followed by the Adjutant's unreasoned orders and directions, he decided to follow his heart and his logic. Taking a deep breath, he decided to meet with the SF Operator again, as scheduled.

***

The Rhapsody
Port of Honolulu, Hawaii
1730 Hours Local Time

Kim had just left Cho's office after enjoying a celebratory toast with single-malt scotch. Earlier that afternoon, they had met with the Acting Commander from Naval Station Pearl Harbor and signed an alliance. The Acting Commander had assumed command over all military forces in the Hawaiian Islands. The alliance was subject to renegotiation if and when military or civilian leadership within the United States was reestablished. Captain Gao had agreed to provide local island government services and to hold elections within six years for major local government offices. The Military would provide support for Gao's new civilian government in the form of personnel and security under the umbrella of the classified Presidential Directive and Continuity of Government protocols. Military Civil Affairs specialists would also lend their help and expertise to Acting Governor Gao in reestablishing a working Island government.

Sitting behind his desk, Cho speculated on whether his plans to return to China would be canceled, delayed or if he would simply take the Rhapsody and sail off to Shanghai. Now that he had gained the support of the military, they might not react favorably to him sailing off, abandoning the alliance. No, he thought, he would develop his power on the Hawaiian Islands and see where that would take him.

CHAPTER 30
THE NEW YEAR – PLUS ONE HUNDRED EIGHTY-FIVE DAYS

Sean and Linda's Residence
Outside of Cronin, Kentucky
0200 Hours EDT

An insistent knock on his front door awakened Sean. The knock was the proper knock-code to identify one of the runners from the communications center. Linda opened the door with her Glock Model 20 .45 caliber pistol pointed at the floor and wearing a bathrobe. The SF Operator standing outside apologized for waking her and asked to see Sean.

Five minutes later, both Sean and Linda were seated on the couch in their living room across from the seated Operator. "General," said the Operator, "I just spoke with our guy Fleishman in Fort Knox and wanted you to get this info right away. I'll type up a written summary when I get back to the Commo Room. Sir Fleishman finished debriefing the Intel Sergeant at Fort Knox about an hour ago. The crazy Colonel was incensed about our detaining the Sniper and Observer and returning them without their weapons and equipment. He's ordered his Adjutant to prepare an assault plan for three weeks from now. One week from now, they expect having a test flight for an assault drone that can carry two Hellfire missiles. Techies to operate it survived and an aircraft mechanic has been working on getting the drone back in service. The Colonel wants to identify specifically where, in the Boone Center Headquarters Building, the National Guard Command offices are located as well as where Mike Broehm lives and works. The Intel Sergeant suspects they plan to use the Hellfire missiles preemptively to take out our leadership."

"Do they only have the two missiles?" Sean asked his question in a soft voice.

"The Intel Sergeant wasn't sure, but he believed so," said the Operator.

"Anything else, Sergeant?" When the Operator shook his head no, Sean said, "Okay, send a message over to Frankfort and ask Captain Dawson, Major Shouse, Lieutenant Ferrell and the CSM to meet me at Mike Broehm's office at 0900. That message delivery can be delayed until either they arrive on duty, or 0700."

The operator laughed, "Ah, General, you take all the fun out of this job!" There was some devilish delight in waking up officers in the middle of the night over something that can wait until morning.

Chuckling, Sean said, "Well, Sergeant, you know how old and cranky most officers are. We all need our beauty sleep!"

"Whatever you say, Sir," the Operator said on his way out the door.

***

Mike Broehm Temporary Office Building
Outside of Cronin, Kentucky
0900 Hours EDT

Sean had briefed Mike on the new intelligence before the arrival of everyone else. It was a crowded conference table with Marc, Sean, Linda, Anna, Suzie, Lisa, and the three officers, plus the CSM, from Frankfort. Mike opened the meeting and looked at Sean. "Sean, want to provide an update for everyone on the Fort Knox situation?"

"Yes Sir, Mike," said Sean. "After the return of Sergeant Ross and his Observer to Fort Knox yesterday, the Post's senior Intel Sergeant debriefed them. They are reported to have accurately described what happened, to the point of not saying we interrogated them, but instead used the word 'interviewed.' That intelligence was then reported to Adjutant Johnson, who brought the Intel Sergeant to report directly to Colonel Briggs. Briggs blew a gasket and demanded to know when the Assault Battalion would be ready for action. The Adjutant informed him they could be ready to execute an assault plan in twenty-one days. It was also reported they do have an assault drone that has access to and can carry two Hellfire missiles. One of our guys got an eyeball on the drone using long-range optics through a partially open hangar door. It is a Predator drone. They want to locate and target the specific office in the National Guard Headquarters building, where our command structure is located. They also want to target Mike Broehm's office or home. Ladies and gentlemen, these people plan to bring war to us in a big way. We should get more intel on their intentions over the next couple of weeks."

When Sean stopped his briefing, the reactions around the room were mixed, from horror on Anna's face to a general attitude of fixed determination on most of the rest. Lisa said, "Sean, isn't there some way we could stop this before it starts?"

Linda responded to the question, "Lisa, I know we would all like to do that and think it's possible, but our experience in dealing with these volatile situations around the world is that short of selective assassination, they can only be managed, but rarely stopped. Mike, would you authorize the assassination of this idiot and traitorous Colonel and his Adjutant?"

The question caught Mike off guard. "Damn," he said, "that came out of left field. No, I don't believe so. Once we were to go there, we're firmly in Banana-Republic territory and where does it end? No, I think that if we can't convince them to not to attack, we just need to crush them, legally and ethically. Now, I've heard there are no rules in war, but I need to follow principles or I have no business being in this position. I believe what we are building here is right and just. We will just have to make it work while upholding those principles. Anyone believe we can't or shouldn't operate that way?"

Mike looked around the table at some of the best minds in the country as they pondered the question. "Anybody?"

Sean and Anna gave Mike an immediate 'thumbs up' gesture and was then followed by everyone present.

"Okay then," Mike said with a determined nod of his head. "Sean, what is your recommended plan to deal with this crisis?"

Sean looked at Linda and said, "Honey, you're the brains of our family. What do you think?"

Linda's face went from annoyed, to appreciative, to pissed off. "Tossed that one off pretty quickly, didn't you, big boy?"

With a wry grin, Sean said, "Leadership."

"All right," said Linda, "I have been working with Jeremy and the CSM on the defense plan for the Frankfort Post. I think we're going to have to include the possibility they may attack the neighborhood as well, but hopefully our intelligence is correct and that will be limited to possibly the Hellfire missile. Oh, and starting today, I've begun a covert four person security team around Mike's office. We're back to not allowing any outsiders into the neighborhood without a known escort. We already stopped and identified two guys from Elizabethtown today that claimed to be looking for relatives."

"Back to defenses," said Linda. "We will want to take down the drone as far away as possible, so we have equipped each of our observation posts with two Stinger missiles. Standard procedure with attack drones is to fly them at high altitude, way out of range of any defense missiles, until they are right on top of the target, so taking down the drone may not be possible. On the day of the attack, and weather may play a major factor in potentially delaying the attack date, we will want to send out six MANPADS units no further than ten kilometers in a semicircular defense pattern covering the 180-degree arc facing Fort Knox from the airport. Two additional MANPAD units will cover the backside of our defense circle, out only five kilometers, in case these jokers decided to burn extra fuel and attack us from the rear. We will station two more at the neighborhood in case they decide to go for Mike first. Fortunately, Stingers are pretty simple to teach people how to use and two of our Operators can do that in only a couple of hours."

Linda stopped for a long drink of water before continuing. "Defending against the expected ground assault will happen in layers. We are presuming they will launch at least one of their Blackhawk helicopters to provide ground support and overhead intelligence collection. When that bird is in the air, we can hope it comes within range of the observation posts and they can take it down with a Stinger. Once the route of their ground force has been identified, at about the distance of Shelbyville, we will begin attacking their vehicles with TOW missiles until they decide to withdraw the attack. We are not out to decimate these attackers like we would an enemy. We need to limit casualties until we can convince their leadership of the futility of their attack. With tin pot dictators, like the Colonel seems to act like, reality doesn't matter much. And yes, we will make efforts to take out their leadership as soon as possible, once their attack has begun. We'll be fine-tuning everything as we get more data and it gets closer to attack day. This entire operation makes me sick to my stomach, but it would be a lot worse if Briggs were to take over."

Mike sat in his chair, feeling extremely uncomfortable. The business-like way Sean and Linda talked about killing Fort Knox soldiers was extremely unsettling. He didn't know how to handle that feeling and looked forward to talking with Anna privately after the meeting.

"What do we need to tell, well, anyone else about this?" Mike asked the question as it occurred to him.

Marc said, "Mike, I know there's a great tendency to want to tell anyone that might be in harms-way. I urge you not to give into that. To reveal to anyone outside this room or outside of the military men and women that need to prepare for it is potentially revealing we know it is coming. Things like adding covert security and neighborhood security is fine, but preparing for the actual battle will tip off Briggs, and his Adjutant that we're getting inside information. I learned in the White House that information is power and extraordinary efforts and, yes risks, are necessary to ensure you continue to get accurate and timely information."

"Thanks, Marc," said Sean. "I couldn't have said it better."

***

Homeless Shelter
Frankfort, Kentucky
0500 Hours EDT

Kerry woke up grumpily with someone shaking his shoulder through the rough, Army-style wool blanket. "Johnny," the man said, "time to get up. You've got to do some cooking this morning."

Through the haze of his awakening, Kerry looked around and remembered he was sleeping on a cot, in the floor of the high school gymnasium. He had arrived two weeks earlier and was told he was welcome to eat, but he would have to work for it. Him! Kerry DuBois! Had to work in order to earn a meal. Outrageous!

Stumbling out of the cot, he pulled up his well-fitting short pants, recoiled at the smell of his dirty t-shirt before slipping on a clean one, slipped on his worn, second-hand running shoes, and walked out of the gym, down the hall, and entered the high school cafeteria. There, a large black woman named Amy saw him enter and said, "Good mornin' sunshine! Another beautiful day the lord has given us, isn't it?"

The first day she had greeted him this way, he had growled at her and found himself planted up against the wall lockers staring at the wrath of God. "Boy," she said softly, "Yo gonna change yo attitude or I throw your mangy ass right out of here. The lord has let you live and find yo way here for a reason, so quit yo snivelin' and be glad yo alive, have a dry place to sleep and food to eat! Now, rejoice or leave!" She shouted the last phrase into his face. Truth be told, she scared the shit out of him.

"Good morning Miss Amy," Kerry said like he used to say to his kindergarten teacher.

Amy just smiled and said, "Johnny, now you go ahead and get started breaking those eggs into that big bowl. The lord found a farmer that had eggs to trade to us!"

Kerry had changed his name when arriving at the shelter. If he played his cards right, he would run the shelter pretty soon.

CHAPTER 31
THE NEW YEAR – PLUS ONE HUNDRED NINETY-FIVE DAYS

Godman AAF Base,
Fort Knox, Kentucky
1300 Hours EDT

Smitty was camped out under a low bush on a slight rise about a kilometer off to the side of runway 18/36 at Godman Army Airforce Airport, Fort Knox. He had been camped out there for the past 36 hours and was relieved to see the hangar at the airfield containing the Predator drone had finally fully opened its hangar doors. While he watched, out rolled the drone, pulled by an airplane tug, to a position at the end of the runway. They had set a table up in front of the hangar with what looked like two laptop computers and related equipment on it. Two young men sat down at the table and within only a few minutes, the engine of the twenty-seven foot long drone with the forty-eight foot wingspan turned its single propeller of multiple propeller blades. Ten minutes later, it rolled down the fifty-one hundred foot runway, becoming airborne half way down. After flying around the airport pattern for twenty minutes, it returned for a soft landing on the runway and rolled up to the hanger, before spinning around back toward the runway.

They impressed Smitty with the controller's ability to fly the drone and the precise landing they could accomplish. Next, a crew of three rolled out two Hellfire missiles and mounted them on the drone. Within a few minutes, the drone again flew around the airport pattern before landing softly. The drone, still bearing its missiles, was rolled back into the hangar. Smitty had taken over two dozen photographs.

***

Mike Broehm Temporary Office Building
Outside of Cronin, Kentucky
1900 Hours EDT

Sean walked into Mike's office after being announced by Anna. Mike had been working late to review a stack of papers with the names and sparse background information for 200 candidates for Judge Executive in Central and Eastern Kentucky. His eyes were watering and his head hurt slightly with the tedium of reading and thinking. Looking up, he said, "Good! I need a break with some good news! What have you got?"

Sean smiled and said, "It's not that good, but one of our guys in Frankfort got a look at their drone and positively confirmed it is a Predator drone. Not sure what type. Since their runway is only fifty-one hundred feet long, we didn't think it would be anything bigger like a Reaper, but it was nice to confirm it being a Predator."

"And why is that good news?" Mike asked with minor confusion.

"A Predator," said Sean, "is smaller than a Reaper and can only fly up to 25,000 feet above sea level and has a top level-flight speed of 117 knots, or 135 miles per hour. Our Apache can keep up with or exceed those speeds and altitude, so we can shoot it down before it gets here. Our guy saw them load two Hellfire missiles on the Predator after the first test flight. They rolled it back into the hanger after successfully flying it with the missiles attached. I think it's safe to say they will try to take out the Guard headquarters offices and probably your office here as well. That day may be a good day for you to be somewhere else, like maybe Peter's house."

Mike said, "I'm tempted to come over to Frankfort and watch you at work, but I know I'd be as useful as tits on a bull, so maybe I should hang out in your radio/com room. Could I do that and not be in the way?"

Sean looked at his Governor and civilian boss. "Mike, you can go anywhere you want to, and no, that wouldn't be in the way and you would be available to consult on any big decisions."

***

Marc and Suzie's Residence
Outside of Cronin, Kentucky
2210 Hours EDT

Marc lay holding Suzie against him in bed after having just blown out the candle. It was still hot inside and outside with the summer heat and humidity, but he just loved to feel her body against his, slippery sweat and all.

"My love?" Suzie asked softly. "Have you considered killing this Colonel before he attacks? I know Mike is against it, but it would save so many lives of good people."

Marc couldn't help but chuckle. "Most gorgeous and talented lover in the world, I'm eternally grateful you aren't mad at me!" His chuckling became infectious.

Suzie giggled, "When I get mad at you, my soon-to-be husband, know that I will never cause you permanent harm or do anything to change the man I love. Now you know, that leaves open a large number of possibilities that will take me the rest of my life to explore. You just get ready for the ride." Her slick, wet body slid against his in a delightful way.

***

Hung and Lisa's Residence
Outside of Cronin, Kentucky
2245 Hours EDT

Lisa walked into the bedroom carrying her single candle in its holder. Hung lay on the bed admiring the incredibly sensual natural form approach him. She said, "What are you looking at so intently, my big Huntsman?"

"Just the most beautiful female form in the entire world," he said with a grin. "I still marvel that you said yes when I asked you to share the rest of your life with me. Yes, I've got some strong points," at which point she couldn't help but look at a rapidly growing point of interest, before going back to his eyes, "but I also know you're smart enough to see the extremely rough spots as well."

Two weeks earlier Lisa had awakened to find Hung with a pillow in his hands, a growl in his throat, and murder in his eyes. She immediately began to softly sing the song lyrics, "I'm so excited, and I just can't hide it. I'm about to lose control and I think I like it," by the Pointer Sisters. Almost as soon as she began to sing, Hung visibly relaxed. He then fell back into a deep sleep. He had awakened her twice since then, starting in on his pillow each time, and had the same reaction to her singing. There was a longer gap in time between the second and third time. He hadn't done that in his sleep for over a week now.

"Come here and remind me why I should put up with you, big guy," Lisa said with twinkling eyes. She resolved to sing him a new, beautiful song each night. He said he loved her singing. She then closed her eyes and also resolved to keep her mind off the possibility of either of them dying within the next few weeks.

***

Mike Broehm Temporary Office Building
Outside of Cronin, Kentucky
2330 Hours EDT

Mike lay in the big king-size bed on the second floor of his office building, enjoying the slight breeze coming through the open window. He was about to blow out the candle when he heard the very soft sound of bare feet walking down the hall, then down the stairs to the kitchen. He could just hear the tinkle of ice cubes falling into two glasses. Anna had virtually moved into the spare bedroom at the end of the hall in her bid to try to keep up with all the hours he worked. When she opened his bedroom door and walked in, she was wearing only a thin, silk robe that barely reached the upper portion of her legs. Her dark hair and eyes sparkled in the candlelight.

"Oh, good," she said, "you're still up."

"I was waiting for you," Mike said in a husky voice.

She handed him the glass of bourbon, conveniently in an insulated steel tumbler that didn't sweat, set her drink down on the far bedside table and, with a flourish, dropped the robe on the floor and slid under the thin sheets. Cuddling up to him, she could tell he was incredibly tense and stressed. "Okay, what's troubling you? I know the list is long, but please tell me what's up at the top?"

Mike stoked her hair, sighed, and said, "Part of me is angry that someone like Briggs is so arrogant and stupid that he'd want to kill us rather than negotiate and come to a consensus. The other part of me keeps wanting to shout out that I am a pussy for not just ordering someone to take him out and spare everyone the potential loss of life. That goes for both sides. I'm doing what I truly believe is absolutely required for people I care about to live and grow the way they should be able to, but I guess I'm feeling sorry for myself for being the one to make these decisions. God, this whole woke culture and communist philosophy has allowed the powerhungry to crush humanity and it hasn't stopped even after killing over 95% of us! Why can't these assholes just see that?"

Anna had a lot she really wanted to say to explain the faults of humanity, especially those that sought power, but wisely said only, "Mike, sweetheart, you're doing the right thing, and we all love you for doing it." She snuggled closer as she felt him slowly relax, and then fall into a deep sleep.

***

Master Sergeant James O'Malley's Residence
Fort Knox, Kentucky
2310 Hours EDT

The Master Sergeant sat on his bed with his head in his hands. Despite having already decided helping the SF Operator was the right thing to do, he still felt enormous waves of guilt for betraying his command. It was a no-win situation for him and he agonized how he could best simply do the right thing. He had thought about it for the past several days without success. When the Adjutant asked him where he thought he should be during the assault to best serve the Command, his answer came to him. After that, he could sleep at least part of a night leading up to the day of the assault.

CHAPTER 32
THE NEW YEAR – PLUS TWO HUNDRED ELEVEN DAYS

Godman AAF Base
Fort Knox, Kentucky
0800 Hours EDT

Smitty was camped out under his familiar bush overlooking the runway at Godman Field at Fort Knox. He saw movement at the airport and observed a pilot, a gunner and what looked like Adjutant Johnson climb aboard a Blackhawk helicopter parked on the tarmac about seventy-five meters from the hangar containing the Predator drone. The Blackhawk lifted off from the airport and, instead of taking the usual departure route to either the practice area or toward the East, it began to circle the field. Within two minutes, Smitty saw the Blackhawk circle back to hover stationary right over his position.

"Shit," said Smitty as he realized they probably had him on the thermal camera. His camo uniform was supposed to provide a small measure of protection from thermal detection, but obviously not enough. Knowing he was toast, Smitty radioed Fleishman, advising him of the situation. He then destroyed the radio, left his weapon and optics under a rock, smoothing the dirt over it for concealment, and walked out from under the bush away from the runway. In broad daylight, it wasn't likely to do him any good to run, especially with the helicopter overhead following him.

For the next twenty minutes, Smitty walked casually away from the airport before a regular Humvee carrying six heavily armed Military Policemen approached him and ordered him to the ground. He complied with their demands and next found himself handcuffed, zip tied, and duct taped around both hands and knees. When he was roughly taken to the MP station, an MP Sergeant demanded to know who the fuck he was and what he was doing there. He hung his head and did not respond to any voice commands or questions, as if he were deaf, dumb and blind. After over a half an hour of shouts and being smacked around, they finally put him into the lockup cell. He was very tempted to ask if he could have his phone call, but quickly quelled that idea.

***

Fort Knox Post Commander's Office
Fort Knox, Kentucky
1000 Hours EDT

The Adjutant walked into the Commander's office, without knocking, to find Colonel Briggs dressed in full field uniform, including pistol belt with non-regulation 9mm pistol with white ivory grips, canteen, ammo pouch containing half a dozen .223 caliber 30-round magazines for the M-4 rifle slung over his shoulder, flak jacket, helmet with Night Vision Goggles, sunglasses, and a pair of very expensive Swarovski binoculars. The Adjutant said, "Sir, I have news to report regarding the assault."

The Colonel stopped after placing the last M-4 magazine into his carrier and motioned for the Adjutant to continue.

"Right after taking off in the Blackhawk for a warmup flight, we circled around the field and spotted someone hiding under a low bush, observing the field. I radioed for MPs to come and arrest the man. He was not armed, but they found an M-4 rifle in .300 Black Out caliber, that's usually favored by Army Special Forces, optics and a radio that had been destroyed and hidden under the bush. So far, the man won't talk to anyone, but we're pretty sure he's one of the Special Forces troops that surrounds LTC Callahan."

The Colonel asked, "Was the drone rolled out of its hanger yet?"

"No Sir," said the Adjutant.

"Good, then this is nothing that will delay our assault today," said the Colonel. "Tell me again why we're launching the assault right after lunch and not at dawn?"

"Sir, my combat tested NCOs have assured me that any military foe would expect and be most ready for us right at dawn, whereas right after lunch may find the traitors slower to react."

"Uh huh," said the Colonel. "By the way, I asked your Intel Sergeant where I might best observe all the action, and maybe take part in some of it. A leader should at least be present, if not in the lead, don't you think?"

"Sir," said the Adjutant carefully, "that is entirely your prerogative."

"I'm glad you think so, Captain. In that case, I think I will ride up front in the Up-Armored Humvee with your Intel Sergeant, leading the way until we reach the Franklin County border, at which time we will fall back and flank the column to the left."

"As you wish, Colonel," said the Adjutant. "Our pre-departure briefing is at 1200 hours. Will you be taking part in that, Sir?"

"Absolutely, Captain. I will be there and will address the troops."

The Adjutant said, "Yes Sir!" He then turned, rolled his eyes and left to get his full combat kit on. He would ride in the Blackhawk.

At 1200 hours, the Colonel and the Adjutant stood in front of approximately 200 men on the Post Parade field. Neither man saw the ironic ridiculousness of preparing to launch a violent military assault on a parade field. The Colonel addressed the assembled Assault Battalion first. "Men, this is the first real military action by our Army since before the Chinese virus struck the world. That event has cost every one of us lives and treasure beyond measure. I lost my wife and two children, and I'm sure each of you has suffered tremendous losses as well. In the aftermath of that event, there have been some that would take advantage of the chaos that has ensued and want to take power and control to which they are not entitled. Under the U.S. Constitution, in the event civilian authorities cannot maintain control and provide Constitutional safeguards to which all Americans are entitled, the U.S. Military is to step in and do so. I am the Ranking military officer in Kentucky and I have asserted that authority. Unfortunately, there are those in Frankfort and the Kentucky National Guard that refuse to recognize that authority and deny our regular, full-time Army is to protect everyone. Those men are, in fact, traitors to our country and must suffer the fate of all traitors. They will be arrested, tried and convicted of treason and suffer the consequences of their actions. Our cause is right and know that you go forth to fight for the side of the Just. May God have mercy on their souls, but we will not. Anyone that does not peacefully submit to arrest is to be shot for treason. You have your orders, your cause is Just and we will be victorious this day! Men, mount up!"

The Colonel did not get the rousing cheer he expected, so he stepped away from the podium and walked toward the Intel Sergeant. "Let's go, Master Sergeant."

Thirty minutes later, right after the launch of the Predator drone, twenty-five vehicles, including four M-1 Abrams tanks, rolled out of the gates of Fort Knox at thirty-five miles per hour heading on a circuitous back roads route toward Frankfort, led by the Commander's Up-Armored Humvee.

Joel Fleishman was in a second story dormitory room overlooking the road to the Post gate and the assault column from above. MSG O'Malley had used a small, encrypted handheld radio to signal him forty minutes earlier that the Commander would be in the lead Humvee and leading the column until the Franklin County line. The roof of the Humvee cab was marked with a white circular spot. Captain Johnson was supposed to be in the Blackhawk, providing air cover. The Predator drone was supposed to launch just before the assault column took off for Frankfort. All of this information was passed on to the Com Center outside of Cronin and distributed as needed.

Fleishman felt strong empathy with the Intel Sergeant and the position he was in. Doing the right thing wasn't always easy or pretty. He said a prayer for the Sergeant, for both during and after the upcoming conflict. He thought it was interesting the way Hollywood created expectations regarding military conflicts. Everything had to happen so quickly with a lot of boom, bang excitement for everyone concerned. In reality, it seemed to take forever for the twenty-five vehicle column to move through the gates. They had delayed it when one of the MRAPS experienced a broken axle. It ended up being pushed to the side, with its crew being distributed to other vehicles. On the road to the Post gate two of Humvees ran into the vehicle in front of them when drivers of those two vehicles felt the need to stop at a Post stop sign. Obviously, they had never been to combat before. Men were cussing each other and twice the column was in danger of stopping all together. Through it all, O'Malley drove slowly and steadily out the gate eastbound along back roads between I-64 to the north and the Blue Grass Parkway to the south.

The Predator had launched as planned except, instead of flying high and slow, it flew very low, around 500 feet above ground level and at a top speed of 117 knots, or 135 miles per hour. Because of the short distances, fuel range was not an issue. The Predator's controllers took it north to the Ohio River, then upriver to LaGrange before turning southeast toward Shelbyville. From there, the controllers followed U.S. 60 straight east toward Frankfort.

****

Helicopter Hanger and Remote Command Center
Boone National Guard Center
1240 Hours EDT

The SF communications specialist manning the encrypted radio system in contact with the Communications Center outside of Cronin, Kentucky, called to Captain Dawson. "Sir, I just heard from our Com Center to the east. The Predator drone was supposed to launch ten minutes ago and our radars here should be able to detect it if it were climbing to maximum altitude. Apparently they are keeping it low, Sir. I have sent warnings to all of our MANPADS units to be on the alert within the next twenty minutes to fire at an instant's notice." Both men knew their shoulder-launched Stingers were unlikely to hit a low-flying drone, and it was nearly impossible to hit an air-launched Hellfire missile.

"Roger that, Sergeant," said Captain Dawson. "Put out the alert on the local radio frequency that the Headquarters building should be completely empty. Also, radio the Apache to launch now, and provide them with all the information you have available."

"Roger that, Captain. Launch the Apache, notify all that the Headquarters building should be empty and advise MANPADS units of incoming." About two minutes later, the radio Sergeant said, "All messages delivered, Captain."

"Copy," said the Captain. It was an antiquated response showing he had heard and "copied" it down, but effectively let the Sergeant know the message was received.

Tension was very high throughout the Frankfort base, waiting for something to happen.

***

Inside the Apache Helicopter
Climbing West near Frankfort, Kentucky
1255 Hours EDT

Lt. Scott Ferrell keyed his intercom microphone. "I got the drone, Major."

Ferrell's heads up display allowed Ron Shouse to immediately lock his own gaze onto the drone. "Damn," said the major. It was almost underneath them and had just launched a Hellfire missile.

Just as he spoke, Ferrell launched an air-to-air, heat-seeking missile toward the drone. He also sent a quick burst from the 30 mm cannon machine gun, while Ron Shouse turned the Apache on a dime and dove in hot pursuit of the Predator. The Predator's internal defenses sent out flares, causing the missile to detonate harmlessly behind it. The Hellfire missile continued on its way toward the target, with two Stinger missiles trailing in vain pursuit. As Ron closed on the Predator, he saw the Hellfire impact into the Headquarters building, right where Sean and Dawson's offices were located.

The Predator continued on past the Boone National Guard Center toward the east, with Ron Shouse and the Apache closing quickly. At a range of one thousand meters, Ferrell opened up on the Predator with a series of 20 round bursts. One burst connected, causing the Predator to swerve violently to the left and veer into the ground at high speed, causing an enormous explosion and fireball. Shouse reported over the encrypted radio, "Predator drone down by cannon fire fourteen kilometers east of the base near U.S. 460."

Frankfort control tower advised, "Birdman, OP spotted the Blackhawk flying approximately seven kilometers south of I-64 heading eastbound, just south of Shelbyville."

"Birdman copies," said Ron, turning the Apache on a course to the south of Shelbyville.

"Birdman, also be advised intel indicates the lead Humvee in their ground column has a white spot on the cab roof and likely contains their Commander. After the strike of the Hellfire missile, you have to green light to fire on that vehicle at any opportunity."

"Birdman copies. Green light for lead Command vehicle."

Ron turned over to the emergency channel on his second radio and transmitted, "Kentucky National Guard Apache One calling Fort Knox Blackhawk helicopter flying eastbound in the vicinity of Shelbyville, Kentucky. Be advised a Fort Knox Hellfire missile fired from a Predator drone originating from Fort Knox airport has struck a building inside of the Boone National Guard Center. This unprovoked, violent action is unacceptable. I have a fully armed and capable bird that will respond to the aggression demonstrated by your Predator drone. Therefore, I recommend you turn around and fly back to Fort Knox. There will be no other warning."

Over the emergency channel, someone responded, "Fuck you!"

Just then Ferrell called out, "got 'em!"

Ron followed his heads up display and instantly saw the Blackhawk just as it launched a Stinger missile from inside the side door. Audible alerts sounded in Ron's headset and he immediately sent the Apache into evasive action, diving to the left while sending out flares to the right. Ron didn't have to tell Ferrell to respond, as he had already unleashed two air-to-air missiles toward the Blackhawk. When the Stinger exploded in the Apache's flares, Ron turned the bird toward the Blackhawk and Ferrell unleashed a one-hundred round burst from his 30 mm cannon. One of the air-to-air missiles reached the Blackhawk at the same time the 30 mm high explosive shells struck, causing the Blackhawk to explode into a ball of fire and fall straight down into a large lake.

When the Blackhawk hit the water, the audible alarm sounded again as Stinger missiles were launched from the assault column six kilometers to the north of where the Blackhawk went down. Shooting flares and chaff to both sides of the Apache, Ron turned the bird hard to the right, behind and just past the flares, and turned and lined up on the column. The magnified display showed the lead Humvee with the white spot clearly, so Ferrell unleashed a shoot-and-forget air-to-ground missile before Ron began to maneuver and put distance between him and the column in case of another barrage of Stingers. Within seconds, the lead Humvee exploded in the road, causing the entire column to come to a halt. Ron then backed off, out of range from the column, but waited for any additional hostile action. There was no further response. Waiting another fifteen minutes, Ron observed the column of vehicles turn around and head back toward Fort Knox.

Watching the column rolling back toward Fort Knox, Ron realized his hands were shaking on the controls. Ferrell keyed his intercom microphone and said, "Major, that was as good a flying as I've ever experienced. I'll happily climb aboard with you anytime!"

Ron climbed higher and moved west over Louisville to watch the column on magnified optics until it had reached the gates of Fort Knox. General Callahan requested they remain within sight of Fort Knox for as long as their fuel held out.

An hour later, Fort Knox airport sent out an unencrypted radio call over the emergency frequency for any National Guard Chopper. After a few seconds, Ron responded with, "This is National Guard One."

"National Guard One, Fort Knox tower. I am directed to advise you the war is over. Do you copy?"

After ten seconds of Ron and Scott hooting, cheering and shouting, Ron responded, "Roger that, Fort Knox. The war is over."

"Fort Knox tower to National Guard One, be advised a single, unarmed vehicle will drive to your Frankfort base tomorrow morning, to arrive at approximately 1000 hours carrying two unarmed individuals plus one of your guys to discuss the way forward. Do you copy?"

"National Guard One copies, Fort Knox tower."

Ron turned the Apache toward the Frankfort Airport and radioed an exact transcript of the conversation with the tower, from memory, to the Com Center outside of Cronin as well as the portable tower at KFFT.

CHAPTER 33
THE NEW YEAR – PLUS TWO HUNDRED ELEVEN DAYS

Mike Broehm Temporary Office Building
Outside of Cronin, Kentucky
1930 Hours EDT

Mike sat at the head of the conference table with a barely touched glass of bourbon in front of him. Sean, Marc, Suzie, Lisa, and Anna were seated at the table, all with glasses in front of them as well. Mike had just made a toast. Not to victory, but to the successful operation. Sitting there, Mike felt hollow inside that he wasn't able to figure out how to resolve the whole mess with no one being killed.

"Sean," Mike asked, "what's the latest?"

"Governor," Sean said, "I just left the Communications Center where I received an update briefing from Captain Dawson, Linda and a few others that are still working in the field. You're all aware that Linda left here to assess damages at the Boone Center, as well as at the site of the Blackhawk crash and the destroyed Humvee. Captain Dawson remained at the Boone Center to organize fire-fighting and to remain in a defensive posture, just in case. The Headquarters Building is a total loss. There weren't any personnel to fight the fire, so when the Hellfire missile struck, it burned and continues to burn until we expect it will burn itself out."

"Turning to the downed Blackhawk," Sean continued, "it crashed into Taylorsville Lake in water over twenty feet deep. There were no survivors, according to a couple of witnesses living on the lake. There were at least three and possibly up to five souls on board that is believed to include Lieutenant, now Captain Jason Johnson, the pilot, and a gunner. I sat in the debriefing of both Major Shouse and Lieutenant Ferrell. The Blackhawk was warned over the emergency radio frequency before someone replied, 'Fuck You' and a shoulder-fired Stinger missile was fired out of the interior of the chopper. Major Shouse apparently made a brilliant evasive maneuver while Lt. Ferrell sent both air-to-air missiles and a 100 round burst of 30 mm cannon fire in response. The Blackhawk burst into flames, having been hit by both missiles and cannon fire, and crashed into the lake." Sean bowed his head in a moment of regret and sadness.

"Linda," Sean continued, "has examined the scene of the destroyed Up-Armored Humvee. Just as the chopper was shot down, the ground column fired several Stinger missiles at the Apache, causing more evasive maneuvers by Major Shouse. Shortly after going airborne, they had been advised of intel that the lead Humvee, with a white dot painted on the roof of the cab, contained the Commander. After the attack by the drone, they had a green light to eliminate that vehicle. With Stingers on the way, Lt. Ferrell located and fired one fire-and-forget missile targeting that Humvee."

Mike interrupted Sean. "Fire and what?"

"Fire-and-forget is the slang description for missiles that are programed to lock on and track a target with no additional outside direction or targeting. They essentially have little targeting computers that identify the target and will guide the missile to that target no matter where it moves. At least unless the target ducks behind some type of obstruction. At the scene, Linda found the remains of the Up-Armored Humvee with two unrecognizable bodies inside. Identification was made by dog tags. One was Colonel Martin T. Briggs, and the other was Master Sergeant James O'Malley. O'Malley was the primary source that allowed us to succeed today. Fleishman said O'Malley was heavily conflicted between doing what he could see was the right thing and betraying his oath. He's the one that painted the white dot on the roof of his own Humvee and obviously decided to sacrifice himself for the chance to take out the Colonel and stop the madness. I'd appreciate a moment of silence in honor of the hero, James O'Malley." Everyone at the table bowed their head in prayer for his spirit and to think about the many ways their own moral principles would be tested in the future.

Mike asked Sean, "So what's up with the Fort Knox tower radio message and waiting until tomorrow morning to come surrender to us?"

Sean shook his head and said, "Mike, I don't think that is entirely accurate, though practically it may amount to the same thing. Fort Knox is now, to the best of our knowledge, being commanded by their senior NCOs, most of whom we believe to have been against the assault in the first place. I'm speculating a bit here, but one of them may have wanted to get their own act together in the new reality of no designated Commander being in place. Also, if they're smart, they will invite Smitty, you know, SF Operator Tommy Smith that is in their custody, to sit in on their meetings and offer some advice. At least that's what I would do in their place. By delaying coming over to Frankfort until tomorrow, they can get a consensus among all those that are left and decide how best to go forward from here."

"General," asked Mike, "how do you think we should go forward with this?"

Giving himself a moment to gather his thoughts, Sean said, "Mike, I think I should offer to take Command of Fort Knox, including all of its personnel and equipment, and use that as the next step in taking command of all available military forces in Kentucky. Essentially, tomorrow I invite the two senior NCOs to join my command with assurances that we will view actions leading up to today as terrible misjudgments by Colonel Briggs and his Adjutant, each of whom are now dead. I would characterize their actions as misjudgments and not treason or anything else and let their deaths stand as unfortunate events. Period. By the way, both Linda and Jeremy Dawson concur with that plan."

"So," said Marc, "you don't expect to have any more problems with Fort Knox trying to kill anyone here?"

"No," said Sean, "the phrase 'the war is over' is a pretty clear indication of their intentions. But we will find out conclusively tomorrow morning."

Marc reached down for his drink and said, "Now I'm ready to toast the successful resolution to this crisis."

Everyone grabbed their glass, nodding a salute around the table and taking a healthy drink.

***

Non-Descript Warehouse
Outside of Cynthiana, Kentucky
2300 Hours EDT

Tank had been disturbed in his exploration of the young girl's talents by Blondi's distinctive knock on his bedroom door. Since moving outside of Cynthiana, Tank had taken an unoccupied house next to the warehouse as his and Blondi's new residence. It was a fairly large stone home with a five acre manicured yard with gardens, at least until the virus struck and killed everyone inside. He had sent Roberto in with four of the women to clear out the bodies and clean up the mess. Five days later, after they had used a lot of bleach, the place was livable. Tank moved into the Master bedroom and Blondi and his little friend moved into the large Mother-in-law's suite off the kitchen. The place did have a whole-house backup generator, so it had been easy for Tank to arrange for propane deliveries to get it fired up.

Tank walked to the door, fully naked, and opened it. "What," he said bluntly.

"Tank," said Blondi, "one of the riders you sent by motorcycle down to Frankfort just got back. I think you're going to want to hear what he has to say."

Tank grunted, then said, "Ten minutes in the Family Room." He then closed the door.

Ten minutes later, Tank walked into the Family Room to see a young, seventeen-year-old boy in a brightly colored BMX leather riding suit sitting down on the couch. "All right, boy," said Tank, "what have you got?"

"Well Mr. Tank," the boy squeaked out, "I rode over to Frankfort like Blondi told me to and learned from an old guy I met at a gas station outside of town, who told me the Army at the Boone Center looked like they were going to war. I used a hand pump to fuel my crotch rocket while the old dude kept tellin' me to avoid going anywhere near the airport. All-a-sudden, like, a weird-assed plane flew over our heads real low. It looked like one of those Predator drones on the video games. Anyway, right after that a loud, mean-lookin' helicopter passed almost overhead and fired a missile and some kind of enormous machine gun at the drone, causing it to crash right next to U.S. 460. Right away after that, the chopper turned and hauled ass toward the west. Me and the old man went inside the gas station to get something to eat off the shelves. I stayed there talking to the old man for a couple of hours. He had a battery radio he kept playing with. After a little while, he found a channel where Fort Knox tower said somethin' about the war is over. And then they were gonna send over a couple of dudes in the morning to talk about what happens next. Me and the old man just looked at each other. The old man said there must have been somebody at Fort Knox that was warring with the National Guard in Frankfort and apparently lost. That's all I know. I came right back to report after that."

Tank sat and thought about it for a couple of minutes before looking at Blondi and said, "Seems like whatever tussle Fort Knox had with the Guard in Frankfort, it's all done now. Maybe that's why nobody has tried to find out where we disappeared to after leaving the warehouse there. Time to sleep on it tonight, Blondi. After, of course, I take care of a little business with that horny little girl upstairs. Damn, she sure is full of tricks! Let's talk about this in the morning."

"Sure, Tank." Blondi just wanted to go to sleep and not have to think about whatever Tank was going to do with his teenaged whore.

***

Sean and Linda's Residence
Outside of Cronin, Kentucky
2330 Hours EDT

Sean finally climbed into his own bed, thankful Linda had just gotten home. They spend twenty minutes discussing the details of the day until jointly deciding the rest would wait until morning.

Snuggling up under Sean's muscular left arm to lay her head on his chest, Linda said, "Baby, you did real good today. Know that?"

"Thank you, my love," Sean said simply. "I've said my prayers for each of those who died today and for what will be the rebirth of our nation. And God, I am so thankful first for my incredible and gorgeous wife, but also for the team Mike has assembled. I truly believe we have a legitimate chance for this grand experiment to be reborn."

Linda squeezed him just before he could hear her breathing deepen with sleep.

THE END, BOOK 3

APPENDIX A: CHARACTERS

Central Kentucky

Mike Broehm (Pronounced Brame and rhymes with frame)
Mike was an outwardly simple man who lived in a nice subdivision in Kentucky. He is married to Lauren. He worked as a research biochemist at a local university before the release of the deadly virus, when he became the recognized leader in Central Kentucky.

Lauren Broehm
Mike's wife and Marc Baxter's older sister. Lauren's parents had died in a tractor trailer/car accident when she was in college. Lauren was 18 at the time and her brother Marc was only 6. Lauren had helped her aunt raise Marc and was later appointed as Marc's guardian.

Marc Baxter
Marc is a Columbia trained Journalism graduate and was a New York Times Junior Political Editor before joining Katherine Fontaine's campaign and then became first Acting Press Secretary, then Acting Chief of Staff after the virus struck the world. He was present during the collapse of the United States and the world. He came to Kentucky with the last 250 doses of the vaccine capable of protecting against the deadly China virus. Marc is also the younger brother of Laura Broehm.

Su Ling, aka Suzie
Suzie is both very attractive and beautifully accomplished in her ability to meet the needs of a man. They trained her at the MSS Charm School located outside of Shanghai to successfully milk incredible amounts of sensitive intelligence

from First Man Walter Fontaine. Escaping to Kentucky with help from her friend Lisa McIntyre, she becomes an advisor for Mike Broehm in his fledgling government. She and best friend Lisa McIntyre are incredibly bright and good additions to Mike Broehm's advisory staff.

Fred Callahan

Fred lives in Mike Broehm's neighborhood and is Chief of Police in the nearby town of Cronin. Fred's Korean-born wife is named Penny. Their son is Sean Callahan.

Sean Callahan

Sean is a Lieutenant Colonel (LTC) in the U.S. Army Special Forces (SF) Command (SOCOM), the commander of a Green Beret company and designated by the President to build and Command an SF Battalion to operate against "subversive" Americans within the U.S. during the expected breakdown in social order. Sean is the son of Fred Callahan.

Linda Sharpe

First Lieutenant Linda Sharpe was a Team Leader in Sean Callahan's Special Forces (Green Berets) Company. She's the orphan of two Army parents and just missed being on the US Olympic swim team. She led an A-Team of operators on a mission in Afghanistan, where she and another female operator were captured by the JOTP terrorist group. Sean Callahan rescued her and lost a leg to an IED in the process. She left the Army to stay with Sean.

Sergeant Hunter "Hung" Jenkins

Hung is a member of Sean Callahan's security detail assigned by the Special Forces Southern Command (SOCOM). He has been a Special Forces (SF) Operator for many years and suffers serious Post Traumatic Stress Disorder (PTSD) due to having killed so many enemies of the United States. He becomes personally involved with Lisa McIntyre.

Lisa McIntyre

Lisa is the daughter of FBI Headquarters Supervisor Hugh McIntyre and best friend of Su "Suzie" Ling. She was a biology Ph.D. candidate before the arrival of the China virus and has become a member of Mike Broehm's staff. She is extremely bright and becomes romantically involved with Hung.

Anna Boesch

Anna, a paralegal, is owner of her family homestead farm near the neighborhood outside of Cronin, Kentucky. The widowed wife of retired U.S. Air Force Colonel Jim Boesch, and mother of two grown sons, she becomes Mike Broehm's executive assistant to help organize Mike's fledgling government.

Peter Worthington

Peter is a university professor of mechanical and environmental engineering. In his mid-50s he is a recognized leader in meeting environmental standards for exotic metals mining, through which he has become wealthy. His large piece of land backs up to Mike Broehm's land. He is married to Elizabeth, also known as Liz, who is a good friend of Lauren Broehm. He also lives in a specially constructed mansion built to survive most potential threats.

Kerry DuBois

Kerry lived in Mike's neighborhood and worked for state government in the transportation cabinet. His background includes a bachelor's in Social Engineering from UC Berkeley. He survived the virus with Tank Monahan and Blondi Blondiac in a survival basement outside of Frankfort, Kentucky.

Jerry 'the Tank' Monahan

Tank is from the mountains of Eastern Kentucky. He accumulated a great deal of wealth from extortion activities targeting the coal companies back in the 1970s. He branched out into marijuana sales before being arrested by federal and state agents. Tank owned the Pen and Ink Saloon in Frankfort, where he met with Kerry DuBois and Mickey Blondiac, among others, for illegal influence peddling activities. Tank arranged for the assassination of the Kentucky

Governor and barely escaped to the prepper basement with Kerry and Blondi as the virus swept the world.

Mickey Blondiac

Mickey, known as "Blondi," was a crony of Kerry DuBois and the political writer for the largest paper in Central Kentucky. He published a weekly column called Blondi's Corner. Blondi is an openly gay man.

Scott Shelby

Scott is a financial advisor who left Wall Street after his heart attack at the age of 32, and opened up a small financial firm in the town of Cronin. He handles Peter Worthington's portfolio and acts as a consultant-turned-banker for Mike's fledgling government.

Staff Sergeant Tommy "Smitty" Smith

Smitty is a Special Forces Operator assigned to Sean Callahan's initial Battalion Staff following Sean's promotion to LTC and assignment as Battalion Staff Commander.

Staff Sergeant Joel Fleishman

Fleishman is a Special Forces Operator assigned to Sean Callahan's initial Battalion Staff following Sean's promotion to LTC and assignment as Battalion Staff Commander.

II. Frankfort

Captain Jeremy Dawson

Dawson is a National Guardsman and ranking survivor at the Boone National Guard Center. He owned and worked full time as the manager for the Lowe's Home Center in Frankfort. He is an Army Ranger and Commander of the Boone Center.

Major Ron Shouse

Major Shouse is a civilian ENT surgeon, as well as the Flight Surgeon for the National Guard Air Wing in Kentucky. He and his family survived the virus in a private survival location outside of Lexington, Kentucky. He joined the Kentucky National Guard to relive his former, active-duty service involving flying helicopters and to fly Army helicopters again.

Lieutenant Scott Ferrell

Scott is the gunner/co-pilot for an Apache attack helicopter assigned to the 101st Airborne Division in Fort Campbell, Kentucky. He is the sole survivor of two two-man teams flying two Apache helicopters that were stranded in Frankfort because of the virus.

Command Sergeant Major Michael Thompson

CSM Thompson was the senior NCO at the Boone National Guard Center after serving for twenty-nine years in the U.S. Army.

George Kessler

Frankfort Vice-Mayor George Kessler was identified by Captain Dawson as a civilian leader. He is recruited by Mike to assist in organizing the civilian portion of the rebuilding effort in Central Kentucky.

Alice Smallwood

Alice is a single, previously obese surgical nurse that takes in Kerry DuBois after his serious knife wound injury.

III. Fort Knox

Colonel Martin T. Briggs

Col. Briggs, the Post Finance Officer, is the ranking survivor on the Fort Knox Army Post. He has chosen himself to take command of all military forces within Kentucky. The Colonel has no combat experience and has spent the vast majority of his career in staff, as opposed to leadership, positions.

First Lieutenant Jason Johnson

Lt. Johnson is an attorney serving in the U.S. Army Reserve as an Intelligence Officer. He was doing a two-week Active Duty for Training assignment at Fort Knox when the virus struck the world. He was named as Adjutant under Col. Briggs and serves as the Colonel's primary staff assistant.

Master Sergeant James O'Malley

O'Mally is the highest ranking NCO in the Intelligence Office at Fort Knox and works directly for Lieutenant Johnson.

IV. Alaska and Hawaii

Cho Chong

Major Cho Chong, aka Captain Gao, is a bright, top-level MSS Officer fluent in 8 languages. A master at manipulating people, Cho coordinated passage of the China virus to Afghan terrorists and survived by flying to Alaska before the virus' spread stopped all travel. Cho wants to gain power in the former People's Republic of China, but must first get there from Alaska in the dramatically changed world.

Michael Kim

Kim is the primary lieutenant to Cho and an ethnic Korean that was born and raised on the west coast of the U.S. He has excellent organizational skills and quickly recognized Cho's abilities to make things happen.

Ho Chin

Chin is a lieutenant for Cho, a friend of Kim's and a Chinese-born immigrant to the U.S. that has unknown connections to the underworld of the seaport docks.

Marla Stapleton

Marla is a Nurse Practitioner that was on a solo Alaskan Cruise aboard the Rhapsody when the virus struck. She has a wide variety of medical skills as well as a quick wit and no-nonsense attitude.

IV. Atlanta CDC

Julie Carrithers

Julie is an American, Arabic-speaking aid girl that had been kidnapped and imprisoned by the JOTP for purposes of teaching JOTP (Jihadists of the Prophet) martyrs enough English and other skills to allow them to be able to travel throughout the world. She survived exposure to the virus and her blood was used by CDC scientists to develop an effective vaccine for the China virus.

Captain Charles Schneider

"Cap" Schneider is the Special Forces A-Team leader that rescued Julie from the JOTP in a raid on their virus development operation in Afghanistan. He also saw the value in getting her out of Afghanistan quickly and to the CDC, along with a terrorist laptop, that allowed for development of an effective vaccine for the China virus.

Appendix B: Forty-Five Goals of Communism

Congressional Record--Appendix, pp. A34-A35 January 10, 1963
Current Communist Goals

EXTENSION OF REMARKS OF HON. A. S. HERLONG, JR. OF FLORIDA IN THE HOUSE OF REPRESENTATIVES

Thursday, January 10, 1963

Mr. HERLONG. Mr. Speaker, Mrs. Patricia Nordman of De Land, Fla., is an ardent and articulate opponent of communism, and until recently published the De Land Courier, which she dedicated to the purpose of alerting the public to the dangers of communism in America.

At Mrs. Nordman's request, I include in the RECORD, under unanimous consent, the following "Current Communist Goals," which she identifies as an excerpt from "The Naked Communist," by Cleon Skousen:

[From "The Naked Communist," by Cleon Skousen]

CURRENT COMMUNIST GOALS

- U.S. acceptance of coexistence as the only alternative to atomic war.
- U.S. willingness to capitulate in preference to engaging in atomic war.
- Develop the illusion that total disarmament [by] the United States would be a demonstration of moral strength.
- Permit free trade between all nations regardless of Communist affiliation and regardless of whether or not items could be used for war.
- Extension of long-term loans to Russia and Soviet satellites.
- Provide American aid to all nations regardless of Communist domination.

- Grant recognition of Red China. Admission of Red China to the U.N.
- Set up East and West Germany as separate states in spite of Khrushchev's promise in 1955 to settle the German question by free elections under supervision of the U.N.
- Prolong the conferences to ban atomic tests because the United States has agreed to suspend tests as long as negotiations are in progress.
- Allow all Soviet satellites individual representation in the U.N.
- Promote the U.N. as the only hope for mankind. If its charter is rewritten, demand that it be set up as a one-world government with its own independent armed forces. (Some
- Communist leaders believe the world can be taken over as easily by the U.N. as by Moscow.
- Sometimes these two centers compete with each other as they are now doing in the Congo.)
- Resist any attempt to outlaw the Communist Party.
- Do away with all loyalty oaths.
- Continue giving Russia access to the U.S. Patent Office.
- Capture one or both of the political parties in the United States.
- Use technical decisions of the courts to weaken basic American institutions by claiming their activities violate civil rights.
- Get control of the schools. Use them as transmission belts for socialism and current Communist propaganda. Soften the curriculum. Get control of teachers' associations.
- Put the party line in textbooks.
- Gain control of all student newspapers.
- Use student riots to foment public protests against programs or organizations which are under Communist attack.
- Infiltrate the press. Get control of book-review assignments, editorial writing, and policymaking positions.
- Gain control of key positions in radio, TV, and motion pictures.
- Continue discrediting American culture by degrading all forms of artistic expression. An American Communist cell was told to

"eliminate all good sculpture from parks and buildings, substitute shapeless, awkward and meaningless forms."

- Control art critics and directors of art museums. "Our plan is to promote ugliness, repulsive, meaningless art."
- Eliminate all laws governing obscenity by calling them "censorship" and a violation of free speech and free press.
- Break down cultural standards of morality by promoting pornography and obscenity in books, magazines, motion pictures, radio, and TV.
- Present homosexuality, degeneracy and promiscuity as "normal, natural, and healthy." Infiltrate the churches and replace revealed religion with "social" religion.
- Discredit the Bible and emphasize the need for intellectual maturity which does not need a "religious crutch."
- Eliminate prayer or any phase of religious expression in the schools on the ground that it violates the principle of "separation of church and state."
- Discredit the American Constitution by calling it inadequate, old-fashioned, out of step with modern needs, a hindrance to cooperation between nations on a worldwide basis.
- Discredit the American Founding Fathers. Present them as selfish aristocrats who had no concern for the "common man."
- Belittle all forms of American culture and discourage the teaching of American history on the ground that it was only a minor part of the "big picture." Give more emphasis to Russian history since the Communists took over.
- Support any socialist movement to give centralized control over any part of the cultureeducation, social agencies, welfare programs, mental health clinics, etc. Eliminate all laws or procedures which interfere with the operation of the
- Communist apparatus.
- Eliminate the House Committee on Un-American Activities.
- Discredit and eventually dismantle the FBI.
- Infiltrate and gain control of more unions.

- Infiltrate and gain control of big business.
- Transfer some of the powers of arrest from the police to social agencies. Treat all behavioral problems as psychiatric disorders which no one but psychiatrists can understand [or treat].
- Dominate the psychiatric profession and use mental health laws as a means of gaining coercive control over those who oppose Communist goals.
- Discredit the family as an institution. Encourage promiscuity and easy divorce.
- Emphasize the need to raise children away from the negative influence of parents. Attribute prejudices, mental blocks and retarding of children to suppressive influence of parents.
- Create the impression that violence and insurrection are legitimate aspects of the American tradition; that students and special-interest groups should rise up and use ["]united force["] to solve economic, political or social problems.
- Overthrow all colonial governments before native populations are ready for self-government.
- Internationalize the Panama Canal.
- Repeal the Connally reservation so the United States cannot prevent the World Court from seizing jurisdiction [over domestic problems. Give the World Court jurisdiction] over nations and individuals alike.

About the Author

The author is an attorney and retired FBI Special Agent. After growing up in the Midwest, he has worked and traveled extensively in the Northeast Corridor. Following college studies, U.S. Army Officer training, and a thirty-one-year career in intelligence, counterintelligence, counterterrorism, and public corruption, he was inspired to write a novel addressing the realistic potential future of America. The author is married with one son, lives in the Midwest and enjoys motorcycling, multiple sports, flying airplanes and service in the American Legion.

THE F RST
CORONATI N
CARLTON JAMES

"James's second novel in this series reflects well his thirty-one years in intelligence work."
-Penny Woods, Kentucky Living Magazine
THE F NAL
PROCLAMATI N
CARLTON JAMES

NOTE FROM CARLTON JAMES

Word-of-mouth is crucial for any author to succeed. If you enjoyed *The Nation Reborn*, please leave a review online—anywhere you are able. Even if it's just a sentence or two. It would make all the difference and would be very much appreciated.

Thanks!
Carlton James

We hope you enjoyed reading this title from:

www.blackrosewriting.com

Subscribe to our mailing list – *The Rosevine* – and receive **FREE** books, daily
deals, and stay current with news about upcoming
releases and our hottest authors.
Scan the QR code below to sign up.

Already a subscriber? Please accept a sincere thank you for being a fan of
Black Rose Writing authors.

View other Black Rose Writing titles at
www.blackrosewriting.com/books and use promo code
PRINT to receive a **20% discount** when purchasing.

www.ingramcontent.com/pod-product-compliance
Lightning Source LLC
Chambersburg PA
CBHW030815210726
48290CB00002B/607